D0276531

McCAFFERTY'S NINE

McCAFFERTY'S NINE

A Jake Hines Mystery

Elizabeth Gunn

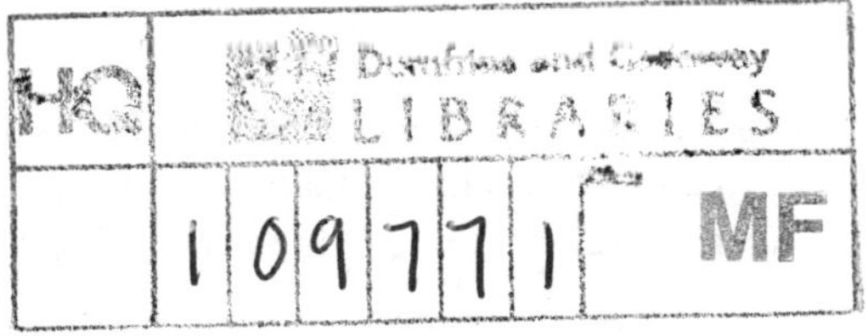

Severn House Large Print
London & New York

This first large print edition published 2008
in Great Britain and the USA by
SEVERN HOUSE PUBLISHERS of
9-15 High Street, Sutton, Surrey, SM1 1DF.
First world regular print edition published 2007 by
Severn House Publishers, London and New York.

British Library Cataloguing in Publication Data

Gunn, Elizabeth, 1927-
McCafferty's nine. - Large print ed. - (A Jake Hines mystery)
1. Hines, Jake (Fictitious character) - Fiction 2. Police - Minnesota - Fiction 3. Detective and mystery stories
4. Large type books
I. Title
813.6[F]

ISBN-13: 978-0-7278-7696-6

Printed and bound in Great Britain by
MPG Books Ltd, Bodmin, Cornwall.

One

A total stranger could have found St Agnes hospital that afternoon by following the lights and sirens from the five-car pile-up on the highway. Three ambulances competed for space in the emergency entrance. I dodged in through the big glass doors, crowded with gurneys and hurrying medics, into a waiting room that for noise level alone deserved a sign reading: 'This room may be hazardous to your health.'

Ray Bailey was waiting against the back wall, looking grim. No surprise there; grim is his natural exprcssion. He looked at me sideways, knowing he was as far off base as he could get, calling out a division captain to look at a mugging. 'Hope I didn't spoil your evening.'

'Nah. I always stop at the ER Friday night before I start to party.' I was blowing smoke. I had no party waiting, and I was about as well off here for the next half hour as eating fumes in the gridlocked exits on the north side of Rutherford. But Ray almost invited ridicule, standing stiff against the wall like that, with his face like a weathered rock. 'What are you doing here yourself? All your detectives call in sick?' The head of my People Crimes section had no business working a purse-snatching.

Ray did not get his job by breaking rules frivolously, so when he phoned from the hospital and asked me to come over and talk to a victim, I just hopped in my pickup and brought my questions along. When he answered them, I had ample reason to know, I would consider this trip worthwhile.

'Remember I told you,' he said, dodging traffic in the noisy hall, 'how I been keeping my eye on this odd cluster of assaults?'

'Muggings, I thought you said.'

'Well, yes. But kind of over the top and freaky. The latest one's in here.'

He held a curtain aside for me. We walked into a bright, aggressively clean space with a high bed and table. It was crowded and woefully short on privacy; the curtains around it were constantly being jerked open and closed by busy technicians in sloppy clothes. Somebody in the next cubicle was moaning.

The woman sitting on the bed was twenty-something, probably pretty when her luck was running better. Just now she was shivering convulsively and crying, and her eyes were swelling shut. She wore a blue sweater, but the lower part of her body was wrapped in the hospital's paper sheet; a pair of jeans, torn at the knee, lay on the cot beside her. Her hands were freshly bandaged so she couldn't clasp them together, but she must have been in the habit of wringing her hands at stressful times. She tried repeatedly, one palm almost touching the back of the other hand before retreating, her hands endlessly seeking each other for the solace of a dry wash. Or not quite dry, I saw – a little blood was leaking through the bandages.

'Janet, this is Captain Hines,' Ray said. 'He's our chief of investigations.'

'How do you do.' Janet Rasmussen's voice came firm and reasonable out of her wet, ruined face. She looked close to hysteria but her voice insisted she was perfectly calm. She probably didn't realize that tears were raining steadily down her face.

'Hi, Janet,' I said, 'I'm sorry you're having a bad night.'

Ray leaned toward her like an anxious parent. 'I know this is hard, but ... we really want to get the guy who did this to you, don't we? So ... I believe it would help if the captain could hear the whole story from you, because you tell it very well.'

She sat up straighter in response to his praise and said, 'All right.' She was trying to look directly at him through her puffy eyes. 'Where do you want me to start?'

This woman needed a champion right now, she was in pain and her purse was gone with all her credentials and cards. Ray Bailey might be sad-faced and balding, but he had come along and offered to help, so he was assuming hero status in her eyes. She looked at him trustingly and tried to do whatever he asked. Down the line, Ray and I both knew, he might feel the backlash of her anger, because if law enforcement percentages held, he would probably never find either the thief or her purse.

'Start where you did before,' he said, 'outside the hospital.'

'OK.'

'Hang on a minute.' Ray stuck his head out of the curtain and said something to an aide, who came in with a soft towel and wiped Janet's swollen face. Getting her face clean somehow enabled her to stop crying, and her hands went still in her lap. She looked into the middle distance, and began to talk.

'My dad had a stroke last week. I've been worried about him so I ran up to see him after work. It was dark by the time I came out of the hospital and the wind had come up a little so I was hurrying along the sidewalk, zipping up my jacket, heading for my car. There was nobody else around.

'I'd walked about a block when I heard somebody running behind me. I turned and saw it was a man in a jogging suit, so I just ... moved over a little so he'd have room to go by on my right. I heard these running footsteps come right up behind me, but then instead of passing on my right he dodged left and squeezed between me and the tree on the verge, and he hit my shoulder so hard I fell down.

'I was shocked, of course ... I mean – he knocked me *down*.' Her voice rose and broke on the last word, a sob shook her and her tears began to flow again. For a few seconds she held her bandaged hands up to her eyes and wept into the backs of them. When she realized she was soaking her bandages she sucked in a shuddering breath and held her hands out to show us. 'I skinned my hands when I fell, that's what I felt first. And then ... my hip hurt. And my knee.' She pulled the paper sheet away from her right leg and I saw the bandage on her knee, and a long scrape above it. 'My head hit the sidewalk too, I guess – when I got in here they said I have a lump up here.' She pointed with her bandaged hand at a great purpling bruise at her hairline. 'They took some X-rays to make sure I don't have a ... what do they call it...? Concussion.'

'You never passed out, though, right?' Ray prompted.

'No ... I yelled really loud. My mother told me once, if you get in trouble, *scream*, it's the best weapon you've got. I've never done it before –' there was a note of wonder in her voice – 'but I did tonight. Naturally I thought the jogger would come running back and apologize ... and help me up. But he kept right on going, and as he turned the corner at the end of the block I saw he had my purse.'

She put her head back and closed her eyes, and a fat tear rolled out of the corner of each eye and down into her ears. She started to put her hands up there, stopped herself and put them back in her lap. Not having the use of her hands augmented her feeling of helplessness and outrage. The pain of her injuries would pass, but this thuggish stranger had dealt a devastating blow to her self-esteem; frustration was rolling off her in waves.

'You hadn't heard anything about a runner attacking people?' I asked her. 'Never saw any of the stories in the paper, about women getting mugged by a runner?'

'What?' She sat back up and looked at me, frowning. 'No. I hardly ever read the paper any more. It's too discouraging.'

'I see. Well ... did you get a look at the guy? Would you recognize him?'

'I doubt it. I mean ... that one quick glance when I turned around and then ... he was running away and it was almost dark...'

'Sure. What about his size?'

'Um ... well, not short, I guess. I'm five-six and he was taller than that. He got past me so fast ... I'm not sure how much taller. Strong, anyway – he decked me with no trouble at all.'

'Tell me about his clothes.'

Now she was sure of herself. 'A blue running suit. Gore-tex, medium blue. A black knitted ... what do they call them? Watch cap. Pulled down low, right to his eyes. Regular running shoes. And some kind of goggles, I think, because when I looked back that one time, the only white I saw was the bottom of his face.'

'No hands? You didn't see his hands?'

'Uh ... let me think.' She tapped her left foot a few times and sniffed. 'I saw him running away with my purse ... but I was so shocked, I didn't notice his hands.'

'Understandable.' I asked Ray, 'Have you shown her an Identikit yet?'

'Andy's bringing one,' Ray said. 'He'll be here in a minute. Probably won't help much, but—'

The curtain parted and a hospital tech said, 'The doctor's coming back now. Let's have another look at that blood pressure before he gets here, huh?'

Ray and I stood in the jury-rigged hall between spaces, dodging gurneys and crash carts. I said, 'So ... does this feel like it belongs in your cluster?'

'Textbook, follows the paradigm precisely. The Sprinter again.' Ray had given his current nemesis a nickname. 'After the third mugging, early in March, I went back and looked up the case notes for the earlier two. It's the same MO in every one, the running gear and the fast approach. Only difference, the first two, he ran up to his victims from the front. Which worked just as well, because nobody looks at a guy running in a tracksuit. But soon as I put that description in the paper he switched to jumping them from behind. Guess he didn't need to bother, goddammit, if nobody's reading the paper.' Frustration was rolling off Ray now too.

'How many is this?'

'Six. In seven weeks. And here's the thing: the first one, he just grabbed the purse and kept running. The second one felt a shove, and the third one got knocked down. Since then each one's been hit a little harder than the one before. Like he's getting off on inflicting pain.'

'Monday morning,' I said, 'we'll figure out how to get him stopped.'

'Let's figure something quick, huh? Because I think this mugger's getting ready to kill somebody.'

Two

The alarm dinged once before I silenced it and slid out of bed, trying not to wake Trudy. She was propped up on a mound of pillows, sleeping for two. Trudy did everything for two now, as anyone could see unless he happened to glance at her from the side, where she appeared to be doing everything for five.

Cold floorboards punished my feet as I hopped to the east window, turned up the thermostat and checked the weather. The horizon was still black, but there was just enough glow from the porch light to see the outdoor thermometer, which read twenty-five degrees. In the last week of March, we were in the middle of a melt-and-freeze cycle that had paved hundreds of square miles of Southeast Minnesota with dirty ice. A skiff of snow had fallen overnight, and was blowing across this enormous skating rink in thin streaks.

A couple of years ago, when Trudy and I decided to live together, we bought this old farmhouse in the country, halfway between my job in Rutherford and hers in St Paul. Whatever flaws went with the house being a hundred years old, we felt, were compensated by its perfect location and beautiful big yard. But living in it for one winter showed us we weren't tough enough to put up with wretched insulation, jury-rigged heating, and electrical wiring that dated from the Hoover administration.

By now we'd almost finished rebuilding it around ourselves, at the cost of all our disposable income for the foreseeable future. Large bank loans were not intimidating, we told each other as we signed them, since we'd agreed not to even think about marriage and a family until the repairs were paid for.

When Trudy found herself pregnant last September we switched to Plan B, which consisted mostly of statements like: 'Stop crying and I'll do anything you say.'

That was what Trudy said. What I said went something like, 'Please, please, please, please, please...' Followed by a string of promises. 'Say you'll have our baby,' I implored her, 'and I'll do anything. Everything. Whatever you want. We'll get married, would you like that?'

'Well,' she said. And after a breathtaking interval: 'Yes.'

Since we were now basically in hock for everything we'd ever earn, we agreed on a private wedding, just a trip to the Justice of the Peace for the two of us. But she told her mother and sister and I told my foster mother and a couple of people at work. All right, I blabbed it all over town. I was too happy to keep it to myself. So when we got back from the JP's office that Saturday, our yard was crowded with off-duty cops and forensic scientists and Trudy's family, which all by itself accounts for a large part of Southeast Minnesota's Swedish demographic bulge. Our private wedding turned into an impromptu all-day bash, in and out of our half-finished house. The pictures, everybody agreed later, were priceless. I mean, Great-Uncle Elmer in a hula skirt? Oof-da.

After that, we only had to recycle seven hundred beer cans and freeze two pieces of wedding cake, and we were ready to start work on the nursery. More than ready, in my case – over the moon. Trudy said, 'It's too bad you're not a dog, you could wag your tail.'

Parenthood was a bigger deal for me than it was for her, because I had no family history. I was found in a dumpster when I was a few hours old and raised in foster homes by the State of Minnesota. Till I found myself becoming one, there was no way I could know that I was born to be a father. You know that double helix thing we've all looked at so many times, the funny twisted ladder with our genes hanging on it? It turns out that on mine there's one big pulsing hummer marked 'Dad'.

In response to the urgings of that tiny, raging node of protein, last September I persuaded this beautiful, sexy blonde, whose thriving career as a forensic scientist already kept her plenty busy, to turn herself into a vast lump of shapeless protoplasm unable to tie its own shoes. And instead of blaming me for that, getting angry and throwing soup cans at my head, this once feisty female had cocooned herself inside a chemical comfort blanket and was doing a lot of smiling and napping.

Which left nobody to do the worrying but me. I was more than taking care of the shortfall, though. I was worrying enough for Trudy and me and the rest of the Tri-State area.

In defiance of my appearance, which is a puzzling mix of light-skinned African-American with an Aztec nose and Asian eyes, I had discovered my inner Greek. I understood about hubris now, it was clear that I had over-reached. With no idea what characteristics I might be passing along, how many sociopaths and deadbeats blazed the hereditary trail to the loser that put me in that garbage can, I had insisted on trying to have a family like other people. To punish me, three weeks ago a large gray wolf had come slavering back into my dreams, reminding me how easily fate can reduce a man's dreams to dust.

I was nine years old the first time I saw that wolf. A few days later, my social worker took me away from the best foster home I ever had. Several times in the years since then, that ominous predator has served as my personal early warning system, stalking through my sleep when trouble's on the way.

You don't want to see a drooling fanged creature in your sleep the month before your first child is due. I spent my nights now trying not to dream about the wolf, and my days waiting for the phone call that would tell me his forecast was right again. I hadn't let myself imagine the specifics, but love had become like a knife in my heart.

Behind me, Trudy yawned contentedly and asked, 'What kind of a day is it?'

'Not bad. Snow's stopped.' I hopped back into bed and scrutinized her carefully while I waited for the heat to come up. Her hands looked a little puffy, was she getting edema? I had read all the literature she brought home from the doctor's office and learned that for the expectant father the world is full of hazards not covered in police training manuals. 'How are you?'

'Mmm.' She raised one hand two inches above the quilt and rocked it. It meant: 'Why waste my energy telling you again that it's hard to breathe and I can't see my swollen ankles and I need two chairs to sit down, but otherwise I'm fine?' She started to turn toward me affectionately, discovered that today it was more work than it was worth, and lay back with a sigh.

'How did that work, sitting up with the pillows?' I asked her. 'You get some sleep?'

'Yeah, hey, that's one of Naomi's better ideas.' Several co-workers at the state crime lab were volunteering coping strategies to get her through the last month. They had no advice for me; they thought my anxieties were a stitch. Over lunch, I could sense, stories about my protective fussing and night terrors fed their mirth.

I had urged Trudy to take this last few weeks off, but she wanted to work to the end of her pregnancy so she'd have all of her family leave time to stay with the baby. It was a sensible strategy, since we couldn't afford any unpaid leave, but now that she was so big and awkward it felt like spousal abuse to watch her wedge herself behind the wheel of her car and pull on to the busy, icy road that ran past our house.

Actually, financial prudence wasn't her only reason to keep working. After a lot of pondering and consultation, Trudy had opted to keep her job in the DNA testing lab, double-gloving and wearing a mask to protect her from the slight risk of damage from the formamide they used in the testing process. She didn't want to lose her place on the team of hot mitochondrial DNA scientists who were feathering the Bureau of Criminal Apprehension's elegant new nest on Maryland Avenue. Most of what she did now in their shiny state-of-the-art crime lab was so complex it made my butt pucker to hear about it, but she was as happy at work as a two-year-old with a clock and a hammer.

So I did what I could for her, started her car and sanded the driveway, fastened her boots that she couldn't reach any more, and did up the bottom button of her coat while she made jokes about how long it had been since she'd seen it. Then I helped her into the car, buckled the seat belt around the six-pound infant currently masquerading as a water buffalo, gave her a cheery wave and ran back into the kitchen where she couldn't see me wringing my hands while I watched her dart into traffic.

A man can't share his ghoulish insights about gray wolves with his pregnant wife, of course, and he certainly doesn't mention them to his colleagues in law enforcement. At least he doesn't in Minnesota unless he wants to be labeled a sissy-pants weirdo and get left out of the office pool. So, as soon as Trudy was out of sight I got in my red pickup and drove to Rutherford, where I walked through the tall glass doors at Government Center and became Captain Jake Hines, a sensible guy using short words to deal with a rough segment of the world's population. For at least eight hours, I would not have time to think about anything but vile crimes and inadequate punishments.

Jesus, it felt good.

Ray was waiting outside my office door, his eyebrows locked across his forehead in a straight line. He didn't even let me get inside before he shared his bad news. 'Janet Rasmussen's got fluid building up in her skull, she's going into surgery this morning.'

'Oh, damn.'

'Yeah. Remember what I told you Friday night? Every purse he grabs, that dirtball gets rougher.'

'We're going to fry his ass, don't worry,' I said. 'Give me an hour, will you? Soon as I finish the Monday morning start-up stuff, I'll call you.'

I had almost powered through urgent phone calls and emails when Kevin Evjan stepped through my open doorway wearing a dazzling smile. He looks like the demo for what Irish and Norwegian bloodlines can do if you mix them just right and add plenty of vitamins. Behind his back, soreheads in the building sometimes call him Kevin Cuteboy, and waste occasional happy hours in bars designing perfect ways for him to get a double dose of humility.

His high self-esteem doesn't bother me, as long as it keeps him drudging away at the head of my Property Crimes division. It takes a full head of steam to keep looking for all those stolen bikes and laptops year after year. Consumer items evolve, but the basic slog of greed and dishonesty grinds on. I figure, if a great self-image keeps Kevin from growing despondent, he's welcome to it.

Of course now and then a shot of extra attention helps too. He loves to get his name in the paper. Kevin's eye, this morning, had the satiny gleam it gets when he smells a chance for a headline. I had a fair idea what his hobby horse was this week and I didn't have time for it, so I finished dialing the number on the slip of paper in my hand before I asked him, 'Whazzup?'

'Cards,' he said. He could hear the phone ringing in my ear so he added, a little louder, 'Credit cards. More bogus charges.'

He'd been nagging at me for a couple of weeks about a wave of fraudulent credit card charges, many of them clustered in the comfortable Rutherford neighborhood around his own home. He was convinced they were the work of local hackers, and he was hell-bent on finding them. The possibility of becoming a hero to his neighbors made him quiver like a dog on the scent.

'Not our job,' I said. 'How many times do I have to say it? Tell them to call the company.'

'They're already doing that. My enraged neighbors, good citizens all, are spending their evenings and weekends talking to customer service reps with Indian accents, while some rotten little pest is living large on their plastic. Occasionally they lean out their windows and shout, as I go by, "Why can't the police ever help with things that bother me?".'

'You're a cop. Get used to criticism.'

'But if you'd let me hire a geek for a month I'd make it go away. The chief would get congratulatory calls and be proud.'

'Especially proud of Kevin Evjan, that's what this is about, right? Hang on.' My ring was being answered, finally, by a message tape. I added my contribution to this round of phone tag and hung up. 'We already have more work than we have budget. Why would I want to add a job that's none of my business?'

'To please your most ambitious sleuth. Because Ray is plundering my staff for his project and I'm entitled to a favor in return.'

'This is not a good week to collect. Go away and quit agitating.'

He turned in the doorway to say, 'One of my neighbors said to me yesterday, "It's getting so identity's a slippery slope."'

'I've always known that. The rest of you are just catching up.'

As soon as he was gone I called Ray. He came in with all his notes and we spent the next hour shamelessly copying Kevin's pitch to try on the chief. Think about the grateful taxpayers, we were ready to say, when we get this pest off the street.

Ray had spent his entire weekend thinking about The Sprinter. He'd marked the locations of all his hits on a street map, and prepared a personality profile of the thief from the victims' stories. 'He's more than ruthless, he's psychotic. He's not particularly large but he's strong and fast and likes to hurt people.'

'I wonder,' I said, 'if this guy's such a hardass, why's he sticking to small stuff like purse-snatching?'

'Well, exactly. That's why I think he's getting ready to escalate.'

'Practicing, you said.'

'Or getting some money together. It's just a feeling I've got, I can't prove it until it happens.' He tapped my desk with the eraser of his pencil. 'He might not even be a user.'

'You think? Almost all muggers are.'

'Seems to me this guy's too well organized to be a druggie.'

'Well ... you ready? Let's see if we can talk to the chief.'

McCafferty had said we could have a few

minutes at ten thirty, but Lulu called back and changed it to eleven. When she cancelled that a few minutes later, she said we could see him after lunch.

'When's that?'

'Well ... About one fifteen. Or a little after.'

'How much after?' I know how Lulu smoothes the work flow for the chief – by keeping everybody else waiting.

'You want to see him or don't you? Make it one thirty.'

As a child, I believe, Lulu became convinced that in the Cinderella story, the cruel stepmother was the heroine. But her job is guarding the chief's office, which is where you need to go to move a project along. So Ray and I walked into his outer office at one twenty-nine exactly. We took along Andy Pitman, the detective who'd run the scene on several of the muggings.

At one forty-five we were still standing there, staring out Lulu's window at power plant smoke being blown around a dishwater sky. We could hear McCafferty in the next room, piling work on his secretary, laughing and yelling at somebody on the phone. The longer he amused himself in there, the madder I got about the holes he was probably going to poke in our plan. I could see his doubting stare, his big red face asking, 'Whose bright idea was this?'

I began to calculate my career total of time

spent in the chief's office trying to get his approval for something. I havc a tendency to exaggerate a little when I'm pissed, so before long I was guessing maybe five hundred hours, and I began repeating silently to myself, Five hundred freaking hours I will never get back. Suddenly I thought, Some day I'm going to have Frank McCafferty's job and I won't have to give a shit what he thinks.

The idea had so much juice, it popped out of my head and went whizzing around the room like a subversive Tinker Bell, throwing off sparks. I looked after it, thinking, Where the hell did that come from?

I'm in no hurry to move up; I like the job I've got. Some day, maybe, but ... McCafferty was my training officer when I joined the department and he has mentored me from the raffish, barely literate rookie I was then, to the (I always hope) able captain I am today. I owe him plenty. Reason enough to be resentful, of course, but ... I turned toward his office door, feeling defensive, just as his secretary walked out with an armload of work clutched to her ample chest.

Maybe I'd imagined the laughter. Lulu looked, if anything, a shade grimmer than usual, and McCafferty, punishing the springs of his big chair behind a desk piled high with paper, wore the pop-eyed expression he gets when too many urgent needs clamor for his attention.

'What's up?' He gave me the hot blue stare. 'You look like you need to confess something.'

'Who, me?' I shrugged off my just-formulated plan to replace him. 'No, we just came for advice.'

He looked us over, his head tilted a little to one side. 'Three of you ganged up on me just to ask for advice?'

'Well, OK, advice and a little bit of help. We have a guy out there doing a series of offbeat muggings…'

'I heard. Sit down. Where are we with that?' His phone rang before I could answer. He grabbed it and said impatiently, 'Yeah?' And then: 'Ask him if I can call him back after this meeting.' He waited a few seconds, moving his lips in some kind of interior dialog, till Lulu came back on with a short, sharp answer. 'Good. Fifteen minutes, tell him.' He looked at his watch as he hung up, and picked up exactly where we'd left off. 'What makes you think there's only one guy?'

'Ray has a list of similarities.'

'OK.' He got Ray in his sights. 'Tell me.'

'Since the third week in January we've been called to a total of six incidents, all on Friday night, all aggravated assaults. In every one the attacker hit the victim fast and hard, snatched her purse and disappeared.'

'That's the basic MO of every mugging I

ever heard.'

'But with escalating violence. The last four got knocked down.'

'Not unusual. I ask again, what makes you think there's only one guy?'

Ray stared mournfully at the chief and said, 'He wears running clothes.'

'So? Plenty of those out there.'

'All his victims have described the same blue tracksuit, one of those all-weather jobs with the stripes down the legs. Track shoes. Collar rolled up – it's been a cold winter, he's had some luck there. He's got a black watch cap that he pulls down to his eyebrows, and I think he's wearing goggles – three ... no, four of the victims have mentioned not being able to see his eyes.' He was flipping through his notes. 'He seems to be able to hide in plain sight.'

'You're saying nobody knows what he looks like?'

'Exactly. Nobody pays much attention to him, a guy running on the sidewalk in a running suit, so what? Guys run on the street every day, all over town. The victim thinks he's going to jog past her, his first victim said she wasn't even thinking about him till he grabbed her purse. The second woman thought she might have tripped on something, didn't realize she'd been hit till she saw him running away with her purse.'

'Huh,' Frank said. 'Cute, huh? But you

said aggravated – what's the weapon?'

'He used a knife to cut the shoulder strap on the purse a couple of times. He's never threatened anybody with it, but—'

'That's all right, he's carrying it, that makes it aggravated.' He pulled his nose. 'You didn't get any physical description at all?'

'I asked about size,' Ray said, 'so far I've got small, medium and large.'

'Typical. What about eyewitnesses?'

'I found one,' Andy Pitman said. His voice made us all jump; he'd been completely silent until now. He looked around at all of us staring at him and added uneasily, 'But I wasn't sure how much to believe.'

'Why?' McCafferty likes Andy, who has more than once done a hard, dirty job for him without complaining. I brought him along partly because I figured McCafferty would find it hard to say no to Pitman.

'He was a really old guy, and he got pretty shook up. He was driving along about ten miles an hour in this beater Ford when he saw an assault taking place, and he got so excited he stopped right in the middle of the street. But he's got arthritis ... it takes him a while to get out of his car. Before he made it a woman ran out of her house with a cell phone, started talking to the victim and calling 911. So the old guy – McClatchey is his name – he decided to follow the runner.

Got to the end of the block, saw him turn right. Turned the corner and the mugger was gone.'

'What, ran into a yard or something?'

'McClatchey swears he was right behind him and he never saw him in anybody's yard. We interviewed people in the first four houses, both sides of the street. They all said the same thing, they never saw anybody run through their place.'

'Doesn't prove he didn't.'

'I know. But McClatchey thinks somebody picked him up. He said one old Volkswagen was driving away, halfway down the block. He didn't get the license number of course, but personally—' Andy scratched his ear thoughtfully – 'I wouldn't be surprised to learn this Sprinter's got a teammate who drops him off and picks him up. We've been doing a lot of canvassing the last two weeks, and we can't find anybody on the streets around the attack sites who's seen a man running.' Pitman shrugged and rubbed his big homely face. 'Seems like he gets in and gets out, boom.' He re-crossed his legs restlessly. 'An organized mugger, go figure.'

Sitting down, Andy Pitman looks pretty much like a beanbag chair that's seen too much use. He's not that much more impressive standing up, but his looks don't matter any more, because he piled up such a legendary record in his years as a beat cop in a rough neighborhood that every rookie in Rutherford wants to be Andy Pitman when he grows up.

'We've been trying to figure out how he picks his spots,' Ray said, 'and we think we've got a read on that.' He spread his marked city map on Frank's desk.

Frank looked. 'Kind of scattered...'

'Well, but these three,' Ray said pointing at the marks on the map, 'are within walking distance of St Agnes hospital, and happened during visiting hours. When we noticed that, we went over our victim interviews again. Two were on the way to visit a patient, and one had just come out of the hospital and was walking toward her car.'

'So the mugger's noticed that a hospital generates foot traffic.'

'And an unusually high percentage of it will be women walking alone.'

'I guess that's right. What about the three farther north?'

'Two fitness clubs and a dance studio close to the college,' Ray said. 'All upstairs, none with its own parking. Customers park in one of the parking lots or walk from the dorms. Andy and I spent a night watching foot traffic. When you know what you're looking for ... it starts a little before seven, a stream of young female students and college employees, carrying gym bags and a purse. They're late, hurrying along the street looking at their watches, paying hardly any attention to who's around them. Perfect marks.'

'Huh. Your mugger's made a study.'

'Looks that way. So we're starting to think...' Ray looked at me.

'We think these two areas are like a cash cow to him,' I said, 'and he'll keep coming back to them till something stops him.'

'OK.' McCafferty stirred restlessly and glanced at his watch. 'What's your plan? I see you have a wants list there.' He made it sound as if the dictionary definition of 'wants list' was 'disgusting slimy creature'. *Economizing is his job. Ours is to get what we need.*

'We want to try a decoy sting,' Ray said.

A cloud began to darken the sun over Frank McCafferty.

Ray charged right along, apparently oblivious. 'Fortunately, the two areas we're talking about are fairly close together.'

'About ten blocks between them,' I said, 'so what we want to do is form two teams...' I described the decoys, our own Detective Rosie Doyle and Patrol Officer Amy Nguyen. 'Both these officers are quick and smart, good team players.'

'And you want these vulnerable young women to stroll around dangling a purse till this dangerous criminal knocks them down?'

'They're not going to get knocked down.

They're going to be wired up so they know he's coming, they'll dodge when the mugger starts his swing, and their partners will be right there to nail him.'

'If you do that he'll claim she misunderstood, he tripped and was just trying to stop his own fall.'

'If we get the right guy, chief, his own DNA will convict him. One of his victims threw her arm up like this—' I swung and showed him— 'and he grabbed her arm. His hand slid all the way down her coat sleeve like this and we got a good DNA sample off a button.'

'A good DNA sample that you haven't been able to match?'

'That's right. He's not in any database.'

I watched while his personal sky brightened a little. He gathered up pens and pencils and stood them upright in a mug. Tidying his desk helps him think. When he got as far as picking up paperclips he said, 'Tell me about the coverage for these decoys.'

'One detective across the street, in scuzzy clothes, with a shopping cart and a bag of aluminum cans, checking out the bushes. Another one half a block behind, walking with a limp and carrying a cane. A third guy in an unmarked car circling the block.'

'And I'll be in the old van,' Ray said, 'parked midway between the two teams, monitoring the radio and the phones.'

'So plenty of security,' I said. I began to list the electronic equipment we would need.

'Uh-huh.' Frank hadn't offered any encouragement, but he hadn't started the doubting stare either. Now, though, he said some discouraging words. 'The gear's not a problem, we've got all that stuff. I'm worried about the overtime.'

'Well, it's not too bad. These attacks have all been between six and nine o'clock, and always on a Friday night.'

'So a three-hour window?' Frank doodled on his desk pad. 'Times two teams, times four people on each team? And he doesn't hit every Friday night, hmmm? You might miss him once or twice.'

'But three or four Fridays in a row ought to do it,' I said.

'And all my guys have offered to trade out hours,' Ray said helpfully.

'Even if they do, it's work that doesn't get done on the day shift.'

'We'll make it up,' Andy said. He was following the plan I'd laid out for him, keeping quiet till we needed him to close the deal.

Frank swiveled his chair a few seconds, whistling tunelessly. When he dropped his pen he said, 'We can try it for two weekends, evaluate it the following week and decide if it's worth one more try.' He looked at us. 'What?'

I said, 'We were hoping to keep at it till we

got this guy.'

He rolled his chair back, putting more distance between us, and looked tragically at the ceiling. 'My budget's tight as a drum. We can't possibly do more than three nights. If that. You want to start this Friday?'

I looked at Ray. He said, 'If I can have Winnie.' Amy Nguyen has that nickname in the department because Frank had trouble with her last name when she started and kept calling her 'Ms Win'. A very small officer of Vietnamese origin who runs marathons and practices martial arts, she was our secret WMD for this plan. We had cackled gleefully over how abruptly the balance of terror would shift if The Sprinter tackled Winnie. 'She's on days, but she'll pull the extra hours if you OK it.'

'I'll put it through,' McCafferty said. He looked at his watch. 'Something else I was going to ask, what was it? Oh, yeah.' He swiveled his chair and fixed me in his laser-blue stare. 'What's happened to my POST list?'

'Coming soon.' I hadn't started it. POST stands for Peace Officers Standard Training. The schedule's due twice a year, one of those bureaucratic tasks that make me want to jump out the window.

'Get on it, will you? I need it yesterday.' Frank knows which jobs I hate, so he usually asks for one right after he's given me something I asked for. It's a hateful trick that works like a charm. He turned his bright stare on Ray Bailey next. 'Is Rosie OK with being the other decoy?'

Ray Bailey's wide mouth flattened out in a thin straight line, as close as he comes to smiling. 'I won't repeat what she said she'd do to me if I gave the job to anybody else.'

Three

Rosie bargained relentlessly for decoy turf. She wanted Ray to give her the route near the college where the last three attacks had gone down. Ray stood firm, insisting she take the sidewalks north of the hospital. He wanted to put Winnie in the area The Sprinter now seemed to prefer.

To get Rosie off his back and teach her some caution as well, Ray asked Winnie to take her to the gym for a couple of lessons in dodging. Winnie said she thought it was a little late in the game for that, but she would do what she could. Rosie came back chastened and quiet from the first session, with red curls sticking up all over her head, and stayed thoughtful all day. She must have been getting her brain around something though, because after the second lesson she was noisy and radiant, pushing all the chairs aside in the meeting room to show us how much she'd learned.

'Here's my Ninja Irish Devil-Girl move, see? Ha!' she shrieked, jumping sideways and planting a kick on Darrell's over-developed right deltoid.

'Hey, that hurt!' Darrell yelled. He was shocked; he's been pumping iron for years and it shows, so people ordinarily try to stay away from his shoulders. 'Do that again, I'll kick you back.'

'Ah, so you want to do battle with babe of steel, eh?' She danced around him, jabbering in some godawful slice-and-dice Oriental accent she'd dreamed up.

The other detectives stood around grinning and taunting her. 'Come on, kick him again,' Andy said, 'what are you afraid of?'

Clint chortled, 'Our money's on you to take this guy, Rosie.'

Bo Dooley poked his head out of his cubicle to see what the noise was about, then stood in his doorway, looking on in frozen disapproval. He's been Rutherford's vice officer for six years, had the same job in St Louis before he transferred up the river looking for a fresh start for his family. There was a tendency in the section to give him a wide berth; he was not a jolly man. His colleagues, behind his back, sometimes called him 'the drug czar'.

Watching him brood over Rosie's antics, I thought, Maybe he's been at it too long.

It didn't help that his personal life afforded no relief from his gritty job. He had waged a long, fierce struggle with his wife's cocaine habit. The last time she disappeared he told me he was filing for divorce. 'I can't let her do this to Nelly any more.' Nelly is his small daughter and for a while he seemed relieved to be raising her in peace. Lately I thought he looked jumpy and unsettled, and I wondered if that meant his wife had shown up again.

His appearance is offbeat, down-at-heel but somehow also elegant, carefully calibrated to be edgy but acceptable anywhere. Today he was wearing clean jeans, boots, and a black T-shirt under an ancient leather jacket. His ice-blue eyes met mine over the top of Rosie's capering shoulders and he shook his head minimally, half an inch each way. The diamond in his earring caught the light and flashed as he turned back into his office. Even allowing for how tight he's usually wrapped, his obvious disapproval of Rosie's assignment worried me some. Bo's not ordinarily a man to dodge a fight.

'Rosie,' I said, 'stand still a minute.'

She turned toward me. 'What?'

'Promise me you won't try to do anything heroic on this job.'

'Aw, come on, I'm just having a little fun with it. Why's everybody so glum? This stuff is very empowering! You want to see me break a chair with my hand?'

She knew I wouldn't say yes or she wouldn't have asked, I was pretty sure. But watching her frolic around like that made me wish I'd never heard of this sting. I asked her, 'You've been practicing your dodging like I told you, right? You and Winnie got your moves figured out so you won't get hurt?'

'We've been over it and over it,' Rosie said. 'I'm cool, Jake.'

'Winnie's good, huh? With this karate stuff?'

'Omigod.' She did one of those don't-ask wave-offs only women can do. 'You know what you guys should say if Amy Nguyen ever tells you to shove it? Ask her politely how far.'

Her male colleagues just grinned and went back to their desks, because it was not possible to imagine the impeccably discreet Amy Nguyen telling anybody to shove it.

The next day after our meeting, Frank McCafferty stopped by my office late afternoon. He jittered awkwardly in the doorway, blocking the light.

'Come in,' I said. 'Please.'

'No, well, um...' He kicked my doorsill. 'I just wanted to apologize for rushing you guys yesterday.'

'Oh ... no problem.'

He went right on as if I hadn't spoken. 'See, I've got this—' he flapped his hands impatiently – '*assignment* I took on ... It's a personal thing and I shouldn't even be messing with it at work but there's no other time. You know Owen Dowd?'

'The insurance guy? A little.'

'He was in my class in high school, we played football together. He's, uh ... he's dying.' Frank choked on the word.

'A young guy like that? Are you sure?'

'Yeah, he's got an inoperable brain tumor. They've done all they can with radiation and chemo but it's growing fast. He's rushing to settle his affairs while he can still talk. I went to see him and said, "What can I do for you?".' Frank wiped his mouth. 'I thought, you know, maybe somebody at the bank I could see, or ... but Owen said, "Wouldn't it be great if we could get our old team together one last time? I don't mean everybody, just the first team, those nine guys that always started, that championship year."'

'Nine?'

'Parochial school. Always short of boys, but they wanted us to play. They made up a league of nine-man teams.'

'Ah. So has Owen Dowd kept in touch with most of them?'

'Hell, no! I don't think we've ever talked about that team since we grew up and got married ... but something about his last days...' Frank shook his head mournfully. 'So, of course I said I'd do it. I mean, the man is dying, it's the least I can ... but it turns out Owen and I are the only ones that stayed in Rutherford! And, do you have any idea,' he asked me, looking desperate, 'how hard it is to find seven Americans who've moved an average of five times apiece since they left home after high school?'

'Is that what you were doing when we came in? I did think maybe I heard you yelling.'

'I bet you did, they probably heard me in Byron. I keep finding telephone numbers where they *used* to live. Even when you find a good number, getting them on the phone ... and then I start telling this guy who can't remember me at all that he was my good close buddy thirty years ago? They all think I'm trying to sell them insurance. I finally convince them we once played football together, I still have to persuade them to drop everything and get back here by the weekend after next.'

'Good thing you kept up your Toastmasters membership.'

'Tell me about it.' He scratched his cheeks. His allergies get aggravated when he's frustrated. 'They tell me they'd love to come see good old Owen, and then they tell me all the reasons why they can't possibly do that. I come back with how much we'll hate ourselves if we don't do this, and we negotiate from there. I spent the entire weekend on the phone! I think I've got four almost definite yeses. But the last three guys are the toughest. I didn't like those three much even when they were young and good-looking.' He gave a short, sharp bark of laughter. 'Anyway, I'm sorry if I was a little short with you when you're just trying to do your job.'

'Hey, not a problem, Frank.' I thought of telling him he was no ruder than usual, but his rash told me this was no time for black humor.

'How's your plan going?'

'Fine. Winnie's on board and Ray's rounding up the extra guys. I put a hold on the old van.'

'Rosie's going to be ready?'

'Getting extra training and totally psyched.'

'Good. Well, keep me in the loop.' His back looked a little stiff and awkward as he walked away. I was touched that he had put aside his middle-aged confrontation with mortality to come over here and offer extra support to his troops when he thought they might be feeling neglected. I remembered then that I had been kind of a putz with Kevin Evjan yesterday, and I got up and walked across the hall.

He was standing in his doorway fishing for the key to his office door. I said, 'You know the new guy on the support staff named John Smith?'

He raised his eyebrows. 'Is this a trick question?'

'No. Although he does look a little like a practical joke, come to think of it. Short round-shouldered guy who never got his teeth straightened? But LeeAnn says he's wicked smart.'

'And God knows LeeAnn is a keen judge of intellect,' Kevin said. 'You want me to fill up this smart lad's dance card, Jake?'

LeeAnn is our steno. She may not be Einstein but she notices the basics. When I asked her recently why she still takes her coffee breaks with the support staff she used to work with, she said, 'They're nicer than detectives.'

My good intentions were wilting fast, so I said quickly, 'John Smith is a particularly adept computer searcher. If you can put your devastating wit on hold for a few seconds I'll tell you how to get a few hours of his help.'

He opened and closed his mouth like a fish out of water and finally said, 'You can do that?'

'Sure. I'm your boss. I have powers I haven't even discussed with you. Also John Smith's supervisor owes me a favor.'

'And you're willing to spend it to please me?'

'No. Just to keep you off my back for the rest of the week.'

Kevin Evjan smiled radiantly and said, 'Isn't it wonderful how that works?'

We went out in the bullpen and made the deal, and Kevin wedged a tiny table and chair into the hall next to LeeAnn's desk. She helped him connect the new guy's laptop to her wireless router. Kevin brought her flowers and candy the next morning and said things that made her neck blush all the way down to wherever.

That whole week, Rosie practiced her duck-and-weave tricks and talked about Friday night. She asked Ray, what did the mugger seem to look for in a target? Should she strut? Wear high heels and a miniskirt?

'Rosie, it's March,' Ray said. 'Nighttime temps are in the twenties. Wear warm pants and boots – you'll be walking for hours.'

She's lived all her life in Minnesota so she gave in easy on the clothing issue. But then she started saying, 'Do I need to pimp my purse? What could I do to make it look rich?' By Thursday afternoon Ray had heard all of that he could stand, and told her to shut up about her purse or lose the assignment.

An hour later I saw Bo in Ray's office with the door closed. When we went over final details Friday morning, Ray told me Bo had made a last-ditch effort to persuade him to cancel the sting. When Ray turned him down, Bo requested assignment to the team guarding Rosie.

'Which I told him he already had. I put him there because I thought they've always worked well together. But this time he seems to think she's not taking it seriously enough and she's likely to get hurt if anything goes wrong.'

'How come he's so negative about this job? Rosie's looked after his drug snitches a couple of times while he was out of town and he always said she did fine.'

'I know. For some reason he's not on board with this one.'

'Well, he has to be. We need everybody we've got.' We were even borrowing detectives from Property Crimes for the first Friday night.

'Oh, he'll do his part, you know Bo. But there's something ... I don't know.'

'Please don't tell me he's having premonitions.' One haunted weirdo in the section was more than enough. My wolf had been back last night, but I was sure it was my personal life he was salivating over.

Ray looked amused. 'No, I don't see Bo with a Ouija board or any of that.'

I was sorely tempted to get in the van with Ray at six o'clock, but it was his show and my job was to stay out of it. I'm a supervisor and planner now, and we'd planned every detail of this operation till our lists were dog-eared. I went home and tried to work off my edge by fussing over Trudy.

'Sit here in the recliner,' I said. 'Put your feet up and tell me astounding facts about mitochondrial DNA while I cook.'

'OK,' she said, 'if you promise not to

explode. What ails you?'

'Nothing.'

'Sure. I always climb the walls too, when nothing's bothering me.'

'Well ... we've got this little sting going...' So instead of listening to her talk about her work I told her all about mine, while I grilled chops and potatoes and made a killer salad. Talking to Trudy while I cooked and we ate and I cleaned the kitchen helped a lot, but it only lasted till eight o'clock. After that I tried to give Trudy a foot massage, but she kept falling asleep sitting up so I had to put her to bed. I did some half-hearted channel surfing for an hour before I gave in and acknowledged my deep need to pace.

I had logged several miles of bedeviled in-house terrain by the time Ray called me at ten o'clock and crowed, 'Is this a great crew or what?'

Relief untangled a couple of knots in my lower intestine. 'It went OK, huh?'

'Never saw better teamwork.'

'The concealed mikes worked OK?'

'Perfect. And with those GPS units in the cell phones, Jake, oh, man, does that make life sweet for the tracker. I knew where everybody was every minute. We're definitely ready...' He came down off his high slightly. 'If only The Sprinter will show.'

'Never saw him tonight, huh?'

'Guess he took the night off.' He sighed.

'Well, we knew there was a chance of this. But listen...' He warmed up again. 'All the guys agreed Winnie and Rosie were perfect. God, Rosie had this fuzzy cap and gloves to match ... I gotta tell you, I almost wanted to jump her myself. If that mugger had seen her, no way he could've resisted.'

'That sweet, huh?' I'd been tense for so long, I was getting muscle cramps from the sudden relief. 'Well ... you're good to go again next week? You're just going to hang on to all the gear, right, keep everything ready?'

'Yeah, why set it up again?'

We'd been over and over all this, there was no need to say it again. But stress was still humming along my nerves, and Ray didn't seem to want to quit talking yet either. 'Remember next week I'm working the concert at the college,' I said.

'I won't forget. I've got your cell number on my pad in the van. You'll be over at the Fieldhouse, won't you? You won't see Winnie and her crew from there.'

'Nope. Few blocks away.'

'We'll call you, though. Well, we've got all week to go over this again, but ... you'll be the first to know when we grab that prick.'

'Let's hope. Nice work, Ray.'

'Thanks. Good night, Jake.'

I'd been pulling extra shifts as a rent-a-cop all winter for money to pay for the baby. It wasn't hard work, mostly providing security and crowd control for big sports and cultural events. It was a little unusual for the head of a section to get back into uniform and do scut work, but the chief was OK with it. He knew the baby had come along a little ahead of schedule while the repairs on the house were still keeping us broke. I hated leaving Trudy alone in the country, but she'd promised me she wouldn't go out the door for any reason.

'Why would I go out?' she said, 'so I can fall asleep in the yard?'

The Minneapolis Symphony concert was a week later. It's a big event in Rutherford, co-sponsored by the Community College and the Chamber of Commerce, and held in the Fieldhouse on campus. Casey and Ganz were the other two off-duty RPD officers working with me, in addition to several members of the regular campus cops. We were busy before the concert, keeping traffic unsnarled in front of the building and dealing with a shouting-match fender-bender. I moved into the lobby as the lights dimmed, to shush the last few season ticket holders who inevitably come late from three-martini dinners and want to keep talking all the way to their expensive seats down front.

Intermission brought a search for lost eyeglasses, the rescue of an early-Alzheimer's victim who went to the bathroom and forgot where he was, and a possible heart attack that the ambulance team downgraded to indigestion. It was a busy evening with a sold-out crowd, and I was glad to hear the last burst of applause and see the lights come up.

The crowd surged out as soon as the doors were open. Alpha drivers who have to be first out of the parking lot headed straight for their cars. Party animals and students drifted out more slowly, mellow and chatting about the music, deciding where to go for a drink. Watching the stragglers, I began to entertain happy thoughts about beer and a snack at home.

Against a background of crowd noise, I heard another sound, louder. It came again, a voice yelling, 'Officer? Over here!' A red-faced man in a classy overcoat, charcoal gray with a black velvet collar, was running toward me, waving his arms. When he was close enough I heard him call, 'A woman's been hurt! Can you ... she's right around the corner here...'

I paged Casey to come and take my spot, and trotted after the sweating red-faced man who was discovering how impractical it is to run in an overcoat. His hat was giving him trouble, too, bouncing off his head so he had to keep jamming it back. But we didn't have far to go. As we neared the end of the block on 14th Street, I saw there was a well-dressed woman waiting for him, and remembered them as the couple with aisle seats in row fourteen.

'She's right around here.' She pointed as I ran up to and then past her. I unsnapped the cover on my Glock and pulled my cell phone out of its holster on my belt. Rounding the corner on to 23rd Avenue, I could see, just ahead, a cluster of people gathered around something on the sidewalk. The crowd leaving the theater spilled left and right on to the frozen grass to get around the growing knot, which kept getting larger as more people got curious and stopped.

There's always an ambulance waiting in the parking lot at these big events. I speed-dialed it, and heard their siren start up within seconds. The group ahead of me broke apart briefly, and I saw the dark shape lying there. *Young female*, was all I got before the knot re-formed.

People turned to protest as I pushed through the close-packed shoulders. As soon as they saw the uniform though, they made way for me. I thought for the hundredth time how much easier detectives' lives would be if they'd put us back in the blue suit.

The woman on the sidewalk was lying on her right side, dressed in the virtual unisex uniform for Minnesota citizens in winter: down jacket, jeans and all-weather boots. Her head was bare and was terribly battered, her nose looked broken and her whole face was bloody; her long mousy hair, spilling over her shoulders and across her chest, was caked with blood. I looked around quickly for a purse. There was none in sight – could this be tonight's mugging scene? If so, for some reason The Sprinter had struck here instead of his usual six-block area farther south where Winnie's team was trolling.

I called Dispatch for back-up. Two squads rolled up in seconds, released from nearby streets where they were waiting to handle problems from post-concert traffic. The ambulance came screaming to the curb right behind them. One of the patrolmen went to work right away dispersing the crowd while the other, at my request, took charge of the scene so I could concentrate on the victim. The paramedics were quiet and quick, tried a defibrillator, shook their heads at me and said, 'We got a "No shock indicated" prompt. We're gonna transport.'

I looked around, asking, 'Where's the person who called me?'

'Right here,' he said, behind me.

'I need to stick with this woman,' I told him. 'I don't know who she is. But will you give your name and address to Officer Hanenberger here, so I can talk to you later?'

'Oh. Sure. Should I know your name?'

'He'll tell you – wait for me!' The paramedics had their patient loaded and were closing the doors.

'Get in then!'

'Hang on one sec till I mark where she was.'

I pulled my pen out of my shirt, but as I bent to the sidewalk the thin medic said, 'We gotta *go*!'

I made one quick swipe where the top of her head had been and hopped in the van. Rolling toward St Agnes, I called Casey to tell him where I'd gone. 'Will you go around the corner—' I described the location – 'and take over the scene from Hanenberger till I can get a detective there?'

'Yeah. OK. I'm working on the college's dime tonight, though, how do we—'

'Just keep track of your time and we'll sort it out Monday.'

I speed-dialed Ray to tell him he could call off the sting because I had the night's mugging victim with me in an ambulance.

Ray didn't answer. I tried Bo's phone, then Andy's. Nothing. What the hell? They'd all have their ringers off, but they should be able to hear the vibrators, working as quietly as they surely were. I tried Ray again.

He finally answered, sounding impatient, just as we were pulling up to the emergency entrance at St Agnes. 'Yeah, what?'

'I've been calling you for some time,' I said, 'to tell you that tonight's mugging happened a block from the concert and I'm taking the victim to St Agnes.'

There was a taut little pause filled with ragged breathing. 'Well, that's goddamned odd,' Ray finally said, 'because Rosie just got creamed a block from St Agnes and we've got The Sprinter over here.'

Four

The paramedic with the shaved head took the driver's seat. I began to wonder if he had some kind of death wish himself, as he careened through stoplights with his siren screaming. He drove on the sidewalk, he drove in the median strip, and he warped around sharp corners without slowing down.

His sandy-haired partner, hips planted firmly on a stool, talked quietly into a headset to somebody back at base while he secured the inert body to the gurney with straps. Without a pause in the conversation, he tried for a blood pressure reading and shook his head, lifted her eyelids and shined a light in her eyes, tried his defibrillator and shook his head again, all as calmly as if we were parked at the curb.

Huddled in a corner to stay out of his way, I got only brief glimpses of the victim. It was hard to judge her looks under so much blood – youngish, I thought, and plain. Her head wounds appeared extensive and had bled a great deal but didn't seem to be bleeding now. Was that a good sign or a bad one? She was utterly still, I couldn't see if she was breathing.

It's strange how fast you get invested in a person you're trying to help. It bothered me that her eyelids were half-closed and her eyes had rolled up in their sockets. I watched her pale face, willing her eyes to roll back down and look at me, but they stayed where they were, only the bottom sliver of her irises showing. Now that I had time for a better look, I saw bruises and a bad scrape on her bare arm. But her hand had no broken nails and it was clean – it didn't look like a hand that had been in a fight.

Three people in green scrubs ran out of the Emergency entrance at St Agnes as we pulled up. They unloaded my still-unconscious victim and rolled her inside while the sandy-haired paramedic ran alongside, yelling stats at them. I followed as close behind as I could, trying to stay out of the way without losing them.

Ahead of us in the hall I saw Rosie Doyle's red curls, bright against the pillow of another gurney. She was talking to the attendants and to Bo Dooley, who was hurrying along behind her. I spend a lot of time trying to get Rosie to shut up, but at that moment I was very glad to hear her voice.

Both patients got wheeled into curtained cubicles by medics who told us to wait outside. Standing beside me in the makeshift hall, Bo said, 'Well, that didn't go quite according to plan.'

'Rosie forgot to duck?'

'She didn't forget, but she wasn't quick enough. And she was dodging when she got hit, so she was off balance and she went down hard.' His jaw muscles jumped. 'Her head hit the sidewalk with a helluva crack, I could hear it clear across the street.'

'But you got The Sprinter.'

'Oh, yeah. Damn near skinned him doing it.' His smile glinted briefly. 'I was going so fast when I hit him, he slid along the sidewalk about five feet with me on top. Soon as I got up, Andy jumped on him. One good way to put out a guy's fire, I guess, have Andy sit on him. He's been pretty quiet ever since.'

'Is Andy taking him in?'

'Yeah. Darrell's got the scene and Ray stayed to help him.'

'So what kind of a predator have we got?'

'Wait till you see him, Jake.' He shook his head the way he does, a fraction of an inch each way with his eyes on the middle distance. 'You will not believe how sweet and innocent he looks.'

'What's that mean? No tattoos?'

'Well, yeah, and pink skin and big blue eyes like a Gerber baby.'

'Wow. You're in love, huh? Anybody you know?'

'Never saw him before. And I have a hunch when we run him, we're gonna come up empty.'

'Oh, yeah? What, uh…'

'The way he acted while we were getting him ready to transport. When I told him to put his hands together behind his back, he put his palms together. Any con knows to do it back-to-back. I don't think he's ever been arrested before.'

'Well, now. Remember that DNA we got at an earlier scene? We never could match that. So maybe this little virgin is our guy.'

'Maybe. Ray's convinced the same guy's doing all these snatches, isn't he? Hard to believe it could be this kid.'

A doctor with a stethoscope stepped out of Rosie's curtained space and we hurried toward him.

'Her eyes are tracking and her speech is not slurred; she can count backward by fives and she remembers her phone number and her mother's maiden name. That's a good-size bump, though, so I'm sending her upstairs for X-rays and probably a scan.'

'She'll stay overnight, then,' I said.

'All weekend, I expect,' he said. 'She's going to have a very stiff neck by morning and we'll see what else. Monday morning we'll decide if we need to do more testing.'

We went inside the cubicle. Rosie was lying flat on a hard little pillow, white-faced with all her freckles showing. She gave me a sheepish smile and said, 'I blew it, Jake, I'm sorry.'

'No, you didn't. The bad guy's in jail. I'm sorry about your goose egg, though.' She looked understandably shaken but undaunted, kind of pleased with herself, actually. I thought she was getting off on the excitement. 'The doc says you can count backward by fives, when did you learn to do that?'

She managed a fairly respectable laugh, better than the joke deserved, and then looked directly at Bo and said, 'My eyes are working right, I can talk, I remember everything. I'm fine.'

'Good.' He was watching her carefully in that coiled way he has.

'I remember *exactly* how he hit me, I'm going to nail this guy in court, Bo.'

'Right.' Bo is never easy to read and today Rosie's behavior was almost as puzzling. They seemed to be settling some argument I didn't understand.

There was a commotion in the hall, the curtain was pulled aside and Amy Nguyen stood there, with Clint Maddox and two other detectives from the second decoy team. 'Oh, Rosie, you hurt?' they all began asking, crowding around her bedside. 'Babe, what happened?'

I eased out of the press of bodies and went back along the crowded hall to the cubicle where my victim had disappeared. I heard someone moving inside, opened the corner of the drape and nearly collided with a pale, fragile-looking young woman in a white coat. Her nameplate read, paradoxically, 'Dr Strong' and her expression said she had no good news.

I held up my shield. 'Hines. I brought her in. How's she doing?'

'Your victim's DOA, detective. Come in here, will you? I need some answers.'

The next couple of hours were filled with the gritty, methodical routine that follows an unexplained death. I woke the coroner out of what must have been a beautiful deep sleep, waited through grunts and snorts and the noise of several items getting knocked over, and finally heard him say, 'Yah?' His name, Adrian Pokornoskovic, is so hard to say that everybody in the department calls him Pokey. He's a dermatologist who's on call to sign death certificates, because Hampstead County's tax base is still not quite large enough for a full-time coroner. Mostly, Pokey signs death certificates for old people who die of natural causes in their beds. The low rate of death by misadventure in Southeast Minnesota only affords him four or five homicides a year to work on, but he loves forensic science so he keeps up.

'Pokey,' I said, 'I have a Jane Doe at St Agnes, Doc Strong says—'

'Right there,' he said, and the phone went dead. He's not a schmoozer.

While I waited for him I called Ray Bailey, who was still working with Darrell at the mugging scene. I asked him to transfer his attention to the crime scene on 23rd Avenue. 'My victim's been declared DOA, so ... huh? Yeah, just now. And as far as I know nobody saw her get hit, so the scene is all we've got.'

'Yeah, I guess ... Darrell can handle the rest of this, sure. How's Rosie?'

'They think she's OK, but they're keeping her in for tests.'

'What does she say? Can she talk?'

'Oh, hell yes, you know Rosie, she's already planning her testimony at the trial. But listen, can you get over to 23rd Avenue ASAP and secure the scene? Casey's there, but he doesn't have any crime scene gear on him.'

'You're going to call BCA, right?'

'Sure, right away. But I'm worried about securing the scene. I only had time to make one little mark on the sidewalk where her head was. I never saw any blood there but there must be some, will you take a good look?'

Ray said, 'I'm on it,' and was gone.

I hit the speed-dial for BCA. A sweet-voiced woman who said her name was Elaine asked me to hold, please. I ground my teeth through several Seventies tunes. Elaine finally came back and took all my information before she said, 'Both our crews are out, and I have three requests ahead of you. So I'll let you know when to expect us.'

'I have an unidentified body and no eyewitnesses,' I pleaded. 'There might be some fingerprints, just possibly DNA evidence if we can pick up a few drops of blood, that's all I've got to go on.'

'I feel your pain,' she said, 'but it's Friday night up here too ... I'll call when I know.' I thanked her politely, because as Trudy often reminds me, the people who work those long night shifts at BCA get yelled at a lot. It's not written down any place and won't ever be, but it's reasonable to hope a little courtesy might get you a boost in the queue.

The rest of the night was basically a phone-tag marathon with email sprints. Ray's elaborate plan for the night's work had to be turned on a dime and most of his crew reassigned. When the dust settled Andy was booking the prisoner, Darrell was folding up the mugging scene by the hospital and going in to write up the report, and Ray was at the new crime scene near the college, with the rest of his crew on the way to join him.

Not wanting to wake Trudy if she was already asleep, I sent her a text message, 'Working late, see you in the morning.' If she woke up, she wouldn't have to wonder. One part of me wanted to be with her 24/7 now; disaster scenarios swirled around my ears every time I slowed down for a minute. Soon as the coroner gets here, I promised myself, I'll go home.

Then Ray called me to say the wind was rising and the temperature had just dropped ten degrees. 'There's a storm's coming in fast,' he said. 'In a couple of hours, everything that hasn't blown away here is going to be covered in snow.'

'I hear you,' I said. 'I'm going to try to find Ollie Green, get him to take samples of that blood on the sidewalk and maybe lift some prints for us, at least.' Another firestorm of phoning began. Ollie's wife said he was at his dad's house. I tracked him from there to an uncle's pinochle game and on to beer at the Elk's Lodge.

By the time I called Ray to tell him Ollie was on his way, Ray said, 'Good. Clint Maddox is here now taking pictures and Bo's walking a grid around the scene.' I turned and saw Pokey coming through the ER door carrying his little brown bag. My phone rang as I went to meet him but I let it take a message.

I was in police work before we all had cell phones, but sometimes now I wonder, how did we do that? It seems to me I live with the damn thing pasted to my ear.

A big cloud of trash and dirt blew through

the door with Pokey; he strode out of it pulling off his red watch cap and muttering, 'Shee, some Spring weather.' He missed about ten years of hot lunches during his formative years in the Soviet Union, so he's not a big guy. A year-long walk across Europe honed his survival instincts and made him an expert at sleeping in culverts and haystacks. Not skills he gets to use much any more, he recently remarked. He's canny, quick and dubious of all authority.

'Very glad to see you,' I said. 'I've got a Jane Doe here with a head wound and no eyewitnesses.'

'Oh, yeah?' He got his foxy look on. He enjoys puzzle-solving.

He was only in the curtained cubicle with my victim for a couple of minutes before he stuck his head out and said, 'What doctor called this?'

'Her name's Strong. Shall I—'

'I'll find her,' he said, and went out to the desk. When he came back he stood looking down on the drab face of the victim. 'You saw her fall down?'

'No, but...' I told him about the man calling me away from the concert. 'He said she'd just been hit, another man saw her right after the attack. And I got to her within two minutes after he called me.'

'So ... this time *you* gonna give *me* time of death, huh?' He's been a US citizen long enough to get a medical degree, a wife and a nice house, but he still doesn't see much need for articles before nouns.

'Ten thirty. Maybe five ... *possibly* ten minutes before.'

'Mmm.' He looked at his thermometer, thought a while, and said, 'Huh. Don't seem right...' He brooded over the facial wounds, glanced at his watch. Looking up after a minute, he seemed surprised I was still there. 'How come you're back in uniform? You get demoted?'

'No.' I told him about the baby fund.

'Ah, yah, is pretty soon, huh? Trudy OK?'

'Hugely successful, as they say.'

He chuckled. 'McCafferty OK with you moonlighting?'

'Oh, he's fine with that. What he doesn't like is me mixing into investigations the way I'm doing now. I keep promising him I'll stay in the office and supervise, but then ten things happen at once and I get sucked back out on the street.'

Dr Strong walked up to us and said, 'Yes, Pokey?' The two of them went back into the curtained space and held a murmured dialog, peering at the wounds, holding the dead girl's fingertips, musing over the thermometer. They reached some kind of consensus, Dr Strong left and Pokey began packing his gear.

When he came out I asked him, 'Will you

let Ray Bailey know when the autopsy's scheduled?'

'Sure.' He snapped his bag shut. 'Man who found this girl – you got his name?'

'One of our officers has it, yes. Why?'

'Better talk to him again.'

'OK. And ask him what?'

'Make him tell whole story again, everything he saw. This body don't match your story.'

'In what way?'

'Wounds all two to three hours old, quit bleeding some time ago. Temperature's ninety-two degrees. Doc Strong agrees, this woman been dead a while.'

Five

I drove north from St Agnes through worsening weather. A booming wind was knocking over trashcans and redistributing dog dishes and bird feeders amongst neighbors. At Broadway, when I should have turned north to head home, I said, 'Oh, hell...' and drove east, instead, to the crime scene. By now, I knew, Trudy would be asleep. I was awake and curious, and my questions were all focused on the campus.

Ray had set up major illumination on the sidewalk where I'd found Jane Doe. His lights flamed up intermittently through the wind-whipped branches of the lofty campus trees, and bounced off the low-hanging clouds. I drove toward the eerie overhead light show and found my crew beneath it.

Two uniforms were stringing flapping crime scene tape in a wide circle. Inside it, Ray had set up two banks of halogen lamps powered by gas-fired generators. Within that circle of punishing super-white illumination, Ollie Green, red-faced and miserable, swabbed samples off the sidewalk. Besides grit and garbage, the gusty wind was beginning to carry stinging sleet. Ray knelt facing Ollie, holding his extra slides and a flashlight.

I hurried over, knelt down beside Ray, and said, 'Here, I'll hold the light.' The two of us sheltered Ollie as he swabbed anonymous-looking dirt and slime off the sidewalk and transferred it carefully on to slides.

'I don't see any blood,' I said.

'We haven't been able to find any,' Ray said. 'Here, shine your light over here.' He pointed down at the ground. 'This is your mark on the sidewalk, isn't it?'

'Looks like it.' I checked the landmarks. Bushes all along the sidewalk, parking lot behind them ... fire hydrant a few steps away, light pole on the corner. 'Yeah, this is where I was. For sure.'

'OK, well, there's no blood here.'

'Tell you the truth I never saw any on the ground either. Which is very surprising because there sure as hell was plenty on her.'

'Right. Strange. So we figured we better try to get some DNA. We're just going on faith that there must be some in this mess, though. And fingerprints...' He squinted as a gust blew dirt in his eyes. 'Probably out of the question. This wind is getting crazy. You hear anything more from BCA?'

'No. I'll call them again.' I sat through another musak concert. When Elaine finally answered I asked her, 'How's Rutherford doing in the queue?'

'You're next in line now, but hang on, I think...' She was off the line through several choruses of 'I'll Give You a Daisy, a Daisy'. When she came back she said, 'That's what I was afraid of, the weather's shutting us down for a while.'

'What weather? It's just spitting a little sleet here.'

'We're getting dumped on. Heavy snow and wind, visibility down to *nada*. Straight down from the pole, probably heading your way.'

'Swell. Will you call us when you're back in business?'

'The minute we're rolling. You'll be at the head of the line then.'

'Thanks.' I told Ray, 'BCA's grounded for a while. We're going to have to do this first part the old-fashioned way.'

'OK. Damn, though, we still don't know who she is, do we?'

Footsteps came fast along the sidewalk and Clint Maddox stepped between us and the lights. His sparse ginger hair and all-over freckles look the same day or night, in any weather. Even in a blizzard, he's a reliably tidy, cheerfully nondescript man. People used to say he looked like Alfred E. Neuman on the cover of *Mad* magazine, but he seems to be aging his way out of that. Now he just looks like the kind of a guy you'd buy a used car from at whatever price he said was fair. 'Maybe we just caught a break here, guys. I found this in the parking lot.' He held it up under the hot halogen lights, a purse made of some dark synthetic fabric.

'Have you opened it?'

'No.'

Ray stood up and said, 'Go ahead.'

I got up and watched too as Clint opened it. 'Whoo-ee.' His triumphant grin flashed in the weird light. 'Jackpot!'

'Wallet and everything,' Ray said softly. 'I don't believe it.'

'I thought this was a purse-snatching,' I said. 'Is there money in the wallet?'

He opened it. 'Eighteen dollars.'

'Cards, too?'

'Full set. Driver's license. Geraldine Lovejoy,' he read. 'Library card, Visa, Master Card ... voter registration, too.'

He held the wallet up under the light with the cards turned to the driver's license. 'Does this look like the woman you found?'

The picture showed a plain, pale girl with no-color hair hanging straight from a left-side part.

'Could be. Yeah.'

'You got an evidence tag handy?' Clint Maddox asked. He was fixated on getting his find recorded.

'What?' Ray looked distracted. 'Oh. Here.' A huge gust of wind made him clutch the card against his chest. When the wind died for a minute, snow began to fall.

'We can't be sure this is our victim's purse,' I said.

Ray said, 'You said it looked like—'

'A lot of girls look like that.' For some reason, I didn't want to give up the idea that I had transported a second mugging victim to the hospital.

'Anybody else lost a purse like this they'd be down here looking for it.'

Standing like a stork with his back to the wind, Clint Maddox was writing the evidence ticket against his knee. 'What kind of material would you say that purse is made out of?'

'Synthetic of some kind. Just put the tag in this bag, we're not going to close it up yet.'

Bo trotted into the circle of light. 'Trash is blowing all over hell down there,' Clint said. 'We better think about winding this up.'

'Wait a minute,' Ray said. 'Now we know she's got a driver's license, she must have a car parked around here close. Anything in the lot?'

'No,' Bo said. 'This lot closes at eleven. The attendant's window's dark, there's a chain across the entrance.'

'There aren't any stragglers left inside?'

'Nope. We already checked that.'

'OK, well ... any other cars you can find parked in the area, I guess, write down their license numbers and I'll check them.'

'I'll take a look.' Bo disappeared into the dark.

'Damn, I found that purse just in time, this damn storm's taking everything to Iowa,' Clint said. 'I'll take one more look soon's I finish this, but then that's going to have to be it, I think, don't you, Ray?'

'We'll see what the weather does.' As if to show him, a punishing gust tore the evidence tag out of Maddox's hands and sent it aloft. Cursing, he watched it disappear above the lights.

Ray found him a replacement and stood thoughtfully pulling his nose. 'It's funny, you know,' he said, 'this is the first time we ever found a purse.'

'Makes you think it might be a different mugger,' I said.

'A mugger who's not after purses? Ollie—' he peered into the dark – 'you there?'

'Over here by my car. Putting my kit away,' Ollie said, sounding defensive. He stepped back into our ring of light reluctantly. 'Whaddya want?'

'Will you leave me a list of the samples you took tonight, so I can make sure BCA takes them all along? If they ever do get down here.' Behind his back, Ollie's eyes rolled in silent protest. Ray noticed his silence and turned sharply toward him. 'What's your problem? Were you planning to sleep tonight or something?'

'It's not that. I ran out on my dad's surprise birthday party, I was supposed to help my wife ... never mind. She's a grown-up, she'll manage.'

'Attaboy,' Ray said, trying to sound as if he meant it. He'd been working on people skills lately, since some of his crew stormed my office threatening to revolt. A bachelor who gets tunnel vision when he's working a case, he finds it incredible that people would sometimes rather think about their personal lives than his investigation.

'OK, well, I'm outa here, then,' Ollie said. He walked toward the row of cars circling the scene. His lights briefly added to our near-daytime effect before they turned away.

'Let's get in Casey's squad,' I said. 'I'll run this license while you go through the purse.' When we were out of the wind Ray laid a paper evidence bag on his lap and began taking items out of the purse one by one, looking at them carefully and listing them in one of the tiny pocket notebooks he favors for fieldwork. He doesn't give a damn how many PalmPilots or other clever electronic devices come on the market; he likes to write it his way, in tiny script only he can read. It's not code; it's just illegible.

The laptop lit up with the result of my search: the license was current and had no warrants against it.

'Damn,' Ray said. 'I was hoping she'd have at least a traffic violation and I might get a phone number.'

'You'd have to go to this address in person anyway,' I said. 'What if she lives with somebody? You'll be delivering a death notice. You can't do that on the phone.'

'Right. What time is it? Just after two. I'd like to wait till BCA gets here...' He checked downtown for missing persons reports and got nothing. 'OK. So she lives alone or with somebody who's unconcerned.'

'Or just a sound sleeper.'

'Or out of town, or – maybe I'll take Clint and go there next. Time I turned you loose, anyway.'

'You're not holding me.'

'Before you go, though, tell me again how you found this woman.'

I told him about the man in the overcoat running toward me and then leading me around the corner to the woman on the sidewalk. 'There were people crowded around everywhere because of the concert. But the squads came right away to control them and the paramedics were right there in the parking lot, so – in spite of all the interference we were loaded up and rolling in about three minutes. I called you a couple of times to tell you I had a mugging victim and by the time you answered we were both in front of the hospital.'

'You get the name of the man in the overcoat?'

'There wasn't time. But he said he'd leave his name and address – wait, here's Casey, maybe he's got it.'

'You ready to turn me loose?' Casey asked, stooping by Ray's open window. 'I'm about due for piss call and coffee.'

'OK,' Ray said. 'Did the guy in the good coat leave his name and address with you?'

'Oh. Yeah. Here.' He had to search every pocket in his uniform to find it. 'This guy was really caught up in the excitement. He wanted to get right on the stand and testify to something.' Casey laughed. 'He said, "Tell them to feel free to call me at any hour. I'm a light sleeper at all times and I probably won't sleep a wink tonight."'

I took the paper. 'Thanks. You want your squad?'

'Well, duh, yeah.'

After we switched all our stuff into the squad belonging to a uniform named Eberly, I sat looking at the paper in my hand. 'I suppose it's too late...'

Ray shrugged. 'He said any time, why not take him up on it?'

I dialed the number. The first ring was cut short by a man's voice. 'Quigley.'

'This is Captain Jake Hines, Mr Quigley.'

'Oh, yes. Um ... how's it going?'

'OK. I'm sorry to call so late, but—'

'That's quite all right. I want to help in any way I can. It's all right, Dodie,' he said, away from the phone, 'it's the police.' He was having a wonderful time, taking part in what he knew would be a front-page story in tomorrow's paper.

'We'd like to find the man you found bending over the victim. Did he tell you his name?'

'No. And I never thought to ask. It was only those few seconds, and then he told me the woman had been attacked and I turned and ran, you know, to get help.'

'I understand. He said it in those words, did he? "She's been attacked"?'

'Uhh ... something like that, yes.'

'Did he say he saw her get attacked?'

'No ... I don't think so.'

'But your impression was that she had just fallen on to the ground right then?'

'That's what I thought he was telling me, yes.'

'What can you remember about the man?'

'Well really, almost nothing, I'm afraid. I expected to see him there waiting for me when I got back, of course, but you remember there were all those people by then. Dodie said – Dodie's my wife – she said as soon as I was gone the man who'd asked us to help jumped in his car and drove away.'

'What kind of car?'

'I have no idea.'

'Would she know?'

'Trust me, no.'

'The man, was he young, old?'

'Quite young, I think. Though I didn't really see his face. But the way he moved—'

'OK. Big or small?'

'Mmmm ... medium.'

'Light or dark?'

'I never saw his hair. Or much of his face, really, he had on a hood—'

'A parka?'

'Yes. And dark glasses, that's the one odd thing I remember, it was dark but he still had on dark glasses.'

'Anything else about how he was dressed?'

'Just ordinary ... what all the young people wear, I guess. Sweat pants and running shoes.'

Six

Ray and I sat in Eberly's squad, watching the world turn white. It was snowing hard and because of the chaotic wind the snow could not settle. It all kept blowing around; the visibility, for a few minutes, was close to zero. I thought I heard a car go by and pause at the end of the block, but the sound was so distorted by the storm I couldn't be sure.

'It doesn't prove anything,' Ray said.

'True. Right now I'm a little loony-tunes on the subject of running gear.'

'Tell me about it. All of a sudden it's everywhere.'

'But it's odd that he was supposedly so concerned and then didn't wait.'

'Yeah. You think your testifying man made him up?'

'And did the lady himself? With his nicely dressed wife helping? Why would he look for a cop to lead back to the body?'

'He wouldn't,' Ray said, 'but none of this makes any sense, so far.'

'In case you do find somebody home at Geraldine's address, by the way, you better have somebody along who can stay and help.'

'I will. I'm working on a list of questions, too ... we want family members, an employer, what else?'

'Friends, enemies, habits, vices, charities ... anything and everything, if you find a talker. What?' Eberly had just opened the door on his side.

'Nothing much more we can do here in this snow, right? Dispatch is screamin' at me about calls stacking up.'

'Yeah. This your squad? Here you go.'

We both got out. As Eberly pulled away Ray asked me, 'Don't you need to get going too?'

'Yeah, I guess I broke enough rules for one night. Let's see, we got The Sprinter on a Friday, didn't we? Damn, you'll have to find a judge tomorrow.' Minnesota gives us forty-eight hours to decide to charge a prisoner or let him go. It probably seems like a long time to the person in the pokey, but it's inconveniently short for the officer making an arrest on Friday night.

'Yeah, we'll need a warrant signed. Buzz Cooper's on duty tomorrow, I'll get him to find a judge. Depending on the storm and what I find at the victim's address, tomorrow I'll either be talking to the victim's family or maybe still waiting for BCA.'

'If you ... uh, find any time...'

'I'll call you later. Or Sunday. When I know some things.'

'Whatever you can do.'

For the first five minutes of the trip home, I wished myself back at the crime scene. Then I was suddenly so tired I was scared to be driving. The storm seemed heavier and wilder out in the country. The last five miles, the wipers couldn't keep up and I drove part of the time with my head out the window. Snow pelted my cheeks and eyeballs like icy needles, which at least made it easier to stay awake.

Trudy was propped up on four pillows, sleeping soundly, so I didn't have to explain why I had icicles in my eyebrows.

She didn't seem to wake up when I eased my cold body into bed, careful not to touch her. But somehow she must have known I got home very late, because it was almost noon when she nudged my elbow and said brunch was ready. The sun was high and bright; snowmelt was running down the driveway and the barn roof was steaming.

Eggs and bacon tasted so good they made my eyes water. After a third coffee I did the dishes while she sat in the rocker folding clothes. We reviewed, once again, plans for getting her to Rutherford from wherever she was when she got ready to give birth.

'You feel like it's close?' I asked her.

'I feel exactly the same as I have every day

for a month. Fat and serene. The doctor says it could be any time now, but probably a week to ten days. Come here. Bend down.' She kissed me. 'Don't look so anxious. Everything's going to be fine.'

'I know.' But I didn't. During last night's heavy sleep, the wolf had slunk along the edge of several dreams. Once he was wearing a well-tailored chesterfield overcoat and light gray fedora. So right now I longed to carry Trudy off to Methodist Hospital and demand an immediate Caesarian section, insist they get that baby out of there and wrapped up warm while I stood guard at the door with my loaded Glock in my hands. I was suffering from two equal and opposite convictions: that I'd get locked up for a certified crazy person if I told people what I was thinking, and that I'd never forgive myself if my premonitions came true and I could have saved my wife and child.

Ray called while I was washing the frying pan. He reported that shortly after six a.m. he had found the door of 4A at the rental eight-plex listed on Geraldine Lovejoy's license, and that his knock was answered by a sleepy young man who said his name was Curtis Brill.

'Claims to be her fiancé,' Ray said. 'I had to tell him the story three times. He went into some kind of deep denial, kept shaking his head and saying no, it couldn't be. Even after I showed him the driver's license we found, he insisted there must be some mistake, why would anything happen to Gerry?'

'Just like that, that's what he said?'

'That's exactly what he said.'

'Huh. Well, you think he's our guy?'

'Off the top? I don't think so, but there's something ... he's a little different.'

'Different how?'

'Well ... after he went back in their apartment and convinced himself she wasn't home, he made me tell the story over again and that time he somehow was able to accept that she was really dead. He started to cry and ... you don't often see a man lose it like that, Jake, he bawled like a baby. Stood right there in his open doorway with the radiators clanking away, and just rained on me for ten minutes.'

'So ... an emotional guy.'

'More than that. He kept saying something like, "I thought I'd prayed enough."'

'Ah.'

'I know. Odd thing to say. But it wasn't quite ... it didn't seem like that kind of guilt. You know how guys, if they really did the crime, they'll try to get you to say the time of death and then start talking right away about where they were, who they were with? He didn't do any of that. Just kind of ... melted down.'

'Survivor's guilt, maybe? Or do you think

he knows he could have prevented her death?'

'Maybe. Hard to say.'

I began to feel a certain amount of sympathy for Curtis Brill. 'Did he say where he thought she was all night?'

'She was supposed to be in Advanced Accounting 253, in the Hugh Fisher building, for a two-hour class that started at eight p.m. He expected her home about ten thirty. Normally he'd wait up, he said, but he'd worked hard on a sermon all evening, he had a heavy schedule of church work and study all day, I'm quoting him here, so when he started to nod off he went to bed. He thought he'd wake up when she came in. Next thing he knew it was six a.m. and I was knocking on his door.'

'So he was alone all night?'

'So he says.'

'So you've got a live-in boyfriend with no alibi?'

'That's right, but...' He breathed into the phone a while. I knew how he'd look, his eyebrows in a straight line across his stern face.

'But his story sounds credible to you, huh?'

'Yeah. He'd have to be one hell of an actor to fake that much shock ... I had to go over the story three times before he'd believe she was dead. And his story about where she was is believable ... the Fisher building he mentioned is right across the street from that sidewalk where you found her body. We can check her class registration on Monday, of course, and why would he lie when he knows we can do that? What I can't figure out is why her car wasn't in the parking lot that's right there, across the hedge from the sidewalk where you found her.'

'Yeah, that's odd. I suppose it could have been full when she got there. Well – you get the names of any other family members?'

'Geraldine's mother. She lives in Dover, works in Rutherford. Curtis didn't seem to feel up to telling her, so I called the sheriff's office after I talked to him, gave them the information and got them to promise they'd deliver it in person, stay with the mother, see if she needs any help, give her my number. She called me a few minutes later, arranged to come in and identify the body. I went with her. She was devastated, but she didn't faint or anything. She's a very sturdy type.'

'She give you anything to go on?'

'Not really. There's a sister, out of town, she'll be in to see us Monday. The three women seem to be tight. Mother doesn't seem to feel friendly toward the boyfriend, but it doesn't seem to be open warfare so far.'

'But maybe there's a wedge there?'

'Yeah, I think there's a lot more everybody wants to say.'

'OK. BCA ever arrive?'

'About daybreak. Searched the scene, did not find anything we missed, but tried some swabs for DNA at the locations we'd marked. They took all our physical evidence. After it got light Bo made one more sweep of the parking lot and the hedge all the way to the end of the block, but he never found any car keys. And we still don't know where the car is.'

'The boyfriend doesn't have it?'

'No. He was adamant that she drove it to class.'

'Maybe the concert filled up all the lots?'

'Maybe. I put it in BOLOs, so the day shift will look for it.'

Hearing how his voice slurred on the last few words, I asked him, 'Ray, have you had any sleep at all?'

'No. Heading home pretty soon.'

'Do that, will you? Right away? Maybe you should get a squad to drive you.'

'I'm OK. Going to be a lot happening Monday, can you—'

'I'll be available. Go home. You're a hazard to everybody around you now, you hear me? Go home.'

'Guess you're right. See you Monday.'

The People Crimes end of the hall sounded like a schoolyard fight Monday morning, everybody trying to tell his version of Friday night's events. I carried my coffee toward the noise as Ray walked out of his office, looking none the worse for his thirty-six hour shift. In fact he seemed stronger than usual, striding to the head of the conference table, yelling, 'Get your notes and sit down! Everybody, right now!'

It was an unusually assertive move for Ray and it worked. When they were all at the table he said, 'We need to review Friday night so we're all on the same page. But we've got to do it fast, we've got two jobs for every hour available today. Turn off your phones, we don't need any interruptions. LeeAnn, any calls, take messages. I'm going to keep this chronological, so shut up till I call on you, and hold comments till later.'

They all looked at him wall-eyed. Usually Ray kept a low profile, almost as quiet as Bo.

To Clint Maddox and the other two detectives who'd been on Winnie's team he said, 'You're clear on what happened with Rosie's team, right? That we got The Sprinter but Rosie got hurt?' They all nodded. 'Then three things happened at once. Bo helped Rosie get to the hospital, Andy took The Sprinter to jail, and Jake called me and said he was coming in with the night's mugging victim. We'll start there. Bo, you go first, how's Rosie?'

'Initial diagnosis was no serious injury, but because of the bump on her head they kept her over the weekend for more tests. She tried hard yesterday to get released, but the docs said no way, she still had some blurred vision.'

'They seem pretty worried?'

'No. But I thought if she got feeling a little better she might just bully her way out of there, so I called her dad. He came up with the brothers and told her to put a sock in it. Them, she listens to.'

I searched his face for some clue to what had brought him out of his emotional ice cave far enough to visit a colleague in the hospital on a Sunday. But he had resumed his normal expression, which is somewhere between super-chilled and flash-frozen.

Ray, for some reason, seemed to think it was Bo's job to stay on Rosie's case. 'Fine, keep us informed. Andy, you next. You booked The Sprinter, what's his name?'

'Jason Wells.'

'What did he have to say?'

'"I want a lawyer,"' Andy said. 'Those are the only words he seems to know.'

Ray frowned. 'Did he call one?'

'Not while I was there. Just kept saying he wouldn't talk till he got one – he knew his rights.'

'Bet he does. You ask him if he's got a partner, if he was getting picked up after his heists?'

'I asked. He wouldn't say. He wouldn't

even say—' Andy looked amused – 'his name and address. He said, "I have the right to remain silent and that's what I'm doing." I guess he thought he was going to be allowed to remain anonymous. We took his clothes off and found his wallet, which was damn near empty but did have a driver's license. He said, "What about my right to privacy?" He's really a piece of work.'

'You run his prints through MINCIS yet?'

'Yup. Got zippo, so I sent an inquiry through the juvenile system ... he's only nineteen, I thought maybe ... but *nada*. This is his first arrest in Minnesota.'

'You find out how long he's lived here?'

'I asked. He wouldn't say. He wants a lawyer.'

'Yeah, well, he'll get one this afternoon when you take him to court. He got any family?' As soon as the words left his mouth he realized he knew the answer, and said, with Andy, 'Didn't say.'

They laughed together, briefly, and Andy said, 'Soon as we're done here I thought I'd go see if there's anybody home at the address on his driver's license. It's a mobile home park out past the airport. I called a couple of times but didn't get any answer.'

'OK. And you're working on school and medical records, right?' Ray frowned. 'He's quite a slugger, huh? For one so young and inexperienced.'

'That's what I been thinking,' Andy said. 'Where's he been? Out back of the barn by himself, torturing cats?'

'Probably. OK, you'll be taking him to court this afternoon. What'll we ask Milo to charge him with?' Admiration for the county attorney was not universal in People Crimes, so the table erupted with noisy suggestions, some quite profane. We finally settled on Aggravated Robbery, Statute 609.245, Subdivision 1, First Degree, which carries a penalty of 'imprisonment for not more than twenty years or ... payment of a fine of not more than $35,000, or both.'

'That ought to wipe the smirk off his face,' Ray said. 'Now, let's get to the big stuff. The second mugging victim, the one Jake brought in, was DOA at St Agnes. The autopsy is scheduled for this afternoon. Bo, can you take that? Good. Two o'clock.'

Ray then asked me to tell the story of being led to the crime scene by well-dressed concert-goers, and we alternated on details of Friday night's search of the crime scene. He told them about his conversation with Curtis Brill. 'So, now we've got the homicide I've been predicting since about number four mugging.'

Clint said, 'You sure this is part of that series?'

'Well ... actually that's a good question. In many ways, it doesn't seem to fit—'

'That's what I mean. A little out of the territory...'

'And the first time we've had a double,' Andy said.

'Not to mention,' I said, 'that the killer didn't get the purse.'

'Well, granted,' Ray said. 'So maybe this is the partner we've been speculating The Sprinter must have. If so he bungled the job; maybe he got interrupted. If it's an entirely separate incident it's a damn odd coincidence. And either way we gotta find the killer so there's a shitload of work to do. Let's get started on the assignments...'

In the background I could hear Lulu saying, in unusually pleasant tones at the other end of the hall, 'Just wait right there.' She came out of the chief's office and started toward us, glaring. As soon as she was close enough she said, 'What happened, did all the phones die at once down here? What is this horse manure, all of you right here and I can't get anybody to answer me?'

I got up and said, 'I'll take care of it, Ray.' I walked back toward her office asking her, 'What's the problem?'

Now that she had my undivided attention she wouldn't even look at me; she kept her eyes straight ahead while she grumped, 'I've got a young woman crying on my desk, says she's the sister of that mugging victim you found Friday night. Will you get her out of my office, for heaven's sake? I shouldn't have to deal with this.' She walked to her desk and said, to the distressed face the young woman turned up toward hers, 'You go with Jake now, he's a detective.'

Her jaw would break, of course, if she called me 'captain'. Or mentioned that I run the division. Lulu's contrary to everybody but the chief, but she's got a couple of special put-downs for me. I've got a puzzling mixed-race face and she seems to feel she shouldn't have to deal with that, either.

Seven

'Is it true?' the tear-stained woman asked me as she followed me into my office. 'Gerry's dead?'

'I'm sorry, yes, she is. Have a seat.' I found my tape recorder in a drawer and plugged it in. 'I need to record this conversation, OK?'

'Sure, OK.'

I started the tape. 'You're her sister? I'm sorry to ask this, but may I see some ID?'

'Uh ... sure, OK.' She dug out her driver's license and passed it across. It said her name was Beverly Keefe, with an address in Rutherford. I read it aloud on to the tape. When I handed it back she leaned forward suddenly under my desk light and asked me, 'You get a lot of people come in here claiming to be related to dead people when they're not?'

I looked up and met a pair of red-rimmed gray eyes in a broad, pale face. Something about the placid set of her jaw said she wasn't the kind of woman who went looking for trouble. Right now though, it was obvious that life had just kicked her hard and she might welcome a fight.

I smiled at her and said, 'You're right, that's kind of an odd habit we have. How did you get the news of your sister's death, Ms – is it Mrs Keefe?'

'Call me Bev, for God's sake, I'm still under thirty. But yes, it's Mrs. My husband's a plumber, Chuck Keefe, he works at Wise's. I'm a waitress, three to eleven, at the IHOP out on the Beltway. Let's see, how did I get the news – well, we both had the weekend off, so when the weather turned nice after the storm we decided to climb on the Harley, meet some friends over by Eau Claire and put some miles on the bike. When we got home last night I found a message on the phone from Ma saying to call her no matter how late it was. Which it was, almost midnight, but I didn't wake her up, she was sitting by the phone crying.' She blew her nose. 'Been quite a night since then.'

'I bet.' I gave her a minute. 'Can you give me a couple of names I can call to verify your whereabouts Friday night?'

'Oh, for Jesus Christ's sake, you think I murdered my own sister?' Anger brightened her coloring and made her more attractive. She had probably once been as drab as her sister, but she'd lightened her hair and curled it, she wore makeup and earrings. She was about twenty pounds overweight but solid, capable-looking and, in a rough-and-ready way, quite sexy.

'Of course I don't think that. But on a homicide investigation, we have to verify everything. That's what you want us to do to find your sister's killer, right? You'd never be satisfied with less.' I watched the fire in her eyes die down a little. 'And we try to eliminate the people we don't suspect first, keep narrowing the field till only the guilty person's left.' It was a radical over-simplification but she seemed to buy it; she simmered a minute longer and then dug some names and phone numbers out of her purse.

When I had them all on tape I asked her, 'Were you close to your sister?'

'Always, all our lives. My dad died the year I started first grade. Mom brought us up out in Dover where housing was cheaper, but she always worked in Rutherford because the jobs paid better. She had to spend a lot of time on the road. Gerry and I always helped with the housework, had dinner waiting for her even when we were little. Both of us worked summers in high school. Gerry graduated two years ahead of me, got a job in an attorney's office here in town and started night school at the college. Her goal was to get a degree in accounting and then go to law school. Soon as I graduated I came to town too, got a waitress job and found an apartment for the two of us. Mom stayed with us sometimes on weekends. My family

... we take care of each other.' A couple of tears leaked out and I waited in silence while she mopped them off her face.

'I did most of the housework so she could study. We refinished stuff from used furniture stores. We even learned how to make drapes together. Believe it or not, it was fun.'

'But you got married...?'

'A little over a year ago. Yes. I met Chuck at an employees' party. He came with somebody else but as soon as we danced together it was all settled. I told Gerry after the first date, I can't let this one get away. She understood, she always wanted what was best for me. I'll never have another friend like her.' Suddenly swamped by grief, she sobbed into a handful of tissue. I waited. After some agonizing sounds she sat up, blew her nose and cleared her throat.

'Gerry met Curtis at some non-profit do while I was planning my wedding. The rest of the do-gooders faded into the background and there he stood. Like it was meant to be, she said.' Her lip curled contemptuously around that idea. 'So when I moved out, he moved in.'

'So that's about a year ago?'

'Thirteen months.' She twirled her wedding and engagement rings, thinking. 'You met Curtis Brill?'

'Not yet.'

'Get ready to be charmed. He's the kind of

guy, when you're fifteen you say, Wow, what a cute guy. When you're twenty you think he's sexy as hell, and by the time you're twenty-five you know he's an empty suit. Or you should. But see ... Gerry was always the studious one, quiet, didn't date. I was a little ... livelier.' She shrugged one shoulder, allowed herself two seconds of a Mona Lisa smile, and the room temperature seemed to rise. 'By the time she met Curt, she'd been working in that same office for nine years, dating only when somebody fixed her up with some nerd. Curt was the first attractive guy who'd ever paid attention to her. And boy, did he ever.'

'He's a divinity student?'

That earned a black look. 'Is that what you call it? He goes to that Bible college out on the west side of town. They crank out noisy preachers for the country churches ... Mom says they used to call them Holy Rollers. I'm sorry, I don't mean to insult anybody's religion, but the idea of anyone taking advice from Curtis Brill about *anything* is way ridiculous. And he wants to tell me how to talk to God? Please.'

'You don't think much of his intelligence?'

She sighed. 'He's a big bag of hot air. He doesn't know anything useful and he'll never improve because he's convinced he already has all the answers. Clichés for every occasion, that's Curtis ... and that little cult he's building around himself, those freeloaders hanging out at Gerry's apartment eating everything in sight, they're even worse.'

'People from his church?'

'They are once he gets his hooks into them. He just charms 'em right in through the door. His "rough diamonds", he calls them. I see the rough, I don't see the sparkle.'

'You mean he recruits street people?'

'Maybe some, but he seems to find most of them at that used car lot where he actually earns a little money once in a while. Only a few hours a week though, because he's convinced Gerry he has to have most of his time to do the Lord's work.'

'He's a part-time pastor too?'

'In training ... he loves to have these guys listen to him practice his sermons. Drives me bananas!' She rolled her eyes. 'Gerry's there cooking and scrubbing after a full day's work, Curt and his merry band of worshippers go in the living room and talk about what the Lord wants. It never seems to occur to them He might want them to do the dishes.'

'But Gerry wasn't dissatisfied?'

The sneer again. 'Happy as a clam.'

'I can sure see why you'd want to put a stop to that.'

Her eyes blazed suddenly greener. 'OK, make fun of me, but if it was your sister you'd be mad too.'

'I didn't mean...' But I had meant it just the way she took it, only now that my mockery had slipped out I was wishing it back. She was biased but she was smart and sincere and we needed what she knew. Or could guess. 'Can you give me the names of some of these friends of Curtis Brill?'

'I only know first names – and most of those are nicknames. Let's see, there's Jay, he's the pretty one ... and there's a strange ugly scarecrow called Pee-Wee. I think they said he's the nephew of the man who owns the used car lot, but boy, if that makes him privileged he has yet to show the signs.'

'Kind of rough, you mean, or...?'

'You'd swear he wandered off the set of *The Beverly Hillbillies*. And let's see, who else? Oh, the cute one with all the freckles ... No-No. I don't know his real name but they call him No-No. He's the one with all the luck, they say. He wins at church bingo.' She tossed her hair back and made a scornful clucking sound. 'Giggling over silly nick-names, like boys in school. When I think of my strong, intelligent sister cooking for that bunch of twinkies...'

'They talk about religion?'

'All the time. And yammer on about their work at that used car lot, too. What's the name of it? Happy Roads. It's owned by this sort of fatherly cowboy named Happy

Rhodes – spelled with an H, get it? So damn cute. The boys get many a chuckle out of Ol' Hap's wise country sayings.' She could express contempt with just the smallest curl of the lip. 'Folks just can't resist Ol' Hap, Pee-Wee says, he's the family go-getter.'

'I see.' I watched while she calmed down from that tirade and said, 'The detective who interviewed Curtis early Saturday morning said that he wept uncontrollably for some time after he learned your sister was dead.'

'I believe it. So?'

'So that seems like the reaction of somebody who was very attached to your sister.'

'Oh, you bet. Like a leech.'

'You don't think he was really sorry she was dead?'

'Sure he was sorry. The world's foremost freeloader just lost his meal ticket.'

She gave me her home and work numbers and the name and number of Gerry's employer. She stated emphatically that her sister didn't smoke or drink, used no recreational drugs and was in perfect health. 'She wasn't pregnant either. I'd have been the first to know.'

'Before Curtis?'

Her eyes wavered. 'OK, these days maybe second.'

What Beverly wanted from me was any information I could give her about where the investigation was headed. Since it wasn't headed much of anywhere yet I gave her boilerplate assurances and promised to keep her informed. Then while the tape was still whirling I sat back and met her eyes. 'You've made it plain you don't think much of Curtis Brill. But you've stopped short of suggesting he might have killed your sister. Do you think he did?'

She thought about it. 'You know, nothing would please me better than to have you prove that, but I don't think you're going to. Why would he?' She re-crossed her legs, pondering. 'Look, Curtis doesn't love anyone but himself. He plays the religion card to get what he wants, and he got everything he wanted from Gerry – board and room and applause and sex.' She thought some more. 'Unless there's something going on that I don't know about. Till last year, I'd have said that wasn't possible, I knew everything about Gerry's life. But now – I've got a new husband myself, I've been a little distracted.'

'Yes,' I said, 'well...' Her improbable heatwave had hit me again.

She stood up and put out a wide, capable hand. 'You seem like a pretty good guy. I'll try not to be a pest, but I am going to keep in close touch.'

'Please do,' I said, 'any time. Anything we can help you with ... your mother, too.'

'Yeah, well...' Her certainty faltered for the

first time, as devastating grief momentarily crumpled her features. 'Ma's pretty much destroyed, however this goes.'

The hall was suddenly filled with clatter as Ray's detectives headed out on the jobs he'd assigned them. Beverly Keefe strode out with the flow, solid and confident, a sister worth having.

I was transcribing addresses off the tape machine when Ray poked his head in and asked me, 'Was that the sister?'

'Yeah.'

'You get anything useful?'

'She bad-mouthed Curtis plenty. Here's the tape. I've made copies of all the names and addresses she gave me. I'll verify her alibi for Friday night, if you like.'

'Good. You think it's solid?'

'As a rock. That and everything else about her, is my impression.'

'OK.' He sat down in front of my desk and yawned.

'Friday catching up to you?'

He nodded. 'Little bit. Things seem kind of ... at arm's length. Let's see, I told you we found Geraldine's car, didn't I?'

'You did? Where?'

'Over on 17th Street, parked at the curb in front of a house.'

'That's more than four blocks from where she was going to class.'

'Yeah, and there are three lots within two

blocks of the Fisher building. Surely she could have used one of them. I mean, she'd have to know how relentless Traffic Control is about ticketing in residential neighborhoods.'

'Did her car have a ticket?'

'No ... and we never found it till Saturday afternoon. Go figure.'

'Shee. My pickup was parked there half an hour, I guarantee you I'd have a ticket.'

'I know. Anyway, I sent Darrell to the impound lot to look it over, but I don't expect he'll get much from eyeballing.'

'You going to have Ollie...'

'No. I decided not to touch it – it's a key piece of evidence that was left in a very odd place, right? Let's not give the lawyers anything more to argue about, let BCA handle it. I'm having it wrapped and hauled to St Paul this afternoon.' He scratched his head, thinking. 'What else? Clint Maddox is canvassing the neighborhood around 23rd Avenue, looking for anybody who saw a jogger. Well, and Buzz Cooper's on his way to interview the dead woman's employer and anybody else working in that office.' He yawned again, flipping through his notes.

'The boyfriend, Curtis, uh...'

'Ah, yes, Curtis Brill. Bo's on his way over there now, to get an exact timeline for his movements Friday night and the names of some people from his church we could talk to, maybe his pastor?'

'Good. The sister, Bev – on that tape – mentions several young men who hang around him a lot, and are kind of – she called them a cult.'

'Oh? I'll call Bo and give him the names, maybe he can get phone numbers.' His cell rang. 'Bailey.' He sat up straighter. 'Uh ... yeah, now is fine. Thanks.' He closed the phone and chuckled softly. 'OK, Jason Wells is all chained up and ready to be brought up for his interview.' The prospect perked him up; he was smiling with his head cocked, looking predatory and pleased, like an amused vulture. 'Two months, I've been stalking this asshole, fixated on getting him by the balls. Friday night we finally got him, and ever since then I've been too busy to talk to him.'

He stood up and began going through his pockets, absent-mindedly, his hands searching for something while he talked. 'This should be kind of fun. Want to meet The Sprinter, Jake? You got time?' He gave up on his pants pockets and began feeling through the pockets of his jacket and shirt. 'Shall we use the big conference room?'

'Why don't you bring him in here?' I said. 'That big space kind of flattens your affect. What are you looking for, Ray?'

'What?' He stopped groping himself and stared at me for a couple of seconds. Then pulled his hands out of his back pants pockets where they had gone for a second search, and held them out in front of himself. 'Holy shit. I was trying to find my cigarettes!'

He sat down in front of my desk, all his manic bounce gone, and frowned as bleakly as only a Bailey can do.

I asked him, 'How long since you quit smoking?'

'Eight years and three months. Well, and five days, but who keeps track?'

I gave him my welcome-to-the-club smile. I gave up smoking years ago in order to train for Emergency Search & Rescue Services. I remember well the despair of letting go an addiction while you're dealing with exhaustion. 'Friday night was a real pisser, huh?'

'After it got to be Saturday afternoon, it had its moments.'

'You need to go home?'

'No, I'm OK. It was just – something about that fresh surge of adrenaline...' He laughed, a sharp ironic bark, but his face relaxed a little. 'I don't really miss smoking at all, any more. But sometimes when things pile up on me, I get to feeling like there's something else I'm supposed to be doing with my hands.'

'Light matches, for instance.'

'Right.' He stood up and shook himself. 'Well – you mean it, about your office?'

'Sure, let's do it. You talk and I'll watch. Are you going to stick to questions about the original string of muggings, or...?'

'I think so, for now. We know The Sprinter didn't do the woman by the Fieldhouse. So if the two events are connected in some way, they're going to come together naturally. I think.'

'Sounds reasonable. Let's see what we've got here.'

Jason Wells was handsome, blond, firmly muscled but with a childish quality about him. The skin of his face was smooth as a girl's, and his eyes were clear baby blue, Ray was right about that. *Not a user, for sure*. His lips were full and pink and turned up at the corners in a kind of permanent smirk.

Ray read him his rights, asked if he understood them. He nodded. 'You have to say it out loud,' Ray said, 'for the tape.'

Jason turned to watch the tape turning silently on the recorder. By the time he turned back, a dimple had appeared in his right cheek. He looked straight into Ray's eyes and said softly, 'Yes,' turning it into something close to a blown kiss.

There was a hollow silence in the room while Ray's sallow face grew longer, gloomier and grayer. For a few vertiginous seconds I thought he might slug his prisoner. Finally in a voice as dry as chalk dust he said, 'Right. Sergeant Pitman will be taking you to Judge

Linderman's courtroom this afternoon, for what's called a preliminary hearing. You'll be charged with Aggravated Robbery, First Degree. Do you have anything to say at this time in answer to these charges?'

'I want an attorney,' Jason said.

'Well, have you tried to hire counsel?'

'No, because I don't have any money.'

'Ask for an attorney when you go to court. The judge will appoint one for you.'

'That's it? I just ask?'

'Yes. Remember, though, that once you get an attorney, we can't talk to you without your attorney being present. So if you have anything to say to us about what went down Friday night, you should say it now.'

'What went down?' The dimple reappeared, deeper, as his smirk turned into a mocking smile. 'I'm what went down. With three or four cops on top of me, so—' he was suddenly indignant – 'I couldn't even *breathe*.'

A shrink could have filled a whole notebook watching this boy's quick transitions, from seductive to petulant, ironic to angry. Did he carry a list in his head, I wondered, and just keep trying different ploys? His personality seemed semi-fluid, like quicksilver.

'Jason,' Ray said, 'do you remember that just before that first officer grabbed you, you attacked a red-haired lady in a blue cap? She's still in the hospital.'

'Why did she jump in front of me like that?

I was trying to run around her.'

'That story's not going to wash. The woman you hit is ready to testify you attacked her, and I've got two other eyewitnesses, plus a video recording of the whole event.'

'Aha, that's what I thought, it was a sting, wasn't it? You were all cops, and you entrapped me. Why me?' He looked so innocent and hurt when he said it, for one crazy second I almost felt sorry for him.

'You trapped yourself when you hit that woman,' Ray said. 'Listen to me, Jason. If you plead guilty now and we don't have to go to trial, you can make this easy for yourself. You can get a lawyer who'll show the court you have no previous record, and you can plead this down to a minimum sentence. Or we can do it the hard way, and then I promise you I'll try you on every possible charge and push for the maximum sentence on each crime.'

There was a commotion in the hall. I heard Lulu say, 'You can't go in there, they're talking to a prisoner—'

Another female voice, younger than Lulu's, louder and shrill, said, 'Don't you try to tell me I can't see my own son, old woman!'

'Aw, shit,' the prisoner said.

'I'm guessing,' Ray said. 'Is that your mother?'

With his eyes closed, Jason nodded.

'Sit still.' Ray closed my door as he went out. I heard him introduce himself to Jason's mother, setting off a firestorm of abuse. When she paused for breath he asked her, What did she need? She told him he could put that shiny badge where the sun didn't shine. She asked him, Did he think she was dimwit enough to let herself get fucked over by some two-bit cop? Ray said her son was being processed right now but she could see him later today. She declared she had kids at home alone, she couldn't be sitting around this dump all day, she didn't need this shit *at all*. Jason's mother seemed to have wind and strength enough to continue yelling and name-calling all day, but I noticed the noise was moving down the hall toward Ray's office, and presently I heard his door close and the storm became a distant rumble.

I had been watching my door, half expecting to have it explode inward and admit an enraged mother showing her fangs. When I heard Ray's door close I turned to Jason and surprised a look of bitter anger on his suddenly adult-looking face. It was just a flash; then the smirk slid back in place on the cool baby mask.

'Sounds like you better stick with Ray,' I said.

'Stick with him for what?'

'He really can help you if you co-operate.'

'Sure,' Jason Wells said, flashing his dimples, 'and pigs can fly.'

After that we sat together silently watching the second hand move around on my desk clock. Finally Ray said, 'In here,' outside my door and rapped once lightly. He walked in with two sheriff's deputies, who went right to work chaining up the prisoner. They treated Jason like an object, moving him into convenient positions without ever talking to him at all.

Ray talked to him the whole time they worked on him, speaking quietly and watching his face. 'You'll have some time now in your cell before Sergeant Pitman takes you to court. I suggest you use it to think hard, because today's your best chance to help yourself. You make a good first impression on that judge, plead guilty and say you're sorry, you and your lawyer can still save most of the rest of your life.' Ray waited for any acknowledgement from the prisoner. When none came he added, 'Your mother will be down to talk to you shortly.'

Jason Wells stood silent, his smooth-skinned face a blank mask over what I now understood was a bottomless pool of anger. Ray looked hard at him for a few seconds. Then he simply put his hands in his pockets and turned his back while the deputies walked the prisoner out.

When the chains had clinked away I asked

Ray, 'Jason's mother change your mind about something?'

'She's a real piece of work, Jake. You mind having a word with her?'

'I guess I can stand it. You better do the talking first, though, you know where you left off.'

Her name was Tammy Knutson. She showed us a driver's license. She had bigger hair in the picture. She volunteered a Teamster's Union card too; she was proud of it. 'From when I drove a forklift.'

'It's made out to Tammy Fisher,' Ray said.

'Yeah, well, my name was Fisher a few years ago. Before that it was Wells. Each husband, I got a new last name and another kid, and that was just about damn-all.'

She had the same handsome head and smooth, unmarked face as her son. The blond hair appeared to be getting a little boost from a bottle now, but the dimple that flashed in her right cheek was exactly like Jason's. Her eyes were that same bright cheerful-looking blue, completely at odds with everything that came out of her mouth. Her anger was not submerged like her son's but right there on the surface, ready to boil up and splash over anything that got in her way.

'I'm a desperate housewife,' she said, 'only I don't get to live in a nice house and wear seventy-dollar T-shirts like those floozies on

TV. I'm out here in the real world living paycheck-to-paycheck.'

'Doing what?' I was hoping to keep her talking till I found out what she was so mad about.

'Right now I'm a cocktail waitress at the Hyatt.'

'Pretty good place to work?'

'About as good as there is in this town. I should move to Minneapolis where the real money is, but hell, it's hard enough raising kids down here. I'd never keep track of them in a big place.'

'You said three...?'

'Yeah, I was just born lucky.' She had a special mean laugh for this subject. 'Three mismatched kids that can't stand each other and treat me like dirt.'

And Jason, she declared, had been out of control for years. 'You probably won't believe me, but I really tried with Jason. He was my first baby, and for a few years after his dad took a powder we were really close. But he hated my second husband and the new little brother was the last straw.' She blew a rueful breath of air up into her bangs. 'Along about fifth grade he just ... quit. Quit studying, quit giving a damn about school, quit listening to anything I said. Started giving me that *look*.' She did a devastating imitation of Jason's dead-eyed smirk.

'He's never been arrested before, though,

right?'

'Absolutely not!' Her hostility came flooding back. 'What is this deal, anyway, why have you got him in jail?'

Ray told her about the mugging.

'Oh, bullshit,' she said, 'that's a trumped-up charge if I ever heard one. Some little bitch got dumped by him and now she's trying to say—'

'Mrs Knutson—' Ray leaned toward her, shaking his head – 'don't waste your breath. I've got eyewitnesses, the victim will testify. Your son did the crime all right.'

'Well...' She looked at me. My face gave her no encouragement so she went back to Ray. 'Well, what am *I* supposed to do about it?'

'Are you here because you want to help him?'

'If I could, but ... I'm sure as hell not going to put my neck in the noose for any bail money, I'll tell you that.' She put her arms around her purse and hugged it close to herself, glaring at us. 'I'm just barely keeping food on the table as it is.'

'I see.' Ray was looking about ten years older than last week and very tired. He said, 'Jason gave us your address. Does he live with you or not?'

'Off and on. I throw him out but he keeps coming back. Mostly, he just stops off now and then to do some laundry and eat everything in the refrigerator.'

'Where does he live when he's not with you?'

'I have no idea.'

'Does he have a job? Do anything for a living besides steal purses?'

'I thought people were innocent till proven guilty, isn't that what they say on TV?'

'OK, point taken. Does he have a job?'

'He worked in a carwash for a few weeks after he dropped out of high school. That was, let's see, about a year ago. He got fired from that job because he couldn't get to work on time. He'd stay out half the night and then come stumbling out of his bedroom at ten o'clock yelling, "Why didn't you wake me up?" I said, "I called you when I called Mike and Tammy, they got up and you just swore at me".'

'So he's been unemployed most of the time for what, a year?'

'Well, he sold used cars for a while. He must have got a friend to vouch for him at some small-timer lot, because he didn't have any of the right credentials, of course. But for a while it looked like he was making a go of it, he came home bragging about how he was making money hand over fist. I said, "Good, then you can pay me board and room." But first he had to get himself a car and some clothes and before he ever paid me anything he picked a fight with me and I threw him out. I think he lost that job soon after, anyway. Now I ask what he's living on, he just says snotty things like, "Oh, I got a couple of things cooking." I said, "I'm not going to support you if you're not in school. Get a job and help me or get out." Three times now, he's moved all his stuff out in garbage bags. Few weeks later back he comes, hungry and with less stuff.' She sighed and sat back, crossed her pretty legs, lit a cigarette and sat holding the smoking match, looking for an ashtray.

'I'm sorry,' I said, 'there's no smoking in this building.'

'Oh, yeah?' In a flash, she was bristling again. 'What are you going to do, put me in jail?'

'Guess I'll have to, if you don't put out the cigarette.' She was staring straight at me with her eyes blazing. I stared back without blinking. 'But it seems like a damn silly thing to make an issue out of, with all the other troubles you've got.' She turned away then and sat looking sullenly at the cigarette for a few seconds. Finally she muttered, 'Shit,' and ground it out on the floor.

When she raised her face toward Ray, one tear was sliding brightly down her pretty cheek. She asked him, 'You pretty sure you can prove he stole that purse?'

'Knocked her down first and *then* stole it. Yes. I've got three eyewitnesses.' He didn't mention his tapes. She was going to start yelling again when she heard about the sting, and I didn't blame him for wanting to put that off.

'Shit,' she said again, but more thoughtfully now. She jiggled one knee, considering. 'Well, what's going to happen next?'

'He's going to court this afternoon. Be a good idea if you were there. A judge will ask him how he pleads. I tried to tell him he should plead guilty and bargain the sentence down, but I don't think I convinced him. You want to go down now, talk to him? Maybe you could make him understand.'

'I'm not interested in making your job easier, why should I be?' The Vesuvian reaction seemed to erupt every couple of sentences, almost regardless of what Ray said. She didn't actually have steam coming out of her ears, but being in the room with her, you got the feeling it was boiling up in there.

'It doesn't affect my job one way or the other,' Ray said. 'I thought you might want to help your son.'

'Didn't you hear what I said? My son hasn't listened to me for years.'

'So you wouldn't know if he had a partner that helps him do these muggings?'

'Oh, now you're trying to say there's been more than one?'

'That's right. A whole string of attacks, since early January.'

'I think you're fishing. This whole story smells like rotten fish to me. And I'll tell you this, Mister High-and-Mighty Policeman, I'm not going to let you railroad my son on some cockamamie charge you dream up. I'll go down and see what he has to say about all this and then we'll see.' She got up, fluffed her hair with quick, angry hands and found her keys. 'I want everybody in this building to know, those guards down there in that jail, too, you hear what I'm saying? Any of you lay a hand on my boy I'm gonna sue your ass all the way to the Supreme Court.'

'It'll be Sergeant Pitman, coming to get him pretty soon, to take him to court. He'll help you all he can, if you give him a chance.'

'Oh, I bet. I can take care of my own kid without any help from Sergeant Pitman, thank you very much.' Her beautiful eyes blazed with futile rage. 'All I want is to get him out of this filthy place.' She rattled the keys in her hand, remembered she wasn't going to her car, and stuffed them back in her purse. Standing there like that with her hand in her purse she flexed a muscle in her jaw and muttered, 'Then I'm gonna take him home and rip his throat out.'

Eight

We sat like survivors in the wake of a hurricane for a few seconds after Tammy Knutson whirled out the door. Finally Ray sighed tiredly and said, 'Well, good to know we brought mother and son together again, huh?'

Buzz Cooper walked by my open door at that moment, saw Ray and came in saying, 'I got some good dirt on that Curtis Brill, you want to hear it?'

Ray said, 'Sure.'

Then my phone rang and a support staffer in the lobby said, 'Is Ray Bailey in your office? Curtis Brill is here to see him.'

'Hold on.' I told Ray who was outside.

'Well, damn,' he said, 'he's here, and Bo's at his place. What is this, all Brill all the time? I'll call Bo and ask him to wait there. But Jake? I'd like to hear what Buzz has to say before I talk to Brill. Could you...'

'Sure, I want a look at him anyway. Come get him when you're ready.'

'Thanks. Come with me, Buzz.' Ray marched down the hall double-time, with Buzz following, moving unevenly because he was having trouble adjusting to his new bi-focals. The little round wire-rimmed specs on his guileless face, with his close haircut and the gap between his front teeth, made him look like a studious Boy Scout.

I called Mary at the desk and asked her to bring Ray's visitor to my office. Bev Keefe's description of her sister's boyfriend had prepared me for a shambling country preacher with a lopsided grin, but the man who walked in behind Mary was six feet tall and handsome, with noble features and an arresting presence – the charisma of a star. Bev had called him a cute guy, but that certainly didn't do him justice.

He actually read the nameplate on my door, too, a tactic that occurs only to the few. So he had my name and title right when he stuck out his hand and said, 'Captain Hines? Happy to meet you.' I took note of his people skills and rich baritone – a little begrudgingly, because I'd been prepared for a simple hayseed and now I had to adjust.

He looked straight into my eyes while he shook my hand, saying, 'Your lieutenant was so kind Saturday morning when I – I'm afraid I kind of lost it when he came to my door with his terrible news. I've asked the Lord to bless him for his help.'

His diction was a blend of evangelical fervor and smooth TV infomercial – Billy

Graham sells the Purple Pill. There was something extra added, a hint of Tobey Maguire diffidence, which I guessed would probably shade more toward Gary Cooper aw-shucksiness for an older audience. I got an immediate inner vision of a cut-and-paste pastor assembling his persona, maybe using mirrors as well as an audience to see what worked. 'You want confidence that stops well short of arrogance,' I imagined his Divinity school teachers instructing him. 'All the understanding and kindliness in the world but just that little hint of distance that makes it clear you're The Leader.' The message he projected as he pumped my hand, his left hand covering our two rights, was, 'I'm here to show you The Way, but I can be a pal, too, if you need one.'

Cops, over time, collect a good-sized set of alarm bells. Curtis Brill rang every one of mine, sitting in front of my desk, earnest and warm, saying in his pipe-organ voice, 'I came down to see if there's any news.'

'One of our detectives is on his way to your house, actually,' I told him.

'Oh? Why, do you ... want something?'

'Well, his orders were to double-check your whereabouts Friday night, get a timeline we could build on for when everything had to happen. Ray Bailey will come and find you in a few minutes and the two of you can go back to your place together, OK?'

'Well, sure, we can do that.' He made it seem he wasn't so much joining my team as enlisting me into his. 'And I wanted to ask, have you found the Toyota?'

'Which, uh ... oh, you mean Geraldine's car?'

'Our car,' he said, firmly. 'Yes. Is there some other Toyota involved?'

'Not that I know of.' I told him where we had found it. 'Why would she leave it way over there? I understand she was attending class in the Hugh Fisher building?

'Yes.'

'Well, there's a parking lot right there, the entrance is at the end of the sidewalk where we found her.'

'Maybe the lot was full when she got there. She would have had a good reason, I can tell you that. Gerry always did the most reasonable thing.' His lips trembled and he turned his face aside, saying, 'Excuse me.' We sat quietly together while he composed himself and I considered the confusing possibility that he had actually cared for Geraldine Lovejoy. Maybe the sister was just jealous? After half a minute he said, 'Where's the car now?'

'It's in impound, unless it's already on its way to the Bureau of Criminal Apprehension in St Paul.'

'Oh? What's that all about?' A little frown grew between his eyebrows. If I was one of his flock and wanted his approval, that frown could worry me a lot, I thought. This guy had a good start on his body language skills.

'They'll examine it for trace evidence, lift any latent fingerprints they find and try for samples of DNA. It's just routine; it's the victim's car.'

'I see. Well, I don't really.' He gave a little self-deprecating laugh. 'I was always hopeless in science classes.' He re-crossed his legs while he thought about his next question. In the end he tried a statement of fact. 'I was hoping to get the car back as soon as possible. I'm pretty seriously inconvenienced without a ride.' He looked at me as if he expected me to fix that.

'Your car is evidence now, I'm afraid. Do you have proof of ownership, by the way? I thought her sister said—'

'Oh, has Bev been here already? I'm surprised you're even talking to me then.' He gave a soft condescending chuckle. 'Bev's favorite hobby is trashing her sister's boyfriend.'

'You don't get along, huh?' *More like it.* People can talk politely all day without telling you much, but get them going on the things that make them mad and the truth comes tumbling out.

Curtis Brill wasn't having any of that, though. He shrugged and said, 'Oh, I get along with everybody.' His composure came back around him like a cloak. 'The Lord didn't grant me my mission so I could waste my time fighting. But Bev...' He shook his head with a condescending smile. 'They were together all those years, you know, and even though she has a husband now, Bev still seems to feel that Geraldine kind of *belongs* to her.' He choked up, momentarily, and turned his head aside again. I waited. When he turned back to me he said, 'Bev and I are both in for some tough times. Geraldine was such a special person, she's going to be very sadly missed.' After the apparent emotion he'd just shown me, his last words sounded shockingly glib. I know pastors and social workers have to have these pat lines ready to lay on families in stressful times, but it was weird to hear him use them on his own situation. I stared at him, wondering if he knew the difference between genuine emotion and ear candy.

Just then Ray walked into my open doorway and tapped on the frame. His face is set by his genetic inheritance in a discouraging expression, so you would have had to know him as well as I did to realize that right now he was quite pleased.

'I was just explaining to Curtis here,' I said, 'that the car, the Toyota that Geraldine was driving Friday night, has been impounded and is on its way to be tested at the crime lab in St Paul. Oh, yes, and you—' I turned back to Curtis – 'were going to show us some proof of ownership.'

'Well, the registration's in the car, of course,' he said.

'Sure,' I said, 'but don't you have a card from the insurance company?'

'Let's see, do I?' He pulled out his wallet with an embarrassed little laugh. 'You're going to think I'm a sap. Gerry handled all the business things, because I'm so absent-minded about ... if I get to studying or working on a sermon I just forget everything. Even the time!' His light-hearted laugh invited us to share the joke. Ray and I watched while he looked through the cards in his wallet's sleeves – a library card, his student card from school, a voter's registration. 'No, I guess she didn't trust me to look after that.' He looked up at us, his expression suddenly bereft, and said, 'Oh, how am I ever going to get along without her?'

Ray said, 'Mr Brill ... it's not Reverend Brill yet, is it?'

'Oh, please, call me Curtis,' Brill said. 'I won't be ordained until next June. And even when I am, I'll always answer to my first name. Doing the Lord's work is supposed to make you humble, not proud!'

Ray has a little what-planet-are-you-from pause he inflicts on people when he thinks they're striking a pose. I'm never sure if it's a conscious put-down or just a little hiatus he needs to take to peer through somebody's smokescreen. He subjected Brill to five seconds of that withering silence now before he asked, 'How did you get here, Curtis?'

'A friend dropped me. People are being very kind.' His eyes grew bright and he blinked several times.

'I see. Sergeant Cooper will give you a ride home, then, and you'll find Sergeant Dooley waiting at your front door. I want you to give the two detectives a precise account of your movements from noon Friday until six o'clock Saturday morning when I came to your door.'

'But Lieutenant,' Curtis Brill said, in his kind-uncle voice, 'I told you all that Saturday morning, remember?'

'We talked about it a little when you weren't crying too hard,' Ray said rudely. Brill was shocked; he blushed bright pink. 'Today I want you to go over it minute by minute till you've remembered every single move, including what you ate, what you watched on TV. Exactly when you went to bed. This is a homicide investigation, nothing is too small. Don't leave anything out.'

'Well...' Brill's bright color faded slowly. 'All right, if that's what you need. Are you sure we couldn't do it here, right now? I have a lot of other things I need to get done,' he pleaded. 'This is a hard time for me, you know.'

'The woman you've been living with has died in mysterious circumstances,' Ray said. He must have heard some interesting things from Buzz; his attitude had hardened while he was out of the room. 'For your own protection, if nothing else, I'd think you'd want to cooperate in the investigation.'

'Of course I want to cooperate,' Brill said. His voice had lost some of its ripe friendliness and grown a shrill edge. He rose to his full, handsome height and looked around, but his magisterial manner had crumbled a little at the edges. 'Where is he, then? This person who's going to drive me? I'd like to go now, and while he's driving me home I'm going to pray on this. I very much need the Lord's help today.' He stared silently into the corner of the room until Buzz Cooper came for him, and he walked out without saying goodbye.

'I think you upset him,' I said.

'Hope so,' Ray said. 'Buzz got some very negative opinions about Curtis Brill at that lawyer's office where Geraldine worked. You got time to listen to the tape?'

'Put it on my desk, will you? I need to check on the rest of my guys.'

I found Kevin in the hall next to LeeAnn's desk, leaning into John Smith's tiny space. He didn't look up when I stopped beside him and asked, 'Howsgoin'?'

'Excellent! But I can't talk right now, Jake,

I gotta stick right here and get max utilization out of my part-time genius. Watch this guy, he takes computer searching into a whole other dimension.'

John Smith was short, nondescript, and cheerful enough when he talked, which was hardly ever. Mostly he pounded relentlessly on a keyboard and made small discovery noises, like 'Mmmp' and 'Hwaah'.

Kevin, mesmerized by the Gatling-gun rattle of his electronic questing, hung over him shuffling lists and urging, 'Yes, try the nine hundred block' and 'Look for the Johnsons, the Johnsons'.

'You know what I call him?' he asked me. 'My über cyber grabber!' He gave me a glittering grin. 'Look at him go!'

I said, 'You know we got The Sprinter, right? So Ray won't be needing to borrow your detectives any more.'

'I heard, yes. Just in time, too. I've got them all out on the street right now, taking reports from enraged citizens about new stuff they didn't buy. My neighbors are waving and smiling again, we're piling up good will all around.'

'Swell. You can have John Smith for two hours a day, for the rest of the week.'

'Well, but if we're close, though—'

'Don't ask for any more. Mary's already giving me back more than she owed. Find your card thieves by Friday, or hang it up.'

'OK. OK, I hear you! What else?'

I opened my mouth to say, 'Nothing,' but before my tongue found a purchase on the roof of my mouth a better idea came zooming in out of the time/space continuum and wiggled its butt. 'Get on the horn with the traffic division ASAP, will you? Find out if either or both of the parking lots nearest the Hugh Fisher building, the one on 23rd Avenue and the one around the corner on Fifteenth Street, were full between seven and ten last Friday night?'

'Is this about Friday's homicide?'

'Yeah.'

'Well, why are you asking me to do it? Can't somebody in Ray's crew—'

'I'm standing here talking to you and I just thought up this question. It's quicker to ask you than to explain it to somebody else all over again. So be nice to me, I just did you a favor. Did you get those locations?'

'23rd Avenue and 15th Street, OK, OK, I'll do it.' He leaned close to me suddenly, his hurry forgotten, and lowered his voice. 'Is it true what I'm hearing, Jake, that Rosie's seriously hurt?'

'Oh, I don't think so, she – who told you that?'

'Every time I go past the break room, I hear somebody whispering that she's still in the hospital and something bad must have happened to her in that fall.'

'How do these things get started? Last I heard, she was getting out this afternoon.' Walking back to my office though, I remembered uneasily how Bo had tried to talk us out of using Rosie on that job.

I'd brought a brown-bag lunch to work and I didn't mind driving while I ate it. Five stop lights and a ham sandwich later, I parked in front of St Agnes hospital. I pulled rank inside, flashed my badge at an admissions clerk and asked authoritatively for Rosie's current room number. Sometimes it works and this was one of those times. I took the elevator to the fourth floor.

The halls were quiet, the doctors done with morning rounds. A few aides were carrying out the last of the lunch trays. The door of 426 stood ajar, so I looked in. The nearest bed was empty. A flimsy privacy curtain hung between it and the bed beyond, but I could see shapes through it. Silhouetted against the light of the big window in the far wall, a man was bending over the figure on the second bed. I took one step into the room. From there I could see, around the end of the curtain, that the man was Bo Dooley. Rosie was on the bed, with her arms raised and wrapped around his neck. She was not giving him a collegial hug; they were kissing each other passionately.

I stepped back quickly, and collided with something soft. A low voice somewhere below my shoulder said, 'Ooh, estop,' and I turned to find a tiny dark-faced Hispanic woman in scrubs, hands raised to fend me off.

'I'm sorry,' I said, because I was standing on her foot. By the time we got all that sorted out and the aide declared her intention of taking Rosie's lunch tray away, my two detectives were spaced discreetly, several feet apart, wearing matching expressions. They looked about equal parts embarrassed, happy and curious, and as I walked toward them I realized my two smart detectives were trying to read my face while I deciphered theirs. I smiled blandly, I hoped, and said, 'Hey there. How's it going, Rosie?'

'Oh, Jake,' she said, 'aren't you nice to come and see me.' It was so out of character for her to say the conventional, appropriate thing that it made us both laugh.

'Well, I better get going,' Bo said, and walked stiffly past me toward the door.

'Don't leave on my account,' I said. 'I'm surprised to find you here, though, I thought you were at Curtis Brill's house.'

He turned halfway back toward me and talked to the sides of my feet. 'Nobody home when I got there.'

'Ray didn't call you?'

'By the time he reached me I was ten blocks away. So he said let Buzz handle the interview, and I said I'd take early lunch, which I just did. Now I'm going right on to the autopsy.'

'Ah, yes, the autopsy.' I looked at my watch. 'Well, you still have plenty of time to get to that.'

'No, I better, um ... I have to check on some...' He waved vaguely at the bed and said, 'See you, Rosie.' His face as he went out the door was almost back to its usual configuration, frozen in neutral.

'Take care, Bo.' Rosie was sitting straight up in bed now, giving me a keen, bright look. When Bo's footsteps had faded, she said, 'OK, so you saw us.'

'Did I say anything?'

'Don't bother looking innocent, I saw you peeking around the curtain like some creepy spy. You ever hear about knocking?'

'The door was open. Is that any way to talk to your boss?'

'It is if your boss sneaks up on you just when you finally get a little action going.' She rolled her eyes up to the ceiling and said, 'Oh, Jesus, what did I just say?'

'Never mind, I'll disregard it. You've probably got an elevated white cell count and don't even know what you're saying.'

'My cell count is fine.'

'How's your temperature? You look kind of feverish.'

'Do I? I'm not. I had a very stiff neck for a couple of days, I couldn't turn my head and my eyesight was a little blurred. So they made me stay for more tests this morning. I'm getting tested for everything in the known world, I think. So far we've established that I don't have peritonitis or tuberculosis or meningitis or Meniere's Syndrome.'

'All good things not to have.'

'Aren't they? I keep suggesting in my mild-mannered way that they just admit I'm fine and let me get back to work. But they can't seem to do that, I think their pride is at stake. A girl got hit on the head, she must need their help. But I *am* fine and I'll be back in a day or two.'

'Good for you.'

She watched my face for a few seconds. 'I want you to know, I never laid a glove on him till his divorce was final.'

'It's none of my business.'

'It will be, though, as soon as word gets around.'

'I won't say anything.'

'It's a police station, for God's sake, gossip circulates faster than air. Not that I'm trying to hide anything. I didn't have anything *to* hide, until a few weeks ago. Even then, when we started, um ... dating, I could tell Bo felt ... uncertain. So I kept it to myself. But when I got hurt ... it seems like that kind of concentrated his mind.' Her smile was a sudden burst of pure radiance, like flowers blooming. Her happiness produced an incongruous glow above the grim hospital gown.

'It makes an unusual courtship story.'

'Yeah, where's a screenwriter when you need one?' Then she was abruptly serious again. 'It's not easy for Bo to be happy, you know. All those years of trying to get a cocaine addict clean, and carrying the whole load with Nelly ... I think he got to feeling like he wasn't ... *entitled* to anything better than just scraping by.'

'He might not be out of the woods yet, Rosie. He seems a little uneasy.'

'And Nelly's going to lay plenty of guilt on him, unless I do everything just exactly right. She's had him all to herself as long as she can remember.'

'You sure you don't want to dodge this bullet?'

She shook her head quickly. 'No. The first time I ever laid eyes on him, I knew that Bo could be ... you know ... *it*, for me.' She turned her hands palms up, in a gesture that said, *Whaddya gonna do*? I shrugged. She turned away and stared out the window, watching the wind whip bare tree limbs against a putty-colored sky. 'But he was always off limits for me. So I made up my mind not to think about him that way, and I didn't. Much. Even the times when his wife ran away I never let myself hope, because what kind of a rotten hope would that be? I just helped him find a day-care place for Nelly, and ... we all tried to help him, Jake, every time, as much as he'd let us.'

'I know.'

'And every time he found Diane and brought her back. Then for a while he'd be wrapped so tight he could hardly breathe. But last summer ... that last time she disappeared he finally said it was too hard, he and Nelly couldn't do it any more.' She turned back from the window, with all her energy and joy of life shining out of her regular Rosie face. 'I made up my mind right then, if he sticks with it ... as soon as he gets his divorce, I'm not letting anybody else get in ahead of me, I'm going to nail this guy.'

'There you go,' I said. It's my inane catch-all phrase for times when I have no idea what might be the right thing to say. 'So, now...' Desperately anxious to get out of the room before she shared any details of how, precisely, she had nailed Bo Dooley, I made a production out of zipping up my jacket, finding my gloves. 'I gotta get back to work. Let me know when you break out of this dungeon, huh?' I found my supervisor voice. 'As for coming back to work, though, don't you be in a hurry. Let's see what the docs say.'

'OK.' She looked confused and a little offended. I could see her wondering, Why did he turn off on me like that, just when we were having such a nice chat? But she recovered quickly and gave me a polite smile. 'Thanks for coming out, Jake.'

'My pleasure. You take care now.' I turned to wave from the doorway and found her watching me with a knowing smile. She had just written off her boss as another one of those males who don't want to talk about relationships.

Little did she know, I couldn't even stand to *think* about this one. In a small staff like mine, a romance between two of my most reliable, hard-working detectives was going to throw sand in the gears, big time. Seriously. There would be firestorms of gossip and jealousy – other detectives were going to worry about pillow talk and secret favors. They would fret about being on the street with the two of them: would they watch anybody else's back as well as they watched each other? In the end one of them would have to go, probably, and wouldn't I be walking on eggs to stay fair to everybody while that happened? *Damn*. Love might be good news for Rosie and Bo, but it spelled disruption and chaos for me.

In heavy traffic creeping back to work, I brooded over a few of the most obvious details. Bo, while he worked with everybody when he was needed, was my one regular vice officer, with drug traffic expertise that would be tough to replace. Rosie had come on board as something of an experiment, the first woman detective in People Crimes, but her energy and humor had made unisex look easy even for Minnesota detectives. If she left under any sort of cloud the next female detective would be harder to recruit, and we were taking some heat from the Equal Opportunity folks as it was. And I dreaded a transition in which we made do with one less detective; we were already too busy to spit. I began to recall that phone on the TV show *Homicide,* ringing endlessly in an empty squad room.

As I parked my pickup I mentally kicked the can down the road. Rosie wasn't at work this week, I reminded myself, and we were staying afloat without her. And Bo looked pretty skittish to me, there was every chance that this ill-starred romance would blow up before it ever got off the launching pad. Not even pausing to admit how shamefully craven that hope was, I decided, Chase a killer today. Do personnel problems later.

Nobody stopped me in the hall and my voicemail only had messages that could wait. I closed my door and slipped Buzz's interview tape in my machine. As soon as I punched it on, I was treated to the astute and drily humorous voice of Aloysius Canfield, the attorney who had employed Geraldine Lovejoy until the day of her death.

'She was one of the greenest girls I ever saw, that day she came in here looking for a job,' he said. 'I looked up her file after you said you were coming to talk to us – it was ten years ago this coming June.

'Even back then, though ... I mean sure, she had a country haircut and dowdy clothes, but there was something about her. Gerry Lovejoy was decent and smart and oh, my God, *determined.* If she decided to do something she *did it.*' A dry chuckle, some paper-shuffling, the heavy breathing of a cigar-smoker past fifty. 'I paid her dog's wages at the start, and that was fair, because although she was a good typist and learned the new computer systems – we were just putting them in and Gerry caught on faster than anybody – still, she had a lot of rough edges to smooth off. The first thing, I remember, she grabbed up the phone when it rang and just said, "Hello?".' He did a good imitation of a naïve girl's voice, and enjoyed another chuckle.

'She never made the same mistake twice, though. Every month she worked in this office, she delivered more value than the one before. I kept giving her raises, I didn't want to lose her. She was earning half again as much as anybody else in the office by the time she—' he sighed, and swallowed a couple of times before he went on – 'and even then, I was getting a bargain. She was one helluva worker.'

Buzz's voice on the tape said, 'Did you

know she was planning to go to law school?'

'Of course – I talked her into it. Ambitious young women, even today, don't usually set their sights high enough. Especially if they come from small towns and poor families, they get used to thinking most things are beyond their reach. I helped her apply for a grant and a government loan, put her on flexitime here so she could arrange classes around her work. It wasn't all altruism on my part – I saw she had the potential to be the junior partner of my dreams.'

'She was that good, huh?'

'It wasn't just her energy and skill. She was the kind of loyal workaholic striver I could see would ease my declining years—' Canfield's voice crackled with a mixture of irony and regret – 'without stealing my practice out from under me.'

'OK, that's a very clear description of Ms Lovejoy, thank you. Did you get an impression of Curtis Brill?'

'Well…' A lot of paper shuffling, a cough, and then reluctantly: 'Oh, well, I guess I better just say it. I thought he was just about the worst thing that ever happened to her.'

'Oh? How so?'

'Gerry Lovejoy had it all, she was on her way to making something of herself. And Curtis – he was just an albatross around her neck! I mean, I could see she was crazy about him – she was a plain girl, I think he was the first real boyfriend she ever had, and he was handsome and paid a lot of attention to her. But it seemed to me that was all he paid.'

'You think he was freeloading?'

'Absolutely. He moved into her house, ate her food, in no time she was doing all his laundry. Then he talked her into that car deal, got her to agree to trade in both their cars for a newer one that he picked out at that lot where he was working part-time. Supposedly he was going to get them this great employee discount because the owner of the lot respected him so much and wanted to do something for the minister – that's what she told me. But Gerry already had an adequate car, a '94 Camaro, and all Curtis had to add to the deal was a ratty old Beetle, as good as dead. I saw what they paid for the Camry and it was a pretty fair price break, but ... Gerry paid the whole tab on the insurance and taxes, yet both their names are on the title.'

'How do you happen to know that?'

'She asked my advice about how to record it. I kept wanting to say to her, "Gerry, wake up." But it was none of my business, of course – and she seemed so happy.'

'You think Curtis had something to do with her death?'

'Oh, wait now, I didn't say that. I said he took advantage of her while she was alive.

Who killed her, that's up to you boys to figure out.' There was another one of the noisy, heavy-breathing, paper-crunching pauses, before Canfield added, 'I'll tell you this, though – you find out that smooth-talking preacher did it, I'll be glad to do the hanging myself.'

Canfield introduced Buzz to his next interview saying, 'This is my secretary, Mrs Manahan.'

She had very flat vowels, said forenoon for morning and called lunch dinner. Her farmer's daughter voice, harsh and uncompromising, said, 'Call me Mrs Manahan, please, none of this Ms stuff for me.'

From where Mrs Manahan sat, Geraldine Lovejoy looked like an entirely different sack of cats.

'That first day,' the begrudging voice said, 'she didn't know *anything*, believe me. I had to teach her everything, even how to answer the phone.' Yes, Geraldine had worked hard and learned fast, the secretary admitted. 'But she was never the sweet little country girl Mr Canfield thought she was. Gerry Lovejoy wormed her way into first place here, just walked right over the top of me and Evelyn – that's my assistant, she's not here today. When she is, you can ask her, she'll tell you the same thing. From the very beginning, Gerry got what she wanted around here.' There was some agitated sniffing, something that sounded like, 'Hmm? So,' and then she added, 'Mr Canfield called her The Over-achiever. Evelyn and I, between ourselves, we called her The Vaulter. If you were in her way, she didn't even bother to push, she just jumped right over you.'

Buzz said, 'You ever meet Curtis?'

'Oh, yes, indeed.' A satisfied little, 'Hmph' and then Mrs Manahan said in a rush of vengefulness, 'The Vaulter was due to get her comeuppance from that one before long or I'm very much mistaken. Minister my foot. That Curtis is nothing but a charlatan.'

Geraldine's image shifted again in the course of Buzz's next interview, with a gum-cracking part-time data processor named Breezy Day. She giggled gloriously when she said her name. 'My ditzy Mom actually *named* me that, can you *stand* it?'

Breezy agreed Gerry was a demon for work. 'But I could never see what Curtis Brill saw in her,' she said. 'I mean, here's this dishy guy hooking up with Miss Drab and Drudgy, what was he thinking?' She did a devastating imitation, dripping with contempt, of Geraldine Lovejoy simpering, 'I get to go home tonight and snuggle with my sweet preacher-man!'

'I mean, too pi-ti-ful, the way she was always going *on* about him. Like, when they bought that car together she said, "He does not really know much about cars but he wants to be the man, you know, so he's always checking the air in the tires!" Even the guy's flaws had to be admired, you know? Like, Barf *City*.' In many ways, Breezy Day was the dream interview. She had strong opinions and a knack for expressing herself clearly, and she didn't hold anything back.

In fact Buzz had brought back, from his short time in the law office, three clear, straightforward interviews filled with specifics. Damn good police work. He has a nice, easy way about him that encourages people to open up. Each of the subjects had a view of the victim that told as much about the person talking as the one described. For different reasons, they all agreed about one thing: Geraldine Lovejoy and Curtis Brill were strikingly mismatched.

'OK, everybody in the law office agrees they were an odd couple,' I said, walking into Ray's office. 'Have you found anybody who thinks they were made for each other?'

He had just finished a call; his outstretched hand was still curled around the phone in the cradle and he was staring at the mug full of pencils that sat beside it on his desk. After several seconds of blinking silence, he peeled his eyes off the writing utensils and shifted them to my face so he could stare through it at something fascinating out in space. I began to understand how a specimen feels in a petri dish.

'Well, maybe Pokey's right after all,' he finally said.

'What?'

He lifted his right hand off the phone and held it out to me, palm up. 'But then everything else that happened makes no sense at all—'

'Who was on the phone, Ray?'

He took a last long look at the planets behind my head before he said, 'The dean of students at the Community College.'

'What did he want?'

'I called him to verify that Geraldine Lovejoy was registered for a class Friday night.'

'Oh, right. And?'

'She was. Advanced Accounting 253, a five-credit course that meets in the Hugh Fisher building on Monday, Wednesday and Friday. It's a two-hour class that starts at eight p.m.' His focus shrank abruptly to my face. 'But last Friday night, the professor who teaches that class went into the faculty lounge a few minutes before class, said she felt like she was coming down with the flu, and passed out. One of her colleagues went down the hall and dismissed the class at ten past eight.'

'Oh. Well, then...'

'That's what I say, oh well then. If Geraldine's class let out at ten after eight, maybe she did get mugged about then. But then where the hell was her body till ten thirty?'

Nine

The new information gave us a whole new set of problems. To begin with, why hadn't Curtis Brill ever mentioned the cancelled class?

'Wouldn't Geraldine call him when her plans got changed?' Ray said.

'But maybe if she loved to snuggle so much, she'd just decide to go home. And got creamed on her way to her car.'

'Maybe. But this was his night to write his sermon.' Ray was poking a sharp pencil through a blank sheet of paper. 'And she was supposed to give No-No a ride home, wasn't she? I'd think she'd call Curtis to discuss a change in plans.'

'Is Buzz still over there, talking to him?'

'Um ... let's find out.'

Buzz answered his cell from a fast-food restaurant. He was just getting started on a BLT with curly fries, which he by God deserved, he said, after that long, teary interview with Curtis Brill. 'Which netted us nothing but a longer and more boring version of the Friday night timeline we already had,' he said. 'Every detail, man, solid as a rock. They had tuna surprise and a salad for dinner, we went over that till I'm pretty sure I could make the whole meal myself. He even told me the prayers they said together before Gerry left for class. I mean, *word for word,* you want me to read 'em out to you?'

'That can wait, I guess.' Ray told him what we'd just learned about Gerry's cancelled class and said, 'Go back there and ask him if it's possible his lady hung out in the library or someplace for two hours instead of going home. Ask him to explain why she didn't call him when her class was cancelled. Or if she *did* call him, why the hell he never mentioned it.'

'Aw, shit,' Buzz said, 'I'm sick of listening to that weepy preacher, couldn't somebody else take a box of tissues over there and ask these questions?' He knew, though, before he even started on that rant, that if Ray Bailey wanted him back at Brill's house he was going to end up there, so after a couple of minutes of half-hearted bitching he agreed to go as soon as he finished lunch.

'Today's lunch,' Ray said, 'not tomorrow's, OK?' He hung up the phone, laid his thin hands along both sides of his nose, up under his glasses, and rubbed. The man was plainly suffering from exhaustion, he needed to lie down.

I had my mouth open to tell him to go

home when Kevin peered into his doorway, saw me sitting there and said, 'Ah, here you are.'

I said, 'What now?'

'Jeez, what are *you* so touchy about? After I chase you all over the building to give you the information you asked for...'

'Oh, you got it already? What about it?'

'None of the campus parking lots ever reached capacity last Friday night.'

'What?' Ray looked at me. 'When did you ask...' He looked back at Kevin. 'You're sure?'

'The gates are automated and they keep the tape, they say, because they have to justify maintenance requests and so forth. You can have a copy if you need it.' Kevin watched while Ray's face puckered up with repressed anger and I, unhappily reminded that I had breached protocol again, examined the backs of my hands. Finally he said, 'Hey, guys, you're welcome. Any time,' and stalked back to his office.

'You're doing it again,' Ray said. 'How many times have we talked about this?'

'I just happened to be standing in his office when I thought of it,' I said. 'He's in touch with those guys all the time, I thought it would expedite...' I took a deep breath and said, 'Aw shit, Ray, I'm sorry. I didn't mean to squeeze your shoes.'

'I know. You never do.' His face looked,

briefly, like the sky just before the tornado hits. Then he kind of sucked up some way, smoothed out his expression to just standard Bailey gloominess and said, 'OK, enough about that! We just found another question for Curtis, didn't we? What the fuck was Geraldine Lovejoy's car doing way over there on 17th Street if the lot right there in front of the Fisher Building had vacancies?' He dialed his phone again, fast, and Buzz Cooper had to pull his face out of his BLT a second time to copy down still another question for Curtis.

While Ray was still busy talking to Buzz I got up and got out of there. I couldn't spare him from the staff over a little thing like fatigue, there was too much to do. And the mood he was in, I thought it was better if he didn't see me for a while.

I've been chief of the investigative division almost three years, and I've got damn-all plenty to do. You'd think I could stay off my assistants' turf. I have a curious nature and I hate to wait, and those are both lousy excuses. I made a new resolution, very similar to several I had made on earlier occasions. This time, I told myself, I was absolutely serious: no more jumping the turnstile between labor and management, ever.

Since that was settled once and for all, I went back into my own office and tackled the mound of paper that continues to grow in the middle of my desk while my back is turned. Requests for changes in days off; a complaint from a woman who claims the investigator who came to her door laid an inappropriate move on her; two reminder notes from Lulu about meeting times and places. Almost certainly, at least one of those meetings would end with a resolution to hold another meeting. Before long I felt so sorry for myself I forgave my own sins.

And the good thing about both Ray and Kevin is they don't hold grudges, they get their bitching done on the spot and get over it. So Monday's turf argument was ancient history by Tuesday morning, when People Crimes detectives mustered at the big table in front of Ray's office. I sat in because I wanted to hear Bo's report on the autopsy.

Watching the crew assemble, noisy and profane with their coffee mugs and stacks of notes, I reflected how much their behavior had changed since last week's meetings. Then they'd all been tense and tightly focused, repeating details of the sting we were planning, anxious to get all the moves memorized so they could be sure of doing their own jobs right. These few days had put a whole new twist on that case and produced a new one. Now we had two virtually simultaneous muggings and one had turned into a homicide. But the detectives, while engaged, were relaxed and happy. They had done what they were asked to do and got the quarry they went after. What was not to like? True, everything we thought we knew was changed now and we had a new set of puzzles to bust our humps over – but hey, no sweat.

'OK, Buzz,' Ray said. 'What did Curtis Brill have to say for himself the second time around?'

'That was even a bigger waste of time than the first interview,' Buzz said. 'He says he never had occasion to ride along with Gerry when she went to that class, so he doesn't know where she usually parked. He always stayed home Friday night and used her class time to get ready for his church duties on Sunday. Last Friday was no exception, he was home writing a sermon. When I asked him who could verify that, he said, "Nobody. You have to be alone with God to write a sermon."' Buzz favored us all with a what-the-hell grin. 'He actually talks like that.'

'What about the time, though? The fact that Gerry got out of class at ten past eight and never came home, how does he explain that?'

'He doesn't. All he'll say is, Gerry always had a good reason for everything she did. He said, "Trust me, when you find out what she was doing Friday night, it'll be perfectly reasonable." He doesn't think it's odd she didn't call. She understood that writing a sermon is hard, serious work, he says, she always tried not to interrupt him.'

'Jeez,' Darrell said, 'some ego, huh?'

'Yeah, he's a pip. He did ask something I couldn't answer, which was, are we sure when she died?'

'Not exactly,' Ray said. He looked at me, so everybody else at the table looked at me too. 'You got the impression she'd just been hit, right? From the—' he cleared his throat – 'the man in the overcoat?'

'Mr Quigley. Yes. He ran up to me like it was an emergency, he was yelling, "Officer!" or something like that and then he said…' I thought a minute. 'He said, "A woman's been hurt." As if it had just happened.'

'Wait a minute,' Andy Pitman said, 'what's this about a man in an overcoat? I haven't heard that part before.'

I told them about the sweating man in the stylish coat and hat, and his well-dressed wife. 'Ray has the telephone number. The trouble with his story is that it's based on the statement of another man he claims he found stooping over the woman when he found her. And that man disappeared before we got back, so—'

'So we're working with double hearsay evidence here,' Andy said.

'Yes, and there's nothing we can do about it, nobody ever got the first man's name.'

'At the hospital, did Pokey verify that she had just died?'

‘No. First he said something like, “This time you can tell me.”’

‘Oh? Because you got there so quick, you mean?’

‘Yes. Quigley called me, I ran after him for less than a block, and there she was, lying on the sidewalk with a crowd around her.’

‘And she was still bleeding?’

‘Uh ... well. There was blood all over her face and her clothes, but I didn’t see any blood flow after I got there. And in the hospital, Pokey conferred with the admitting doc and they both seemed to think she’d been dead a while.’

‘Like how much of a while?’

‘Like maybe an hour or even two.’

‘But you didn’t believe them?’

‘It didn’t fit with what everybody said at the scene. And you know how Pokey is, usually he won’t guess time of death any closer than two or three hours.’

‘What did you think at the scene? And in the ambulance?’ Andy was trying hard to be polite.

‘I never had a chance to form an opinion. I called 911 on my way to the scene, and all the rescue components were right there because of the concert. So the ambulance and both back-up uniforms got there within seconds after me. They were ready to transport within two minutes, and after that I never got close to the victim. I asked Ray to look for blood on the sidewalk as soon as he got to the crime scene, but—'

'I never found any,' Ray said.

'So she could have been dead for two hours.'

'Well, not where we found her. She *might* have been lying on the sidewalk a few minutes before the man found her, but not much more than that. There was a good deal of foot traffic in that area Saturday night.' I looked around the table.

'OK,' Ray said, looking as if he had swallowed something bad. 'The short answer, Andy, is we don't know. *We* think she died just before or just after Jake found her, but the docs think it was earlier. Let's move along. Bo, did the docs at the autopsy decide what killed her?'

Bo read from his notes. '"A massive head injury from some heavy object caused fatal bleeding into the brain and spinal column."'

'OK,' Ray said. 'And no evidence of drugs or alcohol that they could see, right?'

'Tox screen isn't back yet. But that's what they said. And for what it's worth—' his ice-blue eyes swept the table looking for anybody who didn't know what it was worth – 'I agree with them.'

'The mother and sister say the same thing, Gerry wasn't a user, didn't even smoke or drink.'

'Boyfriend agrees,' Buzz said. 'Positively.'

Bo said, 'No sign of defensive wounds, no evidence that she put up a fight, nothing under her fingernails. Looks like a perfect ambush.'

'OK. What else?'

'They said the lividity picture was very confused, like the body might have been moved some time after death.'

'Well, of course it was moved,' Darrell said, 'when we took her to the ER and then they moved her at least twice I bet.'

'Maybe it fits, though,' I said, 'with Pokey's belief that her wounds were a couple of hours old when he first saw them.'

They kicked that around the table for a while, till Ray said, 'OK, we can't settle this now. Till the lab work comes back, we need to fill in some of the other details.'

He assigned interviews to Andy and Clint: the victim's mother and sister, high school and college classmates, associates around town. 'Descriptions of the victim seem somewhat conflicted so far, so get all you can – spending habits, food preferences, what she read. Did she go to her boyfriend's church, by the way? Talk to her teachers at the college. Find out if she was worried about anything, how her grades have been lately. Now, you,' he said turning to Buzz, 'I want you to get me a lot more information on the boyfriend. Relatives, I haven't heard about his family yet. His church seems to be the center of everything for him, talk to some people there. And those friends the sister mentioned ... uh, here—' he found his note – 'Pee-Wee and No-No and Jay. Find them and get them to tell you all about their friendship with Curtis, how long they've known him, what they do together besides pray. Ask them what they like so much at his house besides the big dinners.'

'Besides big dinners what else do you need?' Darrell said, and everybody laughed.

'No last names for these buddies? Just nicknames?' Buzz was sick of everything about Curtis Brill, so he pounced on this excuse to complain.

'Get the full names from Curtis,' Ray said, giving him a don't-try-me look.

'He's going to shit purple if I turn up at his door again,' Buzz said.

'Good,' Ray said brightening a little, 'maybe some of the Viking fans in his congregation will pay attention to his sermon.'

Buzz shook his head at the Minnesota humor and groaned.

'Listen,' Ray said, serious again, 'his lady's dead. He has to talk about it.'

There was still a lot to do on the other mugging. Ray wanted Clint Maddox to call all The Sprinter's earlier victims and arrange for a line-up, see if any of them would pick out Jason Wells.

'A line-up with Jason?' Clint Maddox said. 'Where am I going to find four more guys who look like Britney Spears on steroids?'

'Do the best you can. Andy?'

'Yo.'

'I never talked to you after you took Jason to court yesterday. Did he get his lawyer?'

'Sure did.' Andy is a large ugly man; when he smiles, he looks like Jabba the Hut. 'He got a youngster by the name of Sylvester Melencamp. Nice quiet-spoken boy, had his law degree for a couple of months now.' He leered again and the whole table laughed. 'I guess he decided it was time he showed some chops. Anyway he stepped up like a regular soldier and volunteered to defend Jason Wells.'

'You sure he's a real lawyer? We don't want any legal snafu putting this case on hold forever.'

'Yeah, he's got bona fides. Works for one of the big firms, I forget which one.'

'OK. And they entered a plea of not guilty? Mama didn't talk him out of that?'

'Mama didn't seem to be talking to anybody, just looking around like she suspected all of us had dynamite strapped on our belts.'

'Whatever she's thinking,' Ray said, 'believe me, it's better than if she was talking about it. What kind of bail did they set?'

'Fifty thousand. Milo tried to go higher, but you know, we're only coming in with one mugging so far. So even though it's an attack on a police officer—'

'Yeah. Well, fifty thou ought to hold him till we get some more evidence.'

'That's what I thought.'

'OK, guys,' Ray said, 'let's get at it.'

My desk was piled a little higher than usual that morning. It was near the end of a quarter, so besides the usual clutter of phone messages and so on, I had payroll totals to verify and two new applications waiting for evaluations. Thinking about the Rosie–Bo situation, I decided to get everything else out of the way and give the applications close attention.

I made decent progress on the pile for an hour before Lulu called and said the chief wanted to see me. I put a careful pencil mark on the requisition form I was working on and walked into the chief's office still thinking about it.

As I walked past Lulu's desk she gave me her severe look and said, 'He's got ten minutes, no more.'

'Lulu, you called me, remember?'

'I'm just saying, don't start any long stories.' Lulu's got some pit bull in her, I think; she never backs off.

'Sit,' McCafferty said. 'Fill me in about this new homicide. I'm confused.'

'That just proves you're paying attention. This is one very puzzling crime.' I told him about the victim who was in the wrong place at the wrong time, the car parked in the most unlikely location. 'And it seems like the dead girl's kind of a shape-shifter. Everybody's got a different opinion of what she was like.'

'Huh. Funny. What about the sting, though? You got your mugger, but Rosie got hurt. And there's another body besides? And I don't understand the connection.'

'We're not sure there is one. We could be looking for a new mugger.'

'A copycat?'

'Possibly.'

The chief looked out the window and nodded thoughtfully, swung his bright blue stare back to me and said, 'It's sure swell when you come in here and clear things up for me like this, Jake.' His laugh was sharp and not very humorous.

'We'll have more in a couple of days. Soon as the tests come back.' My watch said I'd been here almost nine minutes and it occurred to me I might run out the clock talking about his hunt for old teammates. 'How's your party for Owen Dowd coming?'

'I got six positive OKs. One to go, that sumbitch Pomeroy. I found him once, but now he's ducking my call. Goddamn quarterback, always was a prima donna.'

'Find his wife and tell her the story,' I said. 'I bet she'll put him on the plane.' It was just a random thought but he seized on it like a drowning man grabbing a rope.

'You know that just might work? In fact, it's sort of brilliant. I'm going to try it, by God.' His phone rang and I heard Lulu reminding him of an appointment. 'OK. Yeah, I've got it.' He was trying to put down the phone but she was still urging him to remember something. 'I know what I said, I'm leaving right now.' He hung up and said, 'OK, I guess that's gotta be it. Thanks, Jake.' He nodded pleasantly, and I got out of there fast.

He's only doing his job, of course, when he asks how a case is coming. But he has a knack for asking at a point when the only honest answer would be, 'Damned if I know.' And you can't very well say that to your chief. So sometimes you have to vamp, throw in a little buck and wing, give it the old razzle-dazzle-doo. That suggestion about the quarterback's wife couldn't have worked any better, I thought, if I'd had on tap shoes and a derby.

I was back in my office, drudging over next quarter's requisitions, when a burst of loud chatter started in the hall. Kevin urged a noisy group into his office. There was more talk and laughter, then quick footsteps came across the hall and his face, excited, appeared in the doorway. 'Jake, got a minute?'

'Sure. What ... uh...?'

'In my office. Julie and Chris came back

with two of the women who have extra charges on their cards.'

We did very quick introductions because everybody in the room was busting to tell me something. Chris Deaver went first, a forty-ish detective with years in Property Crimes, a mild guy, soft-looking, with his pot beginning to spill over his pants.

'Kevin kept telling us to look for something all these people have in common,' he said. His wife gives him awful ties for birthdays and Christmas and he wears them till they're ragged out. His drab appearance seems to reassure many people; he makes even a felony seem ordinary. 'The addresses were all over town, so it wasn't a neighborhood. We ruled out profession, religion and schools on the first phone calls, and went on to sports, hobbies and favorite stores, and got zippo.' The two detectives and their clients chuckled, enjoying the story of the chase.

Julie Rider said, 'For starts, we decided to work with the first twelve families who complained.' She looks like Chris's logical opposite, sleek and buffed-up, shoes polished to a spit-shine, creased slacks and a neat blazer. It's always a source of wonder to me that the two of them work together so well. 'They all had a first set of fraudulent purchases made on the seventeenth or eighteenth of January, so we asked them to list everything they did for a week before those dates.' Julie smiled, becoming softer and prettier. 'One thing quickly jumped out.'

The two victims had been nudging each other and nodding. Now the darker one cried out happily, 'We'd all gone to the same rummage sale!'

'Isn't it crazy?' the gray-haired one said. 'It was the second week in January. That benefit for the two firemen who got hurt when that old hotel burned, remember? They called it the Mother of All Garage Sales, all the families pitched in. It was just a spur-of-the-moment thing for me, I didn't plan it or anything, did you, Muriel?'

'No, I just saw the sign and ... well, Saturday morning, I usually keep my eye peeled. I'm kind of a yard sale groupie – and this was a big one, families from station six and all their friends.' She got a little glow on. 'I got two nice flower pots and a turkey platter, I've always wanted one of those.'

Kevin said, 'How did you pay?'

'Well, with my visa card, obviously,' Muriel said.

'They took credit cards at a garage sale? I never heard of that.'

'Well, this one was huge, they rented a warehouse and went after big bucks.'

'How'd they handle it? Fill it out by hand, run it through a machine, what?'

'Oh, good heavens, I don't remember that.

Let's see, I was talking to Belle Furness there at the checkout table ... seems to me we changed our bridge date from Thursday to Friday, and about then somebody handed me the form and I signed it.' She looked around, a little flustered. 'I've got the copy at home. Or my husband has, he checks the bills. I can find it.'

'That would really help,' Chris said, so soothingly that Muriel looked at him, smiled a little and said, 'Well, sure, then, I'll just go through my stuff till I find it.' Not coming on to him exactly, but you could see she liked him best. In his schlumpy way, Chris has great charm and uses it to make his life easier. We could all take lessons.

'Sounds like you're moving right along, guys,' I said. 'What's the next step?' They all looked at each other and began to talk at once. When I saw they weren't going to stop, I wished them luck and escaped to my office. For some time, I could hear the three detectives reassuring the two yard-sale shoppers that of course they didn't suspect any of those brave helpful firemen, or their wonderful, supportive wives either. The ladies came out of Kevin's office a few minutes later looking a little uneasy. They had opened up this can of worms and now they were dreading what was going to crawl out.

Kevin didn't look as pleased with himself as usual, either, when he knocked on my doorjamb a few minutes later.

'Have a seat,' I said. I watched him fold himself into a chair as if he intended to stay all day. 'So – what *is* next?'

'That's what I want to talk about,' he said. He pulled on his earlobes, a thing he does when he's trying to get his brain to produce. 'It's kind of dicey, when you start to think about it.'

'Uh-huh. Somebody at that yard sale was guilty as hell.'

'And that's kind of sticky. Because here's this wonderful non-profit charity event, the wives baked cakes and cookies to sell, dozens of people worked all day. They got a big turnout and made a lot of money, they're proud as hell of themselves and the nice story they got in the paper. We barge into that group and start asking which one of their helpful pals they think was the thief, we're likely to get stoned.' He added, helpfully, 'Not in a fun way.'

'I got that part. What do your detectives think?'

'Chris thinks we ought to talk to a couple more victims, see if they noticed anything hinky.'

'I've been thinking about the purchases,' I said. 'What did this bandit buy?'

'Oh, uh ... fun stuff, DVD players and cameras and iPods. Xboxes.'

'Electronic toys.'

'That's what I've been hearing, yes. I haven't—'

'Easy to resell.'

'Yes.' Kevin's expression, in the next fifteen seconds, went from cloudy, with showers to sunny and warm. He got up. 'Forget the yard sale for now, is that what you're saying? Follow the new merch.'

'I would.'

'Of course. Absolutely!' He was already out the door on his long legs, calling, 'Where's John Smith? Chris, Julie, anybody else down there? Come talk to me!'

I finished requisitions and started on complaints. I knew nobody from my department had used the n-word or the f-word, or tried to get in a witness's pants. But there they were, the complaints that said so, and they had to be answered. There's a form. It has to be backed up with the tape of the conversation that would take several hours' searching to find. Before I got too frustrated I called Maxine and said, 'What's chances for lunch?'

'Hey, your timing's perfect,' she said, 'I just made goulash soup.' Goulash soup is the get-through-till-payday recipe we invented together when I was about eight; it's made out of whatever's left in the refrigerator with a little paprika and maybe some tomato sauce for cover. Add a little macaroni, it tastes pretty good.

Maxine Daley was my foster mother till I was in fourth grade. She's told me she didn't get me till I was almost three, but since I don't remember any of the caregivers before her, in my mind she's the mother I lost when I was nine. My social worker took me out of her house when she found out Maxine's husband was drinking up the aid money that was supposed to be buying our groceries. Now that I'm a grown-up and a cop, I see a lot more merit in that decision than I did at the time. I put some serious bruises on the people who took me away that day, and for a long time after that, my default emotion was rage.

'You coming now?' Maxine asked.

'I can be there in half an hour,' I said. 'Is that OK? Few phone calls first?'

'I'll go ahead and feed the girls.' She's a day-care provider. You have to be careful where you step in Maxine's house; small people crawl out from under the furniture and careen through doorways.

'How many have you got there today?' I asked her. 'Maybe I can find some ice cream.'

'Well ... apples might be better. Brittany and Brianna both got too many treats last night, I think. They seem to be on a sugar high.'

'Deal.' I did the speed-dial calls first, answering most of my messages by leaving other messages. What wonderful things could we be doing, I wonder, with the time that gets wasted every day with phone tag? When I saw I was running short of time I sent emails to the last two so they couldn't put me on hold, and was out of the building in twenty-two minutes flat. I always get a fresh burst of energy when I'm headed for Maxine's place.

Her charm is a little hard to explain. She has one brown eye and one green one, and most of her wardrobe has seen hard wear since she brought it home from Good Will. Her house is a rundown rental in a poor part of town, on a weedy lot with a gate that sags. After my own house, it's my favorite place to go.

'Ah, here's my Jake-itty Split,' she said, getting up to take the bag of apples. She has a talent for inventing silly names. The two little girls laughed and bounced in their high chairs, banged their spoons on the table and yelled, 'Jake-uddy Spwit' or something close. They're not twins or even sisters, but she's been taking care of them since they were both infants, so even though they go home to different houses at night, by day they function as siblings, fighting over toys and food but defending each other against new-comers.

'Just the Terrible Twos today, huh?'

'Nelly'll be here pretty soon. Kindergarten

only lasts till noon.' Nelly's Bo Dooley's daughter, living proof that a father alone can be enough. 'Sit over there so the girls won't smear you. Let's see, is the soup still hot?' She tasted. 'Yeah. Here you go.' She brought me a big blue bowl.

Losing Maxine kicked a hell of a hole in my childhood. For several years I changed foster parents more often than most kids get new sneakers, because I punished all the people who were trying to help me. I was turned around in middle school by a remarkable teacher who got me to consider studying as a feasible alternative to kicking the crap out of my schoolmates. I was lucky; a tweak or two in a different direction, I could have been one of the bozos I'm chasing today.

I found Maxine again three years ago by a lucky accident. I've kept a careful eye on her ever since; I don't intend to lose her again. She's a rare bird with a skewed sense of humor that keeps a hard world at bay.

Going to her house for lunch is like revisiting childhood; I ate up all my soup so she gave me an apple. I got a whole one instead of a half because I'm big now, as she explained to Brittany, who protests every unfair thing she sees and some she makes up.

'You can both get down and play now,' Maxine said, wiping them off. 'You're excused.'

Brianna ran a few laps around the table, yelling, 'Es-koosed, es-koosed, we're es-koosed,' till Maxine finished cleaning Brittany, put her down too and got them to go play with dolls by promising a story in half an hour. To close the deal, she had to show Brittany exactly where the hands would be on the clock by story time.

'Anybody that thinks bribery is a crime has never raised children,' Maxine said. She sat down with her caregiver's sigh, equal parts sore back and mental fatigue. 'How's Trudy doing?'

'Wonderful,' I said. 'This week, seems like she's got her energy back. She cleaned out a closet last night and re-packed her hospital bag twice. She keeps changing her mind about which books to take...' Maxine had stopped stirring sugar into her coffee and was watching me with her head on one side like a bird. 'What?'

'She's getting close, Jake.'

'That's a sign?'

'Uh-huh. That one last spurt of energy, you can pretty much bet on it. Better stick close to home.'

'Be damned, I never heard that one. Well. Hey.' For one mad moment, I longed to tell Maxine about the wolf. But she had her own heavy loads to carry and I didn't want to add the suspicion that her Jakey might be going around the bend. 'So, are you ready for the granny bit?'

'Absolutely. I might even get my own apron.'

I laughed. Maxine has gone apronless as long as I've known her, allowing the drooling and spills of dozens of children to spread over her nondescript clothing wherever it lands.

'It's easier,' she says. 'Why wash one more thing?'

I never noticed her habit of facing the spattering world unprotected, till I hooked up with Trudy Hanson, who seems to have the wearing of large white kitchen aprons hard-wired into her brain. Maybe it's a Swedish thing. She takes off her coat as she comes in the door, and reaches for the apron on the next peg over. Every time Maxine tries to help her in our kitchen, Trudy puts an apron on her before she'll let her touch a paring knife. I'm careful not to catch Maxine's eye during this laying on of the extra layer, because I know we'd both break up.

'OK, so Trudy's ready and you're ready,' I said. 'I wonder if I am? How do fathers know?'

'I don't think they ever do.' Her mismatched eyes searched my face. I thought I had it in good working order but she knows me well, so she sensed something of what the wolf was doing to me. 'You shouldn't worry so much, sweetheart. Trudy's healthy, she's taken good care of herself. She'll be fine.'

'I know. It's just that ... I keep thinking how we went into this together but at the end she has to take all the risks. It seems so *unfair* to me.'

'You must have a talk with Brittany. I believe she's gathering material for a PhD. thesis on fair and unfair.' She reached across the table and took my hand. 'No use trying to make love come out even, Jake. We all just do what we can.'

'Uh-*huh*.' Coming from a woman who'd let two husbands do her out of everything she'd ever earned, I thought that was probably the straight goods. 'OK, well, I'll be calling you, I guess. Sooner rather than later, huh?' One of our hobbies, when I lived with her, was collecting pretentious phrases, like, 'As it were' and 'If you will'. Lately we'd resurrected the game; our current favorites were 'that said' and 'sooner rather than later'.

I got up and put on my coat, and the little girls came rushing to hug my legs goodbye. They don't have many words yet so they love hellos and goodbyes where they've pretty much got the dialog nailed.

Maxine peeled them off me and I drove straight back to my office, where the next couple of hours felt like darting in and out of a badly organized parade in a rough section of town.

Ten

Property Crimes section was working the phones, schmoozing with victimized card holders. Their research required frequent strategy huddles, so there was a lot of trotting in and out of Kevin's office and excited reports of eureka moments. Word had spread that the police were going after the guy who was wrecking everybody's credit, so Kevin was getting frequent visits from outraged citizens, too. They all needed to vent, so the halls in Kevin's section were lively with stamping and swearing.

By contrast, Ray Bailey seemed even quieter that usual, standing in my doorway carrying an armload of files.

'Come in,' I said, 'and remind me where we're at.'

'Well, it's still Tuesday afternoon. I think. And I'm getting everybody together in my office,' he squinted at his watch, 'in eight minutes.'

'Who's everybody?'

'All the people involved in the Jason Wells case. Both attorneys, all three officers involved in the arrest, and Jason. And maybe, God forbid but maybe, his mother.'

'Sounds like a swell party. You need any help with it?'

'No.' He cleared his throat. 'But after I gave you a bad time yesterday about getting on my turf, now I'm hoping I can talk you into getting on to some more of it.' He smiled tentatively and teetered on the balls of his feet.

'Depends,' I said, not wanting to seem easy. 'What?'

'Well, you know Jason's DNA tests haven't come back.'

'Takes time, nothing I can do about that.'

'I know, but in the meantime we're trying to build enough of a case so we can get Jason to plead, save going to court, right?'

'Sure. So?'

'So, if I left these with you—' he set down the big stack of files as he said it, taking all the *if* out of his question before I'd even considered it – 'could you read through them? See if you see anything the rest of us missed.'

'What are these, the other muggings?'

'Yes. I haven't had time to read them again since we caught him. I thought, maybe fresh eyes – now that we know more about him, what he looks like and that, if you read through the case files you might see a mannerism, something he did – anything about The Sprinter that matches Jason. Maybe if we could show him we've got him boxed, he'd fold.'

'Well ... you need this right now?'

'Could you possibly do it today? While we're all still arguing about what to charge him with, how he's going to plead. I mean–' he gave me a little come-hither smile – 'wouldn't it clear the decks in a hurry? If this little scut would cop to the other six muggings, we could concentrate all our efforts on the homicide.'

'Uh-huh. That would be nice. OK, I'll take a look.' He still jittered in front of my desk. 'What's the matter, you need a hug besides?' He muttered something to his shoes and hurried away.

A couple of minutes later, a sheriff's deputy brought Jason up from the jail in chains, and handed him over to his arresting officer, Andy Pitman, who led him clanking down the hall toward Ray's office.

Andy and Bo came out of their cubicles then, and followed Andy and the prisoner. They'd be at the meeting to provide details of Jason Wells' arrest. Jason had made some noises about police brutality, so Ray was going to make certain both attorneys understood that all the brutal acts were done by Jason, and we had witnesses. Bo was there to tell about the severity of the attack on Rosie. Andy would play the tape he made during his quiet ride to jail with the prisoner, to spike any attempt by Jason to claim he'd been abused during booking. Start-up thugs like Jason don't realize that cops have become experts at protecting against bogus claims. Ray never made a move without thinking about the exposure for his crew and the department, and he was careful about preserving his tapes.

A minute later Milo Nilssen, the county attorney, stepped into my doorway and asked, 'Have I come to the right place to find the most wanted mugger?' He thought he was being funny, casting scorn on our two-bit case.

'Don't laugh,' I said, 'the mugging we caught him at is just the beginning. We're hoping to hang a whole string of assault cases on Jason Wells before we're done.' I told him about the DNA samples working their way through the queue at BCA. 'You can't talk about it yet because it's possible we won't get a match. But in case Jason starts all that horseshit about how Rosie jumped in front of him, rest assured we're looking to toast him.'

'Huh.' Milo sat down and scratched his stomach through his shirt while his crafty lawyer's look blossomed. 'How sure are you he did all the muggings?'

'About ninety-five per cent. Everything about the MO matches.'

'OK.' He pursed his lips and made soft

clucking noises. 'Without getting specific, I could probably mention that we've got some proof in the pipeline that's going to put his nuts in a vice as soon as it gets back from the lab. If he did all these assaults he might start to wonder what he left behind. Usually it doesn't take much doubt to make them deal.'

'Anything short of outright lies is fine with me.'

Milo sneered. 'I don't need outright lies to play hangman's poker with a *mugger*. Spinning the truth a little should be plenty.' He got up and strode out, looking considerably more purpose-driven than when he came in.

He'd barely stepped into the hall when he collided with an awkward kid who was squinting at my nameplate on the door. 'Excuse me!' Milo said. 'Did I hurt – oh, say, you're Jason Wells' attorney, aren't you? I'm sorry, I don't remember your name.'

'Sylvester Melencamp.' Sylvester had a likeable smile.

'Milo Nilssen.' Milo deployed the cordial hand-shaking thing he was learning at Toastmasters, full-bore charm with warm eye contact and his left hand covering their clasped right ones. Maybe he and Curtis Brill were in the same speech class. Sylvester began to lean back from him a little on his skinny haunches, as if he suspected Milo might be sucking up all the air. Milo had a whole set of hair-smoothing and tie-patting anxiety moves when he first got the CA's job, but he's shed most of those. Now if he can just calm down his charm offensive a notch, he might start looking almost as smart as he actually is.

They went down the hall together, collegial, trading markers – schools, previous experience, hometowns. Before they got out of range I heard the pro bono attorney say he was from a tiny town up on the iron range. I nodded contentedly and tackled my reading pile. Milo might not quite be Mr Smooth yet, but he easily outclassed Sylvester Melencamp.

Once Ray got everybody in his office and closed the doors, the section settled down to just the low-level buzzing around Kevin's office, and the stenographic tapping and thumping LeeAnn makes. That much white noise is so familiar, it almost qualifies as silence; I tuned it out and concentrated on reading. I close my door when privacy is important, but when I'm working alone I'd rather tolerate some noise and make sure everybody feels free to come in if they need to.

Scanning quickly through the reports, the first thing that jumped out was how right Ray had been about the increasing severity of the attacks. The first victim was not even sure she'd been hit till she saw her purse was gone. The second described a bump, the third a hard shove. The fourth and fifth got knocked down and the sixth was the weeping, painfully injured woman in the ER, the one Ray called me to see. And now there was Rosie, still in the hospital four days after the attack.

'The Sprinter's getting ready to kill somebody,' Ray had said more than once in the last few weeks. His predictions had so prepared my mind for calamity, I was halfway ready to accept Geraldine Lovejoy's death as an unsurprising endpoint in a sequence of increasingly violent events.

But that brought me to the strange enigma at the center of this case: the mugging that turned into a homicide couldn't have been part of the series. Blocks away from where Ray's crew was grabbing The Sprinter, somebody else killed Geraldine Lovejoy. His partner? We still hadn't proved he had one. A copycat? That could be; the crimes had been fully reported by all the media.

When I finished my initial scan I stacked the files up in order again and began to read through the whole stack thoroughly. I was almost to the end of the top folder when my phone rang.

Jimmy Chang said, 'Jake? I called for Ray but they said he's in conference. So I'll ask you, I guess. What the fuck is the deal with this car?'

'The Toyota we sent up? It's the victim's car. You find something odd?'

'Odd is right. You'd better be ready to assure me this isn't somebody's idea of a joke.'

Jimmy Chang is Trudy's boss, the director of the Bureau of Criminal Apprehension in St Paul. He was overworked when he was running the state crime lab with one satellite. Since they moved into the new building with twice as many scientists and two more adjunct labs, he's up to his eyeballs in Very Important Tasks. He usually skips niceties like hello and goodbye, and I can't remember the last time he called me.

'A joke? What's funny about Gerry Lovejoy's Toyota?'

'It's almost completely clean. There are no latent fingerprints worth lifting. We found a fragment of DNA on a door handle, not enough to work with. You hear what I'm saying? The car's clean.'

'Jimmy, that car's owner was ambushed on the street. There's no way her car could be clean.'

'Jake, I don't have time for games.'

'Who says I'm playing any? Ray took pains with that car, damn it. You got it just as the victim left it. Nobody touched it, we just wrapped it and shipped it.'

'Please don't waste my time arguing.'

Jimmy had climbed on his Chinese–Hawaiian high horse, and was enjoying the ride. All the men in his family are college professors, so he mastered intellectual snobbery some time before he could walk. 'This is intolerable – we moved your car up in the queue because Ray pleaded that you had a homicide with almost no physical evidence. Now we've wasted two highly paid technicians' time – two hours apiece! And the only thing we found to test was that smear on the doorpost, which turned out to be paint. Wretched waste of time, going over and over an automobile that's been washed clean inside and out.'

'Jimmy, you want me to kiss your foot? I'm making a note to talk to Ray about it. I'll investigate, OK? That's what we do here. Are you ready to release the car?'

'More than ready. We're completely out of space here. I'm having your car put on the tow right now. Follow through on this, Jake, I need answers.'

'Well, God, Jimmy, you think you're the only one? I've been talking about this goddamn Toyota every day since—' I had much more to say but the line had gone dead.

Jimmy Chang was always a workaholic with few humorous impulses. But he used to be capable of short civil conversations. Lately most of his utterances sound like they're coming from Mount Olympus. One day soon, I huffed to myself, Jimmy Chang is going to unleash one of those thunderbolts, and fucking Venus will float ashore on a half-shell. That should cause quite a stir on the Minnesota River.

I tried to put his rudeness out of my mind and go back to my reading. It was a few seconds before I could see the print clearly because I was looking at it through a red film of rage. When my vision cleared I found myself staring at an after-report in the Frances McKittridge file. She was the first mugging victim, the file was opened during the last week in January.

Andy Pitman had added a note to her folder on the Friday before last: 'Ms McKittridge phoned, says the Visa card she lost in the mugging (see numbers in file) just sent a bill with several charges to her card for merchandise she never ordered and didn't receive. Admits she's at fault in this – didn't get around to canceling the card for a couple of weeks. Then she was late paying the card this month because her affairs are still a mess. When she found the bogus charges she called the card company, admitted she owed the late charge but protested the charges for the items she didn't buy, and they agreed to remove them. Wanted us to know somebody might still be using the card, asked if we could trace it – I told her we don't do that. Total of over twenty-two hundred dollars charged, she says, online orders for top of the line digital cameras and lenses.'

We'd been talking about bogus credit card charges so much, that for a few seconds this one slid into the ongoing conversation without a wrinkle. I got up to make a copy of the note for Kevin. On my way out to the copy machine it hit me: *Wait a minute, this isn't Kevin's case.*

I stood in my doorway holding the piece of paper, talking to myself.

McKittridge's credit card was lost when she got mugged. Ray's case. Nothing to do with the bogus charges Kevin was investigating. I went back to my desk and wrote another note to Ray to talk to me about the McKittridge file. I started to put Andy's note back into its clip on the back page.

But then I sat back in my chair, propped my left foot on a half-open drawer, and read the note again. Stared at it and tapped it, scratched my head and read it one more time.

Out of all those snatched purses, why would this be the only fraudulent use of the victims' credit cards? If he used McKittridge's credit card to order high-end digital toys he must have some game going. I started through the folders again, looking for any more notes about bogus charges. I found one, again in Andy's handwriting, in the Sandra Mills file, the second mugging in the series. She claimed she had cancelled all her cards on the day after her purse was snatched, but when her Visa bill came it included a charge for a spotting scope for almost fifteen hundred dollars.

Kevin found me there, staring out the door with Andy's notes in my hand. He bent over till his eyes met mine at about his waist level and said, 'Yo.'

'Mmm. What?'

'You look as if you're having an epiphany. Or is it flatulence?'

I gave him my three-days-dead look and said, 'Say what you want in as few words as possible.'

'Julie Rider's found the man who took the money at the firemen's yard sale.'

'Oh?'

'But he can't be our culprit. He's the father of one of the cake-baking wives. He's about eighty years old and looks like a saint. Which he's not; he's a retired CPA who still does a few tax returns for old customers—'

'I'm hearing a great many words...'

'I know, I know, but this is a real breakthrough, Jake. He's over here in my office and he thinks – we all think – that he's got the answer to how this credit card theft happened. If you could just take a minute...?'

'Just one minute, that's a promise? OK, right now, let's go!' Jimmy Chang's bile rolled down on Kevin, who shook it off and led the way.

Inside his dinky office, four Property Crimes detectives were talking to a small man whose white hair did seem to frame his head like a halo. His benign blue eyes added to his air of righteousness; I'd have bought a used kazoo from him and paid his asking price with no haggling. He looked kindly and interested, sitting in front of Kevin's desk between a tall, animated woman in plush sweats and Muriel, the turkey platter lady from the yard sale. Kevin wedged in and I followed with my arms pressed to my sides; Kevin's office had begun to resemble a phone-booth-packing stunt.

'I've been trying to retire for ten years,' the white-haired man said. Everybody called him Mr Herman, except the lady in sweats who called him Dad. 'But I was a CPA in private practice and you know how it is, you have long-time customers who insist they'll go broke if you quit keeping track of their money. So I still take care of a few premium clients, and that's why I kept my credit card machine, even though it's the old manual kind. The bank still furnishes the forms so I never bothered to switch to the new electronic machines with the tape.'

Kevin had wormed his way back to sit behind his desk. He looked across it now, met my eyes and nodded brightly: *You see where this is going?* I did, but the consensus in the room, plainly, was that Mr Herman was owed so much respect he had a right to tell this story at his own pace.

'Cassie's husband is a fireman—' the old man exchanged a fond look with the woman in sweats – 'so when she asked me to help with the benefit sale, of course I said I would. All the wives said, "Oh, you're good with money, why don't you do that part?" I'm afraid I'm the one that suggested they'd sell more if they took credit cards. I said I'd bring my old hand-roller machine to process the cards, I'm used to it.'

Cassie said, 'At the last minute, just as the sale was starting, Dad said that he'd be careful with the carbons so nobody got hold of all those numbers. But I said, "Oh, well, people who misuse credit cards mostly shop online, and for that you need those verification numbers on the back of the card, so I guess we don't need to worry."'

Mr Herman said, 'It was getting noisy in the yard by then, and I thought she said we needed to record those numbers to be safe. So every sale I made, I carefully noted that three-digit verification number in the upper right-hand corner of the card.' He sat back and sighed. 'I've never ordered anything online, I didn't know anything about that. I was focused on making sure I got all my carbon papers in that little wastebasket by my feet. But then, darn it, they started cleaning up before I was done with the last customers, and ... somehow my trash got away. I'm sure sorry, honey.'

'It's not your fault, Dad,' Cassie said, 'we all should have talked it through better.'

'Well, but there was so much going *on*,' the other woman said. She leaned across Mr Herman to smile at his daughter. 'I have to tell you, yours was the best yard sale in *years.*'

'I did think it was quite successful. Although I was hoping we'd get more toys.'

I caught Kevin's eye and ran a finger across my throat. He cleared his throat and said, 'Mr Herman, did anybody help you at the checkout table?'

'No. I told them I wouldn't handle the money if anybody else was going to touch it, and they agreed.'

'So you're sure all the carbons went into that one basket?'

'That's right.'

'Well, then,' Kevin asked Mr Herman's lively daughter, 'you can find out who emptied the wastebasket, can't you?'

'Maybe. We all helped out with the cleanup, I guess. Although come to think of it somebody suggested during a planning session that there'd be a lot of heavy stuff, tables to set up and move around, and why didn't we hire us a helper for the day? Who was it said that?' She looked at her father.

'I have no idea.'

'Well, anyway, there was one boy working there that none of us knew. Except the person who hired him. Why can't I think who that was?' She asked her father, 'Did you pay him?'

'No. I never noticed him, honey.'

'Now this is just going to drive me nuts all day,' Cassie said.

I caught Kevin's eye again, tipped my head toward my office and left. I closed his door carefully behind me, figuring they'd all realize they were suffocating pretty soon, and some of them would leave.

After that hubbub, reading files in my quiet office felt like a rest. I read the entire stack carefully, but there was nothing about Jason's behavior or clothing we didn't already know, nothing that would be helpful to Ray. I put the stack on the corner of my desk and started on my email.

Both meetings broke up a few minutes later. The noisy parade started in the hall again, headed out this time. I thought about Trudy, driving home through freezing slush and crazy traffic, the dark coming down. The need to be driving toward her from the other direction, to see her safe inside our house, became so strong I couldn't think of anything else.

Ray's notes could wait until morning, I decided.

But then he was standing in my doorway, looking tentative, as if he'd come to borrow a cup of something. I told him to come in, wishing he wouldn't. He picked up on my reluctance, said, 'Just for a minute,' and came in and stood two feet inside the door.

I asked him, 'Did your meeting go OK?'

He shrugged. 'Jason didn't fold.' He drove one fist softly into the open palm of his other hand. 'That guy's hard to figure, you know? I know he's The Sprinter, we caught him at it. I'm sure his DNA's going to match the sample from the button, but either he thinks Milo was bluffing about it, or that lawyer he's got—'

'Wait. Milo didn't say DNA evidence, did he? I told him not to.'

'No. But anybody should have known, from what he did say, that he was talking about...' He scratched his head, frowning. 'Why didn't you want him to say it?'

'What if we don't get a match? We look like chumps.'

'You know it's going to match. It's funny, though – it seemed like the lawyer didn't get it. Just out of law school, you'd think he'd be sharp on that stuff. But he didn't confer with his client, made no attempt to get him to reconsider his plea. What's *with* people and DNA, anyway? Do they think we're just making it up?'

'Science is a hard sell to everybody but

scientists. Juries get that look, like, "Oh, here we go again, Frankenstein time."'

'I know. Well, I better...' He turned toward the door; he could tell I wanted him gone. His unease gave me knee-jerk guilt, so I insisted he stay.

'Sit down, will you? I read through the files, I've got a list for you.'

'Oh?' He was in the chair in one quick move, looking relieved.

I picked up my notes. 'Remember how you kept saying, about The Sprinter, "He's getting ready to kill somebody."? You felt like he was honing his skills, was that it?'

'Or getting his nerve up. Something was building.'

'At the time, I thought you were exaggerating. But when I read over the files this afternoon it jumped right out. For at least for the last four attacks, the violence was definitely on the increase.'

'OK. You saw it, huh? OK.' He sat back in his chair, looking gratified.

'Yeah, but that's not how it played out, is it? Geraldine Lovejoy's mugging turned into a homicide, but Jason couldn't have done it. He was a dozen blocks away, getting arrested for attacking Rosie.'

'But if Geraldine Lovejoy died when Pokey says she did...'

'Well. I've been thinking about that. Class was dismissed at eight ten. Is it possible there's just enough of a window so Jason Wells could have attacked both women?'

'I've been wondering. I didn't want to suggest it till I got the lab work back, but ... I'm glad to hear you think it's worth considering.' Fully engaged now, he found a pencil on my desk and started his maddening eraser tap-dance. I wanted to grab the pencil out of his hand but I thought that might seem rude, so I stopped him with the next item on my list.

'I found something else, in two of the files.' He stopped tapping and waited. 'Nothing you missed. Notes Andy added in the last two weeks.' I told him about the fraudulent card charges.

'Oh, I know about those. Andy told me when they called.'

'Oh. You never mentioned it.'

'Well, they weren't asking us to do anything, they took care of getting rid of the charges themselves.'

'But didn't you wonder why just the first two? They all reported carrying at least a couple of cards, didn't they?'

'Yeah, but after those first two muggings we got very insistent about getting victims to get their credit cards cancelled. We stayed right on it because we were trying to control the damage. But the first two, McKittridge and Mills, put off canceling long enough so he had a chance.' He did a short version of the eraser tap-dance, watching me uneasily. 'You have a suggestion?'

'You probably don't know about this, but Kevin's got that John Smith, the computer genius guy? From support staff? Working for him a couple of hours every morning this week. He's got a whole different credit card fraud case going – nothing to do with you – but, why don't you phone those two women, get all the details on dates of purchase and so on, and have Smith find out where those purchases were delivered?'

'Ah.' His eyebrows went up and down a couple of times while he thought about it. He was still a little sore about my parking lot maneuver. It went against the grain for him to get any more help from Kevin's department. But Jason was stonewalling him and he had too much to do. 'OK. That might be ... useful.'

'Good. Here's the whole stack of files. The McKittridge and Mills folders are on top. You can give John Smith the details in the morning.'

He picked up the files, holding them a little away from himself as if they smelled bad.

'One more thing.' I held up my sticky note. I knew what was written on it but I needed a neutral place to put my eyes while I added another smelly scoop to the manure pile of his day. 'Jimmy Chang called and gave me hell about Geraldine's car.'

'What's wrong with Geraldine's car?'

'Hardly anything, that's just it. He says it's almost completely clean. A few smudges of prints on the door handles, no DNA. No blood, no sweat, nothing. Clean.'

'Jake. That can't be.'

'That's what I said. So I was hoping tomorrow you'd get Darrell to figure out how Gerry Lovejoy's car got so clean. Who could have done that?'

'Who? Jesus, what about how and when and why?'

'Sounds a lot like an old Abbott and Costello routine, doesn't it?'

He didn't laugh. 'I took pains to protect that car, Jake. All along it's been the key piece of evidence that didn't fit with anything else. First it was missing, then we found it in a crazy place. I told Darrell, "Don't touch the damn thing, don't even breathe on it. Get the mother wrapped up and carried to St Paul and let them figure it out." And Darrell—'

'Darrell always does exactly what's asked of him. I know.'

'Yes he does. Anyway, Jimmy's not just talking about a few smudged prints, is he? He's saying the goddamn thing is *clean*.'

'That's right.'

'Cleaned *up*. Wiped *down*. Which doesn't make any sense at all.'

'BCA says the car is clean, Ray, I have to

believe it's clean.'

'I know. That's the terrifying thing about BCA, isn't it? They're always right.' He was turning red. 'Goddamn that car. What was it doing way over there in the first place, parked in a residential neighborhood? Why would she leave it there? The whole car thing is so fucking crazy, I can't stand it!' He kicked my desk. He was turning purple.

I looked at my watch. He got himself stopped, somehow, and stood up. 'I'm sorry. Wasting your time, jeez.' He looked at the files in his arms, distractedly. 'Is that the end of your list?'

'Yes.'

'Fine.' He stood up and walked out my door with his lips moving, talking to himself silently. A few seconds later he poked his head back in, looking apologetic. 'Thanks for doing all that work. I didn't mean to—'

'Forget it.' I was already on my feet, putting my coat on. 'Give it a rest tonight, Ray, go to work on it again tomorrow. It's just police work, same old same old. The truth is always out there somewhere.'

'Yeah. But we don't always find it.' He shook his head morosely, said, 'Night,' and stomped off.

Driving home through the early dark, I scrolled through radio stations looking for music. When I happened on a rap station I turned past it as usual, then on impulse quickly back. A thuggish voice began hurling gutter challenges and vile obscenities at the quiet barns and silos along the road. His sound meshed perfectly with the ominous threat that had been haunting my dreams, and I thought for the first time, Maybe these folks are on to something. I turned it up till it rattled the windows. Playing it louder made the words blur together, but that didn't matter, because the meaning of the music – if it could be called music – was unmistakable. Stay out of my way, my noise warned any wolves that might be lurking behind the fenceposts and the big rolls of hay in their white plastic wrappers. I am one very bad dude and I'll kill you if you hurt my lady.

The lights were on in the kitchen, and the little blue Civic stood in the shadow of the house. I smelled beef and onions as my footsteps crackled across the frosty floorboards of the porch. Through the window by the door I could see Trudy's yellow braid moving near the stove. I stood and watched a few seconds while I got my cheerful face on. Then I went in and wrapped my arms most of the way around her while I told her how lucky I was to be married to the smartest and most beautiful forensic scientist and beef stew cooker in Southeast Minnesota. But I didn't say a word about the best part of all, that she had come home safe to me after one more dangerous day.

Eleven

Ray's end of the hall was mysteriously quiet Wednesday morning, his door shut and all his detectives gone from their desks. Kevin's section hummed quietly with phone and computer traffic, but nobody looked up when I walked by.

Good, maybe I can catch up to myself, I decided. I cleared everything off my desk, opened my briefcase, and in one quick and dirty move dumped the detritus of two months' work into the middle of my desk.

Upwards of a dozen people report to me now, and twice that many more provide goods and services to my division. So notes and memos, applications and requests for time off, plans and admonitions and denials fly from all corners of the law enforcement world and attach to me like iron filings to a magnet. Often they reach me when I'm away from my desk, and then they end up in my briefcase.

The only way they ever get out of there is if I take them out. But when I take them out I have to make decisions about them, and I hate that part of my job. Miscellaneous piles of mostly useless paper start a firestorm of protest in my brain. I start thinking about how many more hours of my life will be spent dealing with mounds of mismatched paper, and I feel life ebbing away through the soles of my shoes.

So I put off dealing with my briefcase until I reach the tipping point, where sorting it out becomes less tedious than swearing about things I can't find. Right now I was pretty sure my briefcase had swallowed two training requests I needed to complete the POST list the chief wanted, so I was ready to bite the bullet.

The best way to endure paper sorting is to think about something else while you do it. I wanted to think about Geraldine Lovejoy, her chameleon personality, her pompous boyfriend and their elusive car. The chief wanted me to think about assignments for the POST list. If the world would stay off my back for a couple of hours, I might be able to get both things done at once while I sorted this ugly pile of paper. Double-tasking is supposed to be good, why not try for a triple?

I found a yellow legal tablet, labeled it 'Notes – Geraldine Lovejoy' and lined it up with the right-hand edge of my desk. Below it, I put my printout list of detectives ready for training assignments. Then I plucked two application forms from my pile, clipped them together and set them on the console to read later, saying, 'There!' like it was some big accomplishment. To keep from dying of boredom on a paper chase, I'll even lie to myself.

During the next few tentative jabs at the pile, I paused long enough to write my first notes: 'How good a deal did Curtis get on the Camry? Is it paid for? If not, can he keep up the payments now?' Pondering, I plucked requisitions out of the stack.

The big central mountain had morphed into a lower-lying range of paper goods, plus a sloppy foothill of minutiae – pens, erasers, paper clips and a new toothbrush, still in its wrapper – by the time Milo Nilssen appeared in the middle of my open doorway, impeccably turned out in a fresh haircut and a new blue suit.

'Hey, Milo. Who died?'

'What?'

'You look like you're on your way to a really important funeral.' I tapped a pile of daily report forms together, squaring the corners. It was rude, kind of, but I wanted him to see I was busy. Sometimes Milo gets needy and wants to chat.

'Going to court is all. New clothes have to get started some time.' He came in and closed my door before he thought to ask, 'Mind if I close this?'

'Go right ahead, Milo. Anything you'd like to change about the drapes and furniture?'

'Be nice.' He got comfortable in my extra chair while I smoothed a badly wrinkled, coffee-stained receipt and added it to a pile. 'What the hell are you doing? Don't you have a steno?'

'Sure. First I have to sort out my briefcase and decide what to give her.'

'Ah, yeah.' He peered at the crumpled receipt. 'You wouldn't want LeeAnn nosing around in your coffee break receipts, would you?'

'You come in here and close my door just to sneer at me? Or do you need to wipe your nose on the tail of my shirt too?'

'Actually I'm on my way to see Bo Dooley. He's got another pissant drug dealer he wants me to put in prison so we can waste some more of the state's money. Why can't we just shoot the bastards?'

'OK with me. Shoot their customers too while you're at it and we'll all take a vacation. What else is on your mind?'

'I just wondered if you knew which firm Sylvester Melencamp represents?'

'No, I don't, Milo, and I really don't give a shit. But I see by your beady-eyed expression that you're going to tell me anyway.'

'You get testy about the oddest things.' He picked two ballpoint pens and a Day-Glo marker out of the pile on my desk and began to juggle them. 'I just learned how to do this, watch closely.'

'Why? Anybody can juggle three pens. Add two oranges and you got something.'

'Keep watching while I show you the rest of the trick. Sylvester Melencamp works for Carruthers, Strump and MacAfee.' He plucked all three writing utensils out of the air in front of my mouth, which had just dropped open. 'I see I have your attention now.'

'You talking about Cuddles MacAfee?'

'Bingo. Now will you give Jason Wells a little respect?'

'Not *that* much respect. Not on his best day. Are you sure?'

He nodded brightly, enjoying my reaction.

'Well, what ... come on, they must be just giving their new pup a chance to romp in the yard. There's no way ... what are you suggesting?'

Jeremiah MacAfee got his nickname about ten years ago when courtroom wags noticed that his appreciation for good food and drink was beginning to equip him with the girth and jowls of an old-time movie actor named Cuddles Sakall. When he launches into one of his stem-winder closings, young lawyers claim they stay limber dodging MacAfee's dewlaps.

Opposing counsel would do well to remember, though, that before he got that cute nickname many of his colleagues called him Mack the Knife. Cuddles MacAfee is one of the best defense lawyers in Minnesota. It suits him to keep his office a little out of the mainstream here in Rutherford, but most of his clients are in the Twin Cities. And he does not work for trading stamps.

'No purse-snatcher could pay for the initial consult with MacAfee,' I said, 'and I don't remember ever seeing him take a pro bono case.'

'I know that,' Milo said, 'but the fact remains.' He raised his eyebrows halfway to his hairline. 'So I've been thinking. This mother of Jason's that Ray's so in dread of, does she do any other interesting things besides run her mouth?' The prospect of climbing in the ring with Cuddles MacAfee had Milo all pumped up. In his dreams, I could see, this routine mugging case was crawling out from under a rock and morphing into some big slimy thing with tentacles. Milo was itching to do a Perry Mason on it, dig up what Darrell calls 'the actual facts' and get his picture in the paper in his new blue suit.

'Well, now,' I said, working hard to keep my face straight, 'Jason's mother ... tell you what, Ray has her phone number, if you'd like to visit with her.'

'Oh, yeah? He in this morning, you think? Good, I'll go see him. God, Jake,' he said, getting to his feet, 'how can you work in a mess like this? Look what you've done to my suit!' He went out brushing receipt shavings off his sleeves.

I was still smiling at my empty doorway when my phone rang, and Ray's voice said, 'I need advice.'

'Good morning to you, too. Did you give Milo the mama's phone number?'

'What?'

I became aware of odd noises. 'Aren't you in your office?'

'No. Andy and I are down here in the jail. I got four mugging victims to come in at the same time on a work day, you know how many phone calls that takes? And they're supposed to be looking at Jason Wells in a line-up right now. But two of the guys I was going to use called in sick. Can I run a line-up with only three guys?'

'No. Has to be five. Try some of the prisoners.'

'Today it's all old drunks with pot bellies and beards. I found one deputy here that might do. We got watch caps and goggles for everybody so they just have to be the right body size and not be gray or have facial hair. You and I are both close enough, but these women have all seen me a dozen times. Any chance you could spare some time?'

'To stand in a line-up? Shit, Ray.'

'OK, I didn't think you'd do it. I'll have to

cancel, I guess, and try it later.'

'No, no, don't do that – you'll never get all those victims back again.' I looked at my watch. 'You're all ready to go? No delays?'

'All set.'

'OK.' I sighed once, to keep him grateful. 'I'll be right down.' I arranged the paperweight, staple gun, tape dispenser and in-basket carefully over my precarious piles, and hustled downstairs.

By way of the inside corridor that connects the two buildings, Hampstead County jail's only a two-minute trip from my desk chair. That's a bit too fast for the normal human brain to adjust to the angry human sinkhole waiting on the other side of the locked gray door, so I stood still a few seconds, taking shallow breaths of dead air, till I was ready to walk through the cell block to look for my group. Andy was standing there with a sheriff's deputy, a sleepy street cop just off his night shift, and, amazingly, Kevin's new helper. 'John Smith,' I said. 'You do line-ups too?'

He shrugged. 'Easier than most of my tasks.' That extended to seven the total number of words John Smith had ever directed at me; till now all I'd ever heard from him was 'Hi'.

Andy handed me a watch cap and dark glasses and I put them on. All the other men put their gear on too, and we stood around looking like some weird chorus line in a comedy yet to be written by Mel Brooks. Andy disappeared for a couple of minutes and came back with one of the jailhouse deputies, who led Jason Wells by a chain.

Jason broke up when he saw us. 'Oh, look at this,' he taunted, cackling. 'A matched set of muggers! Ooh, you guys are scare-*eeee*!'

He took much longer to get ready than the rest of us. Andy helped his guard get his chains off, get him out of the orange jump-suit and dress him in something dark and nondescript that looked like a janitor's uniform. Jason co-operated as little as possible, never making a move till he was ordered, 'Lift your foot. Now the other foot.' When they handed him the watch cap he perched it on the back of his head and flashed his dimple in a big smile like he was advertising ski weekends in Banff. Andy jerked the cap down to his eyebrows and Jason wailed, 'Ow, you're pulling my hair, cut it out!'

'Too fuckin' bad. Stand still,' Andy said, and manhandled a pair of swim goggles on to his face.

Jason yelled, 'Your thumb's in my eye! Dammit, you hurt me! I'm gonna report this!' He wasn't really hurt, there was no genuine pain in his voice. But he got off on the anger, and his rage kept building. He huffed around, as noisy and hostile as he'd been light-hearted and humorous a couple of minutes before. The sullen Jason I'd met in my office two days ago had turned volatile. Jail seemed to have tapped into a deep streak of instability in him.

A few seconds after he blew up at Andy he took another turn through Mood Swing City and found his mean side, mocking John Smith for his small stature and the way his cap fit. 'I hope you don't think anybody's going to mistake this little creep for me,' he ranted. 'I mean, look at his ears, for Chrissake – he looks like his head's got sails. You must have to be careful on windy days, don't you, Dwarfy?'

We went into the cubicle when we were told to, did our standing and turning thing, stepping forward when we were ordered. When we were done and back out in the hall I handed my cap and glasses to Andy.

Jason said, 'Well, shit, lookit here, it's the loo-tenant.'

'Captain,' Andy said. 'Watch your smart mouth.'

Ray appeared in the doorway to the viewing room, met my eyes, shook his head quickly and ducked back inside. Andy saw him; his face was grim as he and the deputy began the tiresome process of getting Jason back into his own gear and back to a cell.

He muttered as I passed him, 'Ray said ask you if you'd save some time for him later on?'

'Sure, tell him any time.' I watched him tug at Jason's coverall, stooping, running out of breath. Red in the face, he kicked the kid sharply on the ankle and said, 'Lift your foot, numbnuts.'

Andy meant it to hurt and it did; I heard the crack of shoe on bone as I passed them, and Jason's obscene protests followed me out. The last six days had given Andy and Jason a chance to get better acquainted, and their initial dislike had blossomed into full-blown hate.

John Smith followed me up, went past the support staff bullpen without pausing and into the investigative section, where he walked into Kevin's office without knocking. They came back out in the hall together almost at once, Kevin carrying a pile of credit card bills. In a few seconds they were both crouched over the littered desk next to LeeAnn's station, talking excitedly.

I tuned them out while I shuffled paper and made notes. I found the two training requests I was looking for, scribbled on odd-sized pieces of paper, and added them to the POST list. Added to the two I'd written this morning, now I had four. Triple-tasking had turned out to be a lot harder than double. If I stopped to research the training database I lost focus on the other two jobs, so the POST schedule hadn't grown for some time.

My Gerry 'n' Curt list was growing fast, though, covering most of a page on my long yellow tablet. They were an offbeat couple even before she was killed; now, questions about them clamored for attention. How had Geraldine, the dowdy workaholic, been able to launch this red-hot love affair with the handsome preacher, apparently without changing anything else? I had a string of questions like, 'Has G made any efforts to change her appearance? Anybody looked in her closets? Did her school plans change after she met Curtis? Has romance changed her relationship with her mother?'

Curtis's situation suggested more sinister questions. Where had he lived before he moved in with Gerry? Did he have any means of support besides her? We hadn't found a criminal record, but had we searched the military?

I was starting a fresh line about their car when Kevin's footsteps hurried up to my door. He vibrated on the threshold, saying, 'God, Jake, you gotta come talk to my guy.'

'Something big?'

'Beyond big. Major major major.' I followed him across the hall to where John Smith crouched inside a sort of paper fort. His tiny desk had stacks of paper teetering and fluttering all over it, as did the seats of the two straight chairs he had turned into side tables. Around the desk and chairs, towering piles of paper grew like stalagmites up from the floor. Apparently untroubled by the prospect of drowning in paper goods, John Smith beamed like a lamp over it all.

'Tell him,' Kevin commanded.

'All the contested items I've found so far were delivered to the same address,' John Smith said.

'Fact?'

He nodded, smiling sweetly.

'Someplace in Rutherford?'

'Mail Boxes store in the Mohawk Mall.'

'Mail B ... oh.' They both watched me figure it out. 'All to the same person?'

He shook his head. 'Four names so far. Four box numbers.'

Kevin was doing a happy little dance by my left shoulder. I asked him, 'Anybody you know?'

'No. Let's see if you do.' He read off a list. 'Edward Kyle, Lee Evert, Oscar Amundson, Neil Flynn.'

'Nope. None of them.'

'There may be more, of course. I still have a couple dozen items to go.' John Smith looked as if he'd just announced he still had a full quart of double fudge ripple in the freezer.

'Shall we, uh...?' I nodded toward Kevin's office. Inside, I asked him, 'You figure this is your yard sale helper and three buddies?'

'Or one yard sale helper and three names

he made up. Who knows with a crook? Next thing I'm going to do is send somebody to talk to those Friends of the Firehouse people again. They have got to come up with the name of that helper. And some idea how to find him.'

'There you go,' I said. 'Be firm with the saintly Mr Herman.'

'Indeed,' Kevin said, 'and even firmer with his ladies.' He did a Groucho Marx thing with his eyebrows.

'And then figure out how the Mail Boxes connection works,' I said. 'That's kind of tricky, isn't it?'

'Yeah, but I'll figure it out.'

'Good. That might keep you busy for the rest of the day, don't you think?'

'Let's see, it's the middle of the morning, isn't it? So yes. Maybe not, though, because by a rare piece of luck, I used to date the woman who manages that store.'

'Oh, that is rare, isn't it?'

Kevin tried to look modest. Twenty-nine years old, randy and ridiculously handsome, he has dated most of the females anywhere near his age range in the greater Rutherford market area. 'Her name is Shelley, uh ... well, it's changed now anyway, she got married. You know, there can't be many employees at a small store like that. I'm sure she'll give me the list, she might even guess who's the black hat.'

'What if it's Shelley?'

'It won't be. I squandered several frustrating hours of my youth, finding out how straight Shelley is.'

'Well, but sex and stealing are two different things.'

'Ah, God, Jake, now see, that's what we all rely on, those sophisticated insights of yours.'

I flipped him the bird as I left. He gave me a gleaming smile and began punching numbers into his phone. From the hall, I heard Chris Deaver answer in his cubicle, and Kevin say, 'Find Julie. The three of us gotta hit the road.'

I rode Kevin's big wave of happy energy back into my office and cleared my desk in a firestorm of decision-making. If LeeAnn had been anybody else she'd have protested my suddenly dumping a load of filing on her, but being LeeAnn she pretended to think I was doing her a favor. LeeAnn needs two weeks at self-esteem boot camp, but that's on the long list of things I can't do anything about.

A ragtag rubble of receipt forms were all that remained on my desk by the time Ray came back upstairs, disgusted, already grumbling as he came through my door. 'That was a complete waste of time, Jake, I should have known. I'm sorry.'

'Not to worry, you had to try it.' I knew he

wanted to talk about Geraldine and so did I, but seeing him made me remember something else. 'Did you give those fraudulent credit card charges to Kevin's helper yet?'

'What?' He slapped his forehead. 'No.'

'Why don't you take it over there right now? John Smith seems to be having a lot of luck today. And then come right back,' I called after him as he went out. We'd been totally concentrated on Kevin's credit card search, so I hadn't had time to think where Ray's would take us, and I didn't want to think about it now. My notes had got as far as Geraldine Lovejoy's car, which was beginning to seem like the nine-hundred-pound gorilla in the middle of her case.

'Ray,' I said when he got back, 'we've got to quit spinning our wheels now and figure out that frigging car.'

'OK. But every time I think about it my brain turns to jelly.'

'Sit down. Let's bombard the damn thing with logic. Wait, though.' Terrified by the realization that I was about to sneeze and blow just-sorted paperwork all over my office, I clamped my lips together and hummed, pulled rubber bands around the receipts in panicky haste and tossed them on to the console behind me. Then I sneezed.

Ray's expression changed from anxious to tolerant. 'Bless you. I thought you were going bananas.'

'Not quite yet. OK, now – is the car back yet, by the way?'

'Yes. In the impound yard. Jimmy phoned me this morning, too, by the way. Did he rake your back with spurs like he did mine?'

'Uh-huh. He's even more lovable than usual this week.'

'Tell me again.' Ray's face settled into the Bailey mask of tragedy. 'Why we can't yell back?'

'He runs BCA, he might as well have blue long johns and a cape. Don't get me started on Jimmy, I'll get too mad to stay focused. One more time, now: why wouldn't Geraldine park her car in the parking lot nearest her class, if there was room in the lot?'

'No reason. She would.'

'Fine. Next question: after she in fact parked it in the most unreasonable place, several blocks away in a residential neighborhood where it was unhandy and sure to get a ticket, why did she wipe it clean?'

'And not just why, but how? There wasn't time. She wouldn't have the right tools along. She was on her way to *class*.'

'All right then! Suppose we quit asking why Gerry did any of that with her car and assume somebody else did it?'

'OK.' He looked relieved. 'That's about where I got to last night.'

'Little trouble sleeping?'

'Quite a bit. Rightly so, since I wasted all

that time having a temper tantrum in your office because you wouldn't change the evidence for me.' His eyebrows expressed irony and contrition equally.

'OK, but don't let guilt slow you down, now. Say her attacker took it. Why would a mugger take Geraldine's car away and clean it?'

His eyes glinted. 'Well, see, there you go, that's what I played with all night. The car business just doesn't fit into the picture with a mugger, does it?'

'No. So let's skip over him for a minute. Why does anybody wipe a car clean?'

He shrugged impatiently. 'To get rid of trace evidence.'

'Exactly. And since the car's owner is dead the trace evidence probably concerns her murder, right?'

'Isn't that the most reasonable assumption?'

'Yes it is. Keep going, you're doing great. Who do you like for her killer?'

He rubbed his cheeks, re-crossed his legs and sighed, 'I feel like I have to start with Curtis Brill.'

'Why?'

'We always start with significant others if we can. And Curt's a moocher who everybody says was taking advantage of her.'

'OK, and dependency breeds anger, so ... anyway he's easy to despise, let's despise him together for a while. So ... he'd move the car and clean it because...?'

'He just killed her in it?'

'I like that answer, in a way. Except—'

'Don't bother, I got a whole list.' He pulled his little spiral notebook out of his pocket. 'The timing's a terrible problem, unless everything we've been told is a lie. He was in an apartment, what, fifteen blocks away? He'd have to walk over there. And he could not have known her class was going to be cancelled.'

'Bingo. It seems to me that's the linchpin we should swivel around – he could not have known, nobody knew, that the class would be cancelled.'

'She could have phoned him with the news,' Ray said, tentatively, putting one thought in front of another like a man feeling his way across thin ice. 'Or gone home and picked him up.'

'Only that scenario doesn't seem to fit with her being found dead in front of her classroom, does it? With her car parked elsewhere? And her purse all the way down the block, why would Curtis do that?'

'See, that's what's driving me nuts about this murder. Nothing fits with anything else.'

'I don't exactly like Curt's personality for the job, either.'

'You don't? The self-centered gasbag, pretending to love his fellow man?'

'Can you prove he's pretending? Just because you're not religious—'

'If I was, I sure as hell wouldn't want to be preached at by a phony like Curtis Brill.'

'But if you believed what he said it would not sound phony, would it? Also, if you're convinced Geraldine would not know how to get a car wiped down, try to imagine Curtis doing it.'

'You got a point there.' He pulled on his nose awhile and finally said, 'Except, you know, I think Curtis makes his helplessness work for him. And passive aggressive manipulators, I always like them for nefarious deeds.'

'Well, shit, Sherlock, that's pretty sophisticated.'

He did the thing with his eyebrows again. 'I won't tell if you won't.'

'OK.' I stared at the shadow my ceiling light cast. 'Her boss ... Canfield? On that tape Buzz brought back from her office ... didn't he say he thought Curtis pushed Gerry into buying that car?'

'From the used car dealership where he worked. And they supposedly got a great break in the price, but Canfield didn't think the car was such a bargain.'

'Yeah, well, that's one of the questions I've got on my list here – why was Curtis so hot for this new car? You know what I think you should do? Find Curtis Brill and take him to the impound yard. Get him to walk around the car and explain what he liked about it, what kind of a deal he got, and then after you've got him talking get him to say why Geraldine might have parked it where she did. There's something damned odd about this whole car deal and it's time Curtis took some heat about it.'

'Yeah.' He sat bouncing his knees, thinking. 'Yeah, I guess that might be a good thing to do next. I'll go see if I can find him.' He started to get up, sat back down and said, 'And then, depending how that goes, I think I'll take him home and go on out to the used car lot – what's the name of it? Happy Roads, that's it. See how big it is and if everybody's busy. Interview the guy that owns the place, Happy Somebody, he seems to be everybody's Big Daddy. Find out how much of a car salesman Curtis is.'

'Ray, would you buy a used car from Curtis?'

'No, but I wouldn't consult him on matters of faith and morals either. If he's no good as a salesman why would they keep him?'

'Good question. You should get all the records from the car deal, too.'

'That'll be a fight.'

'Well, that's why God made subpoenas.' My phone rang. Ray looked at his watch and stood up, made a vague waving motion and began walking out.

'Wait!' I tore off my list of Geraldine/Curtis questions and held it out. He took it and left while I was saying hello.

Rosie said, 'Hey, I'm home.'

'Good for you. How many fingers do you have?'

'Back down to ten. I kind of miss all those extras.' She rapped out one happy laugh before the hard charger came back. 'I could still put in half a day, if you want me to? I can be there by one.'

'Rosie, if I see you in this building before Monday I'll fire you.'

'Jake, even the docs say I'm fine now.'

'Good. Anybody there with you?'

'My folks brought me home and stayed to baby me. My dad's checking the air in my tires and my mom's making lunch. Can you believe this? I keep saying I'm perfectly OK but nobody—'

'Sergeant Doyle, it's the twenty-first century now. We have this enlightened thing called sick leave. I want you to take some of it, so I can quit feeling bad about getting your head smashed.'

'Not your fault. If I'd done my job right—'

'Listen, thanks to you we got that mugger off the street. Now I want you to rest up so you can come back and do some more good stuff.'

'OK, you put it that way.' She sighed. 'How's The Sprinter doing in the slammer?'

'Getting testier every hour. We need to keep him there, and your testimony's going to be key. Wait'll you see the pictures we took of your shiners. How are they now?'

'Green and purple. I'm a raging beauty. Listen, Jake…' She cleared her throat. I waited. Hesitation sounds from Rosie Doyle are rare as tulips in January. 'OK, maybe I didn't duck fast enough, but I need to make sure you understand something. When he caught up to me I was off-balance and I had my purse in the hand nearest him, with no strap over my shoulder, nothing to stop him. He could have grabbed the purse and kept going.'

'So?'

'So I want you to remember he went out of his way to hurt me. Maybe these muggings were about the purses to begin with, but by the time that guy got to me, the money was incidental. He was getting off on hurting women.'

'I hear you, Rosie. And Ray agrees with you. So, don't worry, Andy got bail set as high as it would go, fifty thou. The Sprinter's not going anyplace.'

'That's good. Oh, somebody's at the door. Never mind, Dad's got it. Oh—' she dropped her voice – 'it's Bo. Watch my mom, now, pretending she has no idea it's lunch time and she doesn't have soup and fruit and cookies all over the kitchen.'

'Your mother isn't crazy about Bo?'

'My female parental unit would gladly watch my new significant other sink slowly into a tar pit. She won't be rude about it, though, that's not her style. She's just doing this sweet and vague thing, like, "Who's this, again?" I better go.'

'Good luck with all that.'

Now I was ready to start on the chief's POST schedule, as soon as I finished my own expense voucher. I ran a tape, typed up the form and attached the receipts. When it was ready I double-checked all the items, which is a sneaky way of dawdling. I needed the money, as usual, so I wanted to submit the claim right away. But I hate the process; Lulu keeps the petty cash accounts and she always gives me grief before she'll write the check. She loves to lecture me about how I should hand these things in promptly at the first of every month. Once I said I thought catching bad guys was more important than tidying up our desks, and Lulu remarked that, as far as she could ever see, I wasn't doing much of either.

So I had my jaw clamped shut as I carried the claim form to the chief's office. Lulu was not at her desk, though. Her space, and then some, was being filled by Frank McCafferty's large behind. He was bent double, rooting through the papers in her in-basket.

Feeling awkward about addressing my

boss's posterior, I said, lamely, 'Oh.' He straightened up and I added: 'Hi.'

'Hey, Jake. Ah, is that your POST list?'

'Expense vouchers. POST isn't quite ready yet.'

'You're working on it, though, right? Time's getting short.'

'Sure.' I held up my expense sheet. 'Shall I just leave this or—'

'Yeah, put it in the basket here, Lulu'll take care of it. She's taking a personal day—' he shrugged – 'to keep me humble, I suspect. She said she'd leave the minutes of the last city council meeting on her desk, but I sure as hell don't see them.'

'Maybe that blue folder—' I pointed – 'on the blotter?'

'Oh.' He opened it. 'Be damned, there it is.' He started toward his own office, turned back and said, 'Been to lunch?'

'I brought my own. I'm sticking close to the phone, Trudy's due to pop any minute.' I knew that didn't make sense; I had my cell on my belt, she could reach me anywhere. But these days I was happier eating a sandwich at my desk, waiting for the phone to ring, with the quickest way to Methodist Hospital all figured out. I knew it wouldn't help to get there before Trudy, but I also knew if anybody was late arriving, it wasn't going to be me.

'Oh, right,' Frank said. He has five children

of his own and roomfuls of nieces and nephews, so he knows better than to clutter an expectant father's mind with logic. He just nodded and said, 'Why don't you eat your lunch in my office? Bring the list along and we'll talk about it.'

'You're brown-bagging too?'

'Drywall and water till the end of the month.' Frank's battle with his weight is ongoing and fierce. When his nightly sessions on the Stairmaster fail to keep blubber at bay, he limits his lunch to a hundred-calorie granola bar he calls drywall. 'I hate these damn things but what else can I do? All these lean and mean athletes coming to town—' he unwrapped his skimpy snack carefully, trying not to spill a crumb – 'they'll all be bragging about their golf and skiing and SCUBA, probably, and here I sit behind this desk swelling up like a blimp.'

'Show them your wall full of shooting trophies,' I said, 'that'll get you your edge back.' I was already sick of his reunion, and it hadn't even happened yet. Over the years, I'd seen McCafferty's self-esteem hold up fine in the face of firefights, demanding taxpayers and ranting editorials. Now this little get-together with long-lost teammates was making him crazy.

Living in a hundred-year-old farmhouse with a pregnant perfectionist had kept me hopping all winter, so I wasn't concerned about calories. My lunch was a big roast beef sandwich, heavy on the mayo. I was still working on the first half of it when Frank crunched through the last of his oats, brushed off a few crumbs, and said, 'OK, lessee your list.'

'Well, it's not finished yet, but here...' I handed it over with one hand while I fished a juicy dill pickle out of its baggie with the other. I took a big crunchy bite and maybe, come to think of it, I might have squirted a little juice around. It was way beyond good.

So maybe it was the juice, or the smell of garlic and dill coming off my pickle. Something darkened Frank's mood about then, and soured his reaction to my list. He read through my plans for the four detectives I'd assigned courses to, turned the paper over to see if there was anything on the other side, put it down and fixed me with a blazing blue stare. 'This is all you've done?'

'I told you it still needs work.'

'Needs work, hell, it's hardly started.' He rocked back in his chair, torturing the springs. 'Damn it, Jake, POST credits are not just busy-work! Licenses are at stake, you know that! I swear, getting paperwork out of you is like wringing blood from a stone.'

'Aw, come on, Frank, when have I ever missed a training deadline?'

'You're damn close to missing one right

now. I have to submit the whole package Monday, training and promotions and budgets for all the divisions. I need half a day to review it and make sure everything fits. And from Friday noon on I'm tied up with this group coming in. Besides, what if Trudy goes into labor, who'll do my POST list then? Damn it, quit procrastinating and give it to me this afternoon.'

'Well ... I can't. I've got interviews...'

His face grew dark as his blood pressure rose; the room itself grew darker. How does he do that?

'I can switch those,' I said quickly. 'I'll do the POST list next.'

'Do that,' he said.

I rolled up my brown bag and got out of there, feeling his eyes hot on my back. In my office, I called the two officers I'd intended to interview and put them off to Thursday. Then I laid my list of investigators in the middle of the desk, spread course lists all around it, pulled up the running tally of points I keep on my computer and started the complex time/points/budget waltz that the training schedule involves.

Wagers have to be made, because each part affects all the others. Was Rosie back for good? I decided to bet she was, and put her down for diversity training and a Taser course. But if Rosie stayed, would Bo be forced to move? Not in the next six months,

I promised myself, even if food fights erupt in the hall. I set him up for a three day update on the latest permutations in meth labs.

The trick is to get everybody scheduled for courses they haven't taken before, without having more than one People Crimes and one Property Crimes investigator off the duty list at a time. Night courses and Saturdays help, but they put a bruise on the budget for overtime. I love to see competitive shoots coming up because I get to count that time against the required training hours, but the only pay anybody gets is in trophies. I usually have one or two requests waiting in the folder, too – this time I was giving Darrell the two-day seminar in blood-borne pathogens he'd asked for.

POST math gets complicated as hell. To keep their licenses, they all need forty-five credits every three-year period. That has to be balanced against keeping the duty roster covered, and staying inside the budget. It's like juggling two spatulas, a rolling pin and an umbrella – and I was doing this trick with one eye on the clock. Kevin put his head in my door once and got as far as, 'Could you—' before I raised my right hand in a claw and bared my teeth, and he backed out.

At three thirty I carried this triumph of guesswork past Lulu's empty desk and into Frank's office. I was hoping for at least a mild 'attaboy' when I laid the schedule in front of him, but he was on the phone and just pointed to a spot on his desk.

I checked Lulu's desk on the way out. Somebody had placed another document on top of my expense claim form. I switched it back to the top.

Back in my office, wired to the eyeballs after three hours of sweaty concentration, I sat through a weird quarter hour of twitching solitude while nobody asked for help, nothing popped up on my email and my phone didn't ring. I filled my paper clip holder and dusted the clock. Ray Bailey probably saved my life when he walked in and requested a favor.

'Sure,' I said. 'What?'

'I've spent all afternoon tracking down Curtis Brill, now I've got him headed for the impound lot and every detective on my roster is out of the building.'

'You need help finding the impound lot?'

'I'd just like to have a second set of eyes on this guy when he looks at this car. But if you're busy...' He eyeballed my desk, which was clean and bare.

'Promise me there's no paperwork involved,' I said, 'and I'll follow you anywhere.'

We took a car from the pool. Coming up out of the underground garage, we drove into a trash blizzard – a blustery wind blowing garbage and a little light snow over dirty ice. Squinting into it, we grouched about changeable Spring weather for ten blocks, leaving the ambient air substantially unchanged. Why do we waste our breath like that?

I parked by the litter-strewn chain-link fence of the impound lot and watched Curtis Brill climb out of the squad car Ray had sent for him. Hunched against the cold and frowning, he seemed to be losing some of his magisterial calm.

'I was teaching a Bible class for seniors.' His lips trembled a little with indignation. 'I got kidnapped out of my own church.'

'Sorry if we caught you at a bad time,' Ray said, not sounding sorry. 'We need to talk to you about your car.'

'Oh, is it back, finally? Are you going to let me take it now?'

'Not quite yet,' Ray said. 'We need the answers to a few questions first.'

'Well, not from me, I hope.' Curtis had a sharp little laugh today. 'I seem to know less and less about more and more.'

We walked together into the cold little office shack. Ray signed us in and got the keys to the Camry from a man in a plaid wool cap with ear-flaps. 'Out there in the lot.' He pointed.

'Let's go sit in it,' Ray said. There was really no choice, we would all be too cold to think if we stood in the lot.

Ray opened the driver's-side door and told Curtis, 'Get in.' He was being coldly neutral, not nasty but not friendly either. I was doing my best to be invisible. We had agreed we'd like to keep Curtis a little uncertain. But it seemed to me he was already pretty strung out, and I was hoping Ray would not do much bullying. We wanted him nervous, not explosive.

Ray walked around to the passenger side. Curtis still stood by the car with the door open, looking down. 'What's that?' He stooped, brushing at something on the door post.

I walked up beside him and looked. 'Some kind of a stain,' I said. 'Might be paint?'

'It wasn't there before,' he said. 'What have you been doing with this car?'

'Get in, Curtis,' Ray said. I stayed beside Curtis till he got in and closed the door, then I got in the backseat behind him. Getting out of the wind helped, but it was still very cold in the car. I tucked my gloved hands in my armpits and leaned forward to hear Ray above the whistle of the wind.

'We sent your car to the crime lab in St Paul,' Ray said, 'where they discovered that it had been wiped clean. They couldn't lift any usable fingerprints off this car. How do you account for that?'

'I don't account for it,' Curtis said. 'I don't even know what you're talking about. What did they do to the volume control?'

'What, on the radio? Where?'

'That's just it, it isn't there. The volume control knob is missing off my radio, Mr High and Mighty, how do *you* account for *that*?'

'Are you saying it was there before?'

'Well of *course* it was there before. This car was in excellent condition, the radio had all its knobs and there was no paint smear on the door post, I assure you. And what's become of my cup-holder?' He described his black plastic slide-out cup-holder, perfect for coffee or a water bottle and it fit right *there* ... He was still talking about it when Ray got out, walked around the front of the car and began peering in through the windshield. When he came around to Curtis's side he opened the door, leaned down to the door post and rubbed a little at the dark smear there.

'Jake?' He met my eyes. Ray's mood had changed. He was secretly pleased and excited about something, and as I got out of the car I realized what it must be. We stood together looking at the paint smear.

'Looks like somebody did it on purpose, doesn't it?' he said.

'Now that you mention it,' I said.

'Take a look at the VIN plate,' he said.

I peered in through the windshield, squinted, looked again. When I raised my head I met his eyes, and we both nodded. One of the things Ray and I have in common is that our first assignments after we made investigator were in Auto Theft. I stared at the VIN plate for a few seconds longer, feeling the universe rearrange itself around Geraldine Lovejoy's murder. 'I don't suppose the documentation's in the glove compartment, is it?'

'Back in my office, in Geraldine's file. I'm going to call Kevin and see if one of his Auto Theft guys is free.' He spent five minutes in the cold with his back to us, talking on his cell. I got back in the backseat and listened while Curtis complained that the dome light cover was cracked and the brake pedal felt too stiff.

Ray got back in the passenger seat and said, 'Joe Shively'll be here in a couple of shakes.'

Curtis showed him the crack in the dome light cover. 'This doesn't even hardly feel like my car any more. What on earth have you people *done* to it?'

'Curtis, in a few minutes my auto expert will be here, and we'll figure out exactly what somebody did to this car. Are you going to be ready to tell me, then, who wiped it so clean it didn't yield any of Geraldine's DNA at the lab?' He turned his moody brown eyes on Curtis and left them there, and for a few seconds it felt as if his long-faced, gloomy stare was drilling a hole in the front of Curtis's head so he could peer in there and get his answer.

Curtis puffed up and turned red. 'I don't know anything about your shiny DNA lab and what they can find. What I do know, Lieutenant Bailey, is that I'm sick and tired of being treated like a criminal. I'm the bereaved party here, *I'm the one* whose life has been trashed! And maybe you've forgotten that I will soon be ordained a Christian minister, entrusted with the well-being of my parishioners' *souls.* Do you understand the responsibility that entails? Any number of quite eminent people would be willing to testify – oh, for heaven's sake now who's that?'

Joe Shively's round red face was grinning in the window on Ray's side of the car.

Ray and I got out and shook hands. Shively was carrying Geraldine's file. He handed it over and Ray found the registration for the Toyota. Joe and I peered through the windshield while Ray read the vehicle identification number.

'Yup, that's a match,' Joe said.

'OK, but look at the plate,' Ray said. He wedged in between us and pointed. 'Doesn't the upper right-hand corner look a little scratched? See there, just above the last three digits?'

'Uhhh ... yeah, I see what you mean. Kinda looks like the marks from a needle-nose pliers, doesn't it?'

'That's what we thought. Just what you'd leave if you switched the plate.' Ray opened the driver's-side door and showed him the paint smear on the door post.

'Ah, yeah.' Joe turned on his Streamlight. 'Let's get a better look at that.'

'What is it?' Curtis said. 'What are you all talking about?'

Joe said, 'This is what, a '97 Camry? That's the Fed sticker under there.'

'That's what I thought,' Ray said. 'So where's the third stamp on this model?'

'Under the car somewhere. Bitch to find, though. Hang on, I'll phone my guy at NICB.' He groped a cell out of his overcoat and began punching numbers, hunched over the phone with his back to the wind.

'His guy at what?' Curtis said. 'Why do you all talk in code?'

'He's calling the National Insurance Crime Bureau,' Ray said. 'There's an office in St Paul.'

After a few minutes of muttering, Joe put the phone against his chest and said, 'Fella says he can be here in an hour and a half, and if we'll have the car up on a hoist, he can find the number in a few minutes. OK?'

'Fantastic,' Ray said, 'I'll go see our man about getting some heat on in the bay.' He headed for the office.

Curtis walked around the Camry once,

stopped in front of me and looked into my face. 'Captain Hines,' he said, 'I don't understand police work at all. But this is my car and my life, so will you *please* tell me what's going on?' He had veered back again from outraged to plaintive. He couldn't settle on an attitude because, I was beginning to believe, he really didn't understand what we were talking about. But how could he not? I was still watching him, trying to decide how much if anything to tell him, when Ray came back and said the hoist bay was warming up, they could put the Toyota up in a few minutes.

The NICB man was named Mel, a solid confident man with outsize hands and feet. He didn't hurry but he didn't have any time for small talk, he made plain. He arrived at the impound yard in just under an hour and a quarter. Four minutes later he was under the chassis of the Camry with Joe Shively.

The bay was heated just enough to keep the hydraulic hoist working, so we were all half-frozen by the time Mel sang out from under the Camry, 'Found it!' Joe called out the numbers off the registration. Mel recited another string, and then they both came out. Joe's face was streaked with dirt but triumphant when he said, 'Not even close!'

'What does *that* mean?' Curtis said.

I looked at Ray and said, 'I really don't think he knows what we're talking about.'

'Maybe not,' Ray said. 'Why don't you take him in the squad and warm up while I get these guys under way?'

I turned the heat on high. Ray joined us in a couple of minutes, got in the backseat with Curtis and asked him, 'You understand what a vehicle identification number is for? It's like the DNA of your car.'

'Like I'd know what *that* meant,' Curtis said.

'OK, it's information,' Ray said. 'The numbers you can see up there on your dashboard are code for the make and model of your car, where it was made and when. That label on the door post carries the same number plus a certification label that says it meets the emission standards. There's a matching VIN that's stamped out of sight on car bodies, somewhere underneath. It's so hard to find that most people never see it. Owners usually don't know it's there and even car thieves don't bother with it. They're usually only going as far as the nearest chop shop anyway. But it's there for cops like us when we need it. What we just established is that the VIN on your dash doesn't match the one that's underneath.'

'Are you saying Happy sold me parts of two different cars? I don't believe that. Hap's a good man, he's been like a father to me.'

'That's not what I said. *Your* car didn't have paint on the door post, did it? Or a missing radio knob? No. I think what you've got here is a re-tag.'

'Now what's *that*?'

'The VIN plate's been changed. After you said it didn't feel like the same car I took another look and saw some very faint scratches, where somebody switched the dashboard VIN plate out of your car into this one. Switched the license plates too, of course. By then it looked like the Camry Geraldine drove to class that night, except for the bar code on the door post, so they smeared some paint on that. Why they parked it so far away from the lot, I still don't know. Anyway we picked it up believing it was yours. It could have worked, except they got too clever and wiped the car clean. If it had just come back to you – the paint annoyed you but you didn't know it was covering up the second copy of your VIN, did you?'

'Never paid any attention to it,' Curtis said.

'Most people don't. Ah, Sweeney's here.' A squad was parked at the curb and the uniformed officer was at the gate, looking in. 'He's going to take you home.'

Curtis got out saying, 'So I still don't get my car?'

'Haven't you heard anything I said? *This isn't your car*. And when we find your car it's going to be impounded till we figure this whole mess out.' Ray went on in that barely civil tone he'd been using to Curtis all afternoon. 'I'll call you in the morning, we'll talk some more. Maybe by then you'll be ready to tell me what you're involved in that makes people want to switch cars with you, hmmm?'

'I'm not involved in anything but the Lord's business. How many times must I tell you that? I'm going to go home,' Curtis said, blowing his nose, wiping his eyes, 'and ask the Lord for a little help with *my* business.'

Ray and I were mostly silent on the ride back to the station. There was a lot to figure out but the cold had sucked all the energy out of my brain. It was well after six, already dark. Ray dropped me at government center and went on home.

I went up to my office to check messages. The only papers on my desk were the applications from the cops I'd intended to interview this afternoon, two equally qualified officers who were trying for the same job. On paper, there was no way to decide between them. Everything would depend on the interviews.

'This time tomorrow,' I promised myself, 'I'll know which one I want.'

But I didn't. Because at four o'clock Thursday morning, Trudy poked my shoulder and said, 'Jake? Wake up. Hear me? Time to go have a baby.'

Twelve

The first half of the morning went pretty well. Trudy said we didn't have to hurry, she was just getting started. 'And it's probably going to take all day,' she said, 'so we better eat something.'

I tried, but the cereal seemed to stick in my throat. I rinsed the bowl in the sink, took her suitcase out to the pickup and started the motor to warm up the cab. The moon was barely a sliver in the west, the rest of the sky inky black with a billion stars blazing. I found the Big Dipper and Cassiopeia, and for a few thrilling seconds imagined myself teaching my child the names of constellations.

Then my foot slipped on the ice, reminding me that my function in this enterprise was to do the worrying. I got the porch light on, brought the bucket of sand from the shed and made a safe track for Trudy. She was in the kitchen, buttoning her coat as best she could, checking her watch. I said, 'Ready?'

'Couple of minutes,' she said, matter-of-fact, looking at her watch.

'You called the hospital?'

'Yes.' We were both talking in short, quiet bursts, like guys on a SWAT team gearing up for a raid. 'They said come in when contractions are about twenty minutes apart. I'm timing.' We stood side by side, watching her digital watch flip numbers. 'Ah, there,' she said with a little groan. I held her hand and we panted together the way they taught us in class. 'That was nineteen minutes and thirty seconds, let's go.' I walked her out my narrow sand path, belted her into the truck and crunched carefully out our frozen driveway on to the empty road. I'd timed the trip to Methodist Hospital several times: forty minutes average. That morning I made it in thirty-eight.

The OB/GYN ward was quiet, the night shift winding down. The nurses who'd be helping us weren't on duty yet, and Trudy's doctor wasn't expected for some time. An aide found her a room and a gown and told me where to find coffee. When I came back with a cup Trudy was standing by the end of the bed in a skimpy shirt that opened in the back, looking thoughtful.

'They asked me how far apart my contractions are and when I said still twenty minutes they seemed kind of disappointed. I hope I haven't ... *Oh*!' She grabbed my arm and held on like a vice-grip on steroids.

'Breathe,' I said. We breathed together and after a while she quit giving my arm free tourniquet service. 'Well, that answers *that* question,' she said. 'Today's the day.' She got into bed, looking cheerful.

'I think while you're resting I'm going to call Ray Bailey,' I said, 'and tell him I won't be in today.'

'Why don't you do that?' she said, 'and then—' she gave me the look that makes her resemble her mother – 'turn off your phone.'

Ray answered on the first ring. When I told him where I was he said, 'Aw, hey, this is it, huh?' He chuckled uneasily the way childless people do at such times, hoping – I've done this many times myself – they won't have to hear much more about this episode but dismally afraid they probably will. 'OK, listen, now, Papa Hines, just don't worry about a thing down here today.' His voice took on energy as he thought about being top dog for a while. 'Kevin and I'll keep the shop open, no problem.'

'Good. You're going to work down the list we made together yesterday, right, the car questions and that?' I knew he was. I just had to tug on his reins a little.

'Right, just like we planned.' His voice went a little dry, suggesting he thought I should give it a rest.

'Good. Oh, and say, do me a favor, will you? Go in my office and get the two applications off my desk, take them to LeeAnn and tell her I said cancel their appointments for today, tell them I'll reschedule as soon as I can.'

'Two applications, gotcha. Anything else you need? You got plenty old magazines to read?'

Men who haven't been paying attention, including me before this year, still think fathers sit in waiting rooms looking pitiful while their wives have babies somewhere down the hall.

That's not the way it works any more. Trudy took me with her to prenatal classes, where energetic interns with loud voices taught me how to time contractions, help regulate breathing, give neck-rubs. With that preparation added to the fourteen-plus years the Rutherford Police Department had spent training me not to wilt under fire, I was hoping not to disgrace myself as a cheer-leader at this event. The wolf had been absent from my dreams for several days, and this morning I was shoring up my mental firewall, determined to keep him out of my thoughts.

A round-cheeked young woman with mouse-colored hair in a bun was standing by the bed in Trudy's room, writing on a chart. 'Jake,' Trudy said, 'this is Franny. She's going to be our chief nurse.' They were smiling at each other like friends.

I have always been a little suspicious of the quick and easy camaraderie that women achieve – are they really that trusting, or just better at putting a shine on things? One of the things I liked about Trudy when I met her was that she seemed to have a little space around herself that people had to earn their way across. But Franny had evidently won immediate approval.

Trudy's opinion was the one that counted, of course, but for the first hour Franny seemed to me to be a lot more like Big Nurse than Mary Poppins. 'Sit here,' she said, and put me through an oral exam of what I'd learned in birthing school. As soon as I'd spilled the entire contents of my brain on this subject, she began telling me firmly which things we'd be doing differently in here today.

I was listening to her carefully, trying to remember every word, when Trudy said on a rising note of distress, 'Oh, here comes a big one, Oh, *hold my hand, Jake!*'

Franny was by the bed in one quick move, her hand on Trudy's heaving belly as she read her watch, urging me, 'That's good, hold her hand, rub her arm a little.' Then she was telling Trudy, 'Do your breathing now, remember how to breathe?'

I don't happen to be one of those cops who've been called on to deliver babies in taxis and bus stations – that just never happened to me. Still, somebody must have pointed out to me, from time to time, that giving birth is not an easy task. Till Trudy got pregnant I paid that information about as much attention as I allot to pork belly futures and decorating tips from Martha Stewart. I didn't doubt it, it was just information for somebody else's playbook.

After we started birthing classes I got very interested in the process and read everything I could find. But my whole emphasis was on identifying things that could go wrong and guarding against them. Every time Trudy passed one of her tests with good marks I breathed a happy sigh of relief and said, 'There now, that worry's over, we're going along great here, hot dog!' What I never quite understood till it happened was this: childbirth, even for a healthy mother having a normal child under ideal conditions, hurts like hell.

Once, during the classes we took together during Trudy's pregnancy, our instructor handed me a half-dozen ice-cubes and told me to hold them till she said I could drop them. She waited two minutes to say, 'Now,' and by then I thought I knew quite a bit about muscle cramps. 'Oh, thanks,' I said, 'that was very uncomfortable at the end, but now I understand.'

Wrong. By early-afternoon Thursday, when a blameless orderly rattled in with a pitcher of fresh ice water, Trudy yelled, 'And let me tell you where you can put those stupid ice-cubes, Jake Hines.' Franny and the orderly looked us over carefully, wondering what pit of marital discord that could be coming from, but I understood her perfectly; cramps in the hand were chump change compared to the pain she felt now.

I was a street cop for years. In the line of duty I have been bitten and kicked, had my nose flattened and my finger broken and my foot frozen, got shot with a .45 caliber bullet and cut with a hunting knife. But that day, as Trudy changed from the serene, happy Earth Mother I'd been living with all winter into a wailing termagant trying to get this terrible agony out of her belly, I thought I finally understood the wolf's message. He had come to warn me that in childbirth, there is no get-home-free pass you win by doing everything right. Even perfectly normal is hazardous and scary. And the danger wasn't coming from outside, so I couldn't guard against it or chase it away. Terrible suffering was the unavoidable price of the course we had chosen.

Given no other option, the three of us became a team. Franny was the captain, unflappable and smart; Trudy was the hero, brave and strong beyond belief. I was the willing slave, a spear-chucker who did as he was told, wished he could do more, and longed for the whole thing to end. In time, a doctor came in and added himself to our team; I thought of him as The Commander. Respect was due him, he was a master any slobbering slave would be proud to claim, but he was not the source of all the world's solace that Franny was. This plain, bossy young woman, as the day went along, commanded me to count, rub Trudy's shoulders, breathe; to fetch and carry; to 'hold on to that leg now, hold it firm!' Resourceful and tireless, as we needed her more Franny became attractive and then beautiful, and by mid-afternoon when my son was born I was almost as in love with Franny as I was with my wife.

'Help her push, now, this is it. *Come on, Trudy, good girl, push,*' Franny said.

Trudy gave one last huge screaming push that scared me pop-eyed, and the doctor said, '*There*. Good, good, good, here it comes. OK now, baby's here, relax. Rest, now, sweetie, you're done.'

'How does it look?' Trudy whispered. Chalk-white and soaking wet, she was not being secretive but simply too exhausted to speak out loud. I was wiping tears and snot off her face, my hands were trembling with relief. It was over and she was still alive. Who the hell cared what the baby looked like?

Then I looked, and almost lost it. Tears started in my eyes, my throat closed and my heart seemed to fill my chest. 'My God, Trudy,' I said, when I could talk, 'he's a regular little ... *person*.'

'Well, *that's* good,' she said, with a shaky laugh.

Then Franny came carrying him, saying, 'You've got a beautiful boy here, Trudy, congratulations,' and plunked him down beside her. We stared at him in mutual surprise. He didn't look like anybody we'd ever seen before. He was lighter than I am but darker than Trudy, but then he was also redder and more wrinkled than most human beings, so who knew? Anyway he was hollering his head off, not at all glad to see us.

He hated being born. Yanked out into the cold and the light like this, he seemed to be yelling, Who needs it? He didn't have any words yet so he was adjusting the volume on the vocal effects he did have, to make sure we understood how pissed off he was. I thought he was doing a helluva job with the little he had to work with, and I watched him wave his tiny fists, admiring his nerve and style and the way he got his message across. After about a minute, though, I began wishing for the noise to stop.

'Why is he crying like that?' I asked Franny. 'Is something wrong?'

Our team bond was already breaking up; she gave me her Big Nurse look, the one that says you're a waste of skin. 'He's a baby,' she said. 'That's what babies do, sleep and eat, poop and cry.'

'Any way we could switch him to one of those other activities?'

'Jake, for God's sake,' Trudy said. 'He just got born, give him a minute.'

'Already, you're on his side?' I kissed her. She smelled like all the sweat in a roomful of laundry workers. Her color was coming back, though. I said, 'God, you're beautiful.'

She laughed and said, 'Oh, I bet.' But she pushed her hair back.

For the first time in hours, I looked at my watch. Four thirty. 'OK if I go out in the hall and call the department?'

'Go ahead,' she said. 'I'm going to drink about a gallon of water and talk to this boy here.'

Ray was in his office. We helped each other through the congratulations as best we could, both of us awkward because we had almost never talked about anything but work.

'All the fingers and toes are in the right places, so Trudy's happy,' I told him. 'Any surprises over there today?'

'Yeah, we've had one or two. Let's see, what first?' He seemed to be moving things around on his desk. 'I talked to Curtis some more. He still claims he has no idea who'd want his car clean. He must be faking but he's so damn dense in some ways, it's hard to tell. Joe's helping me put a manufacturer's trace on the secondary VIN, the one on the chassis, to see if we can find the last owner of that car.

'Then Kevin found out ... wait, he's sitting right here, why don't I let him tell you?'

After some stretching and breathing noises, Kevin said, 'Hey, Daddy. Boy or girl?'

'Boy.'

'You got a name yet?'

'Oh ... uh...' The small creature yelling in Trudy's arms already seemed so insistently his own person, I was beginning to feel we should have waited and let him decide. But we'd already picked it. 'Ben.'

'Just Ben, no middle name?'

I took a deep breath, anticipating Kevin's mockery, and said, 'Benjamin Franklin.'

'You serious? What, you've got a thing for Founding Fathers?'

'Not all of them. Just that one.'

'The mottoes, you mean? Poor Richard's Almanac?'

'No, the kites ... and the stove. We both identify with problem solvers.'

'I'll be damned. Benjamin Franklin Hines. That does kind of roll off the tongue, doesn't it?'

'Glad you approve. So tell me, did you find your old flame at Mail Boxes?'

'Oh, yeah. Shelley. Still very attractive and

less accessible than ever.'

'Maybe there's a correlation. She give you the names of her employees?'

'Indeed she did.'

'Well, is one of them the kid who helped at the sale?'

'Not sure yet – I haven't been able to reach any of those people. But Shelley thinks maybe it's the part-timer who opens the shop for her three mornings a week. He's so quick and clever, she says, she's been wondering why he settles for a dumb little pickup job. Ambitious, too – sometimes comes in on Saturday afternoon just to see if she needs any help.'

'Have you seen him?'

'No, but I've got his name, Noel Utley. He'll be opening tomorrow morning, so I'm sending Julie and Chris to meet Shelley there at eight. They're going to see if he receives any packages addressed to one of those four names I showed you.'

'What'll you do if he doesn't?'

'Shelley's got another reason to want him brought in for questioning. Most of those box numbers the stuff's been coming to are rented to other customers. She figures Noel's been doubling up on her addresses and doing an intercept. She wants to help us to protect her license.'

'Slick. Have you figured out where he's selling the merch?'

'Maybe a swap meet for small stuff, but we figure he must have an eBay account, we're looking for that.'

'How much of this can you prove?'

'Oh, thanks to John Smith I think we can prove it all. The bad guy used the same computer for all the transactions. John showed me the IP addresses. If my hunch is correct that he used his own computer, it's almost too easy. Even if he used somebody else's, there's still the eBay account. And the money, there has to be a money trail.'

'Always. Well, hey, we all made progress today, huh?'

'Well, wait, Ray's got some more good news and some bad news. I'm going to pass you back to him.'

'BCA called,' Ray said when he got the phone back, 'and said Jason Wells' blood matches the smear we lifted off that button – remember the button he inadvertently grabbed, on the third mugging victim?'

'I sure do. So we've got him, right? He's toast now for at least that mugging and Rosie's.'

'Yes. Which makes it completely infuriating that he got out of jail this afternoon.'

'*What?* Somebody made bail?'

'None other than Mommy Dearest.'

'Mrs Paycheck-to-paycheck? How could she do that?' Milo's wry smile came back to me, behind his voice saying, *This mother of*

Jason's that Ray's so in dread of, does she do other interesting things?

'If I'd had any idea she could come up with the money,' Ray said, 'I'd have tried to get him bound over for trial.'

'Don't beat yourself up, you could never have made that case for a purse-snatcher.'

'I suppose not. Jeez, I hate to think of him out there on the streets.'

'It won't be long. We'll get him a trial date soon.'

'Yeah. Well, are you going to take another family day tomorrow?'

'No, no, I'll be in. Trudy got her doc to harass our insurance rep into a day's R&R for her in the hospital. She worked right to the end, and today was no picnic, so she needs a day of bedrest.'

'Good. Well, there's plenty to do here, for sure. Among other things I never did get to that used car lot.'

'That used...? Oh, yeah. Maybe I can give you a hand with that.' My son had already wrought a miracle – for hours, on a week day, I had completely forgotten about my job. 'Oh, and remember, tomorrow's the last day we have John Smith's help, so be sure you get him to find out anything he can about your two charges, Ray. Are you talking to Kevin about that?'

'That's what we're doing here, talking about it,' Ray said. 'See you tomorrow.' I was folding up my phone when his voice came out of it, smaller, saying, 'Hope you'll come up with an idea for how to get Jason Wells back in jail.'

Thirteen

Driving to work Friday morning felt like the start of a long-delayed holiday. With Trudy and Ben safe in the hospital, I had enjoyed ten hours of restful sleep untroubled by toothy carnivores. And at the job I was driving toward, everybody knew what to do next. Kevin's detectives would keep after the credit card thief, and Ray's section would be busy all day getting the answers on Geraldine's car. I was going to try and reschedule the interviews for those two applicants, finally, and decide on my pick for the next job opening.

Aside from that, I looked forward to preening around the building handing out cigars and bragging about my new son. After yesterday, it seemed to me, I had an easy day coming.

Whistling, I put the cigars in the pickup and headed for town early. I had the fix in at the hospital for a short visit with Trudy before work.

The first faint wail of a siren reached me as I passed the storage sheds north of town. By the time I got to the 55th Street overpass, the screams of emergency vehicles had swelled into a symphony of distress. Patrol cars were converging from all sections, two ambulances shrieked out of midtown and the big fire truck for the paramedics bullied its way through downtown with the reverb on high.

They all seemed to be headed south. I called Dispatch.

'There's a stand-off in a mobile home park south of town, Jake,' Schultzy said. 'Nothing for your guys yet. There might be, though, as soon as they talk the shooter out of there. All the chatter so far says maybe one fatality, but it could be more.'

It was seven fifteen. 'You called any investigators yet?'

'Nah. They'll all be here by the time I'd get around to them, my board looks like a Christmas tree.'

I hung up and called Ray. 'I need to stay off the phone, Jake,' he said. 'Something big's going on, I'm expecting Dispatch to call.'

'Just talked to her,' I said, and explained what little I knew. 'I thought you might like to go in a little early and get a jump on things. If this is what they think, you're in for a busy day.'

'Thanks. On my way.'

The direct-dial system at Methodist Hospital involves more numbers than I can hold in my head. I read it off a paper in my wallet at a stoplight on North Broadway. 'I figured you'd be calling,' Trudy said, 'I heard the sirens. What is it?'

I shared my skimpy news again. 'I haven't got any details yet, but there may be multiple casualties, so I better go on in.'

'Sure. Don't worry about me today, Jake, I'm just going to sleep and talk to this handsome young man who keeps getting into bed with me.'

'Oh, is he there now? Did I interrupt a feeding?'

'No, they moved his crib in, we're roommates.'

'Oh? Will you get enough rest like that?'

'Yeah, we've both been snoring like hogs.'

'What, Ben finally quit crying?'

'He cries when he's hungry, the rest of the time he's a serious sleeper. He's got a blue knit cap now and he looks determined, kind of like you when you shovel snow.'

'Oh, now, come on, Trudy, didn't we have a deal? This kid's got to look like you.' It was a joke, sort of. She comes from handsome blond Scandinavians with perfect teeth. I have no idea what my parents looked like, but between the two of them they left me with a very odd face, so my advice to Ben is to grow up looking as much as possible like his mama.

The wind had picked up and the cloud

cover was darkening. Occasional snowflakes drifted down from a lead-colored sky. Sirens were still screaming all over town; the day was taking on an ominous, jumpy feel. Damn. I felt like I'd had enough ominous and jumpy yesterday to last me for years. Today was supposed to be fun.

A freezing gust blew snow down my neck while I locked up my truck. Andy Pitman came wallowing across the slippery ice of the parking lot, grumbling, 'Hell's going on, anyway? Sounds like a war.'

'Just a little domestic, Dispatch says.'

Andy snorted. 'Domestic, maybe. Little it ain't.'

Cold air and commotion blew in behind us at Government Center. As we reached the top of the stairs, Ray came in the tall glass doors below us, bringing another burst of freezing air and more noise. I let Andy go on ahead and waited for Ray.

We walked together toward the glass cage marked 'Dispatch'. The lieutenant was in there, moving intently around the three workstations where Schultzy and two other operators, talking into headsets and typing nonstop, faced boards alive with dancing lights.

My card wouldn't work in the slot. The double lock was on and a hand-lettered sign taped to the inside of the glass door read: 'Too Busy – See shift captain.'

'Looks like a lively day,' Ray said. We walked across to the patrol side of the floor, where Ed Gray was running the shift.

'Kinda lucky the way it broke,' he said. He'd been almost done briefing the day shift. 'Just finishing BOLOs when the call came in. Domestic in a mobile home park south of town. What else is new? I sent Casey. Soon as he got there he asked for back-up and I sent Hanenberger. Casey said the neighbors heard yelling and then gunshots, before he got there. When he knocked, a young man's voice said, "Go away, we don't need any help." Soon as Hanenberger got there and got set up by the back door, Casey knocked again, but nobody answered – and he hasn't been able to get a word out of anybody in there since then.'

'You know if there's any casualties?'

'Casey looked through a crack in the front curtain, thought he saw the tip of one toe on the floor. SWAT team's on its way, they're going in as soon as they get all the equipment in place.'

Andy, coming up behind us, said, 'A prebuilt out south? Where?'

'Mobile home park on 26th Street – out by the airport.'

'Ray, that's—'

'McKay Meadows,' Ray said. 'Shit.' He turned away, looking sick.

'What?' I asked Andy.

'Sprinter's mama lives there.' He asked Ed Gray, 'They give you a name yet?'

'Neighbor said Tammy Knutson. Casey's calling the manager of the park, trying to confirm.'

I said, 'Is there a negotiator out there?'

'Working on it. Haven't found one yet.'

'Well, if the shooter's in Tammy Knutson's house, all three of us think we know him.'

'Hell you say. You offering to help?'

'We could try.'

'Fine. Whichever one of you knows him best, why don't you get out there right now?'

'I'll go,' Ray said quickly. 'I still got my coat on, I can go right now. What's the house number?'

Ed gave him a number and said, 'I'll call my team and tell them to hold off till you get there.'

Ray hustled away toward the stairs. Andy watched him go with a dubious expression on his big ugly face. 'Actually Jason Wells was my collar,' he reminded me as we walked back toward our section.

'Did you want to go? You should have said.'

'Nah,' he said, 'Jason Wells would rather eat worms than talk to me.'

'I thought I noticed some hostility between the two of you.'

'Yeah, well, the better you get to know that kid the more you want to kick his ass. Anyway, just now – you could see for yourself –

I would've had to put a headlock on Ray to keep him from going.'

'He thinks he should have stopped Jason earlier,' I said.

'Because he had this *feeling*,' Andy said, 'that The Sprinter was working his way up to a murder.' He shook his head disapprovingly. 'Hell business does a cop have getting *feelings*? Take one day at a time and work with what you got, ain't that right?'

'Sure,' I said, 'although Rosie said the same thing, that Jason was getting off on hurting women. And she ought to know.'

'Yeah, well ... but that's Rosie.' Andy shrugged and gave me a little, secret smile. He liked Rosie Doyle, he wished her well, but he was old school and would always see women in the department as a not quite harmless joke.

Kevin's section, as we walked through it, sounded like a whole different police department, full of happy noises. Julie and Chris were already out at Mohawk Mall, expected to call with an update any minute. The rest of his investigators were making phone calls, dashing in and out of his office, comparing lists.

Down at Ray's end of the hall, People Crimes detectives had just hung up their coats and turned on their computers. Now they were coming out of their cubicles, looking for a cup of coffee and asking each other, 'Hell's going on?' As soon as Andy Pitman reached Darrell Betts and began telling him what he'd just heard from the duty sergeant, the rest of the crew clustered around him like ants on a doughnut. They had driven in through all that siren noise, expecting to be put to work the minute they came in the building. Now here they were with adrenaline pumping and everybody too busy to talk to them? Forget that. They were detectives, they were going to get information. I walked down the hall toward them with my arms out, saying, 'Let's take this to the meeting room, guys. Come on, you're jamming up the hall.'

Andy led the way to the conference table at the end of the hall, and I turned into my office to answer my ringing phone. The chief said, 'Can you come in here a minute?'

I put two cigars in my breast pocket and headed his way.

Lulu was already busy at her high-piled desk. As I passed her she said, 'Here's your expense check,' and handed it over. I reached to take it from her, and … she *smiled* at me. I was so shocked I barely heard her say, 'How's that baby?'

'Oh,' I said, which is hard to say with your mouth open. 'Um … he's fine.' I tossed a choked, 'Thank you' back over my shoulder and walked on toward the chief, who was yelling out the door, 'Jake? That you?'

His pop-eyed blue stare was already aimed at the doorway when I walked in. He said, 'Tell me about it.'

'Ed thinks it's just a domestic gone sour. But Ray's very concerned because he thinks it might be that guy that...' I stopped because he was shaking his head. 'What?'

'Didn't you have a baby yesterday? I heard that's what you were doing.'

'Oh. Yes, well, *Trudy* had a baby yesterday, and I helped as much as I could. Did you know that police work is actually quite easy and pleasant compared to giving birth?'

'I believe my wife mentioned that a time or two. Is Trudy OK?'

'Fine. She seems slightly deranged about the kid, but I suppose that will moderate, huh?'

'Don't count on it.' He leaned toward me, his voice confidential. 'Benjamin Franklin, that was a joke, right?'

'No, no, that's his name.'

'Fact?' He cleared his throat, tried to look neutral. 'Kevin said you're into kite-flying?'

'Kite-flying, jeez – *science*, he experimented with electricity, remember? Also started a library and a fire department – he was a problem solver. We're both hoping Ben will be like that. Also, since we've been taking on all this debt, Trudy's begun to admire the classy way Franklin borrowed money. She says he even went to France and Holland for it. She wants to raise her son to think like that.'

Frank loved it; he had a nice big laugh, rocking in his chair. When he settled down he said, 'Now, tell me, why's Ray so alarmed about this domestic?'

I told him about Ray's premonitions about escalating violence, and about his disappointment when the purse-snatcher made bail.

'Well, hell, we can't help what judges decide,' Frank said. 'How many times do I have to say it? Just work with what you've got.'

'We will. We are. We've got most of the uniforms on duty out there right now, though, can we call in some extra help? I know the budget's tight, but—'

'I've got an emergency fund for days like this. Yeah, I'll authorize it.'

'Good. I wish we didn't have this distraction right now. I think we were getting close to some answers on last week's homicide. Anyway—' I got up – 'have a cigar, huh?'

'Oh, thanks, but – you know I don't smoke. Never have.'

'That's OK – take two, pass them out to your friends at the reunion. It's still on for this weekend, right?'

'Yeah. Boy, will I be glad when *that's* over.'

'What? You're tired of your old buddies before the party even starts?'

'Nine guys who haven't seen each other since they were kids, and the guest of honor is dying? What was I thinking? That's not a party, that's a goddamn *wake*. Here, on second thought I will take your cigars. A fake nose and a whoopee cushion might be good, too, if you could find them. You're right, Jake, there's plenty of things in this world harder than law enforcement.'

LeeAnn said both my applicants had the next three days off and would be out of town until Monday. Yes, she had made a note to try to reschedule them then, and no thanks, she didn't want a cigar. But she wanted to hear all about the baby. I saw her write 'card' on her to-do list as I walked away, and I bet myself it would have a stork flying, with a baby dangling in a diaper from its beak.

I was answering email when Julie and Chris got out of the elevator with a prisoner between them. He looked so young and so awkward in his handcuffs, I figured this was probably his first arrest. They walked him briskly past my office and into Kevin's. I heard Kevin say, 'Noel Utley,' before the door closed. A few minutes later Kevin came across the hall and said, 'All my guys want to sit in on this interview. Any chance we could use the chief's conference room?'

'Uh, sure. I'll go make sure it's clear.' But as I stood up, my phone rang.

'Oh, God, Jake,' Ray said, in a strangled voice, 'he killed the whole damn family.'

I sat down. 'Where are you, Ray?'

'In Jason's house, in the mobile home park. He never answered me on the bullhorn, so they threw in the flash-bang and broke down the door...' He swallowed, then said, 'Excuse me,' and put the phone down hard. I heard some choking noises.

To Kevin, who was standing there, I mouthed silently, 'Wait.'

Ray came back on the phone in a few seconds with his voice under control. 'There is nobody left alive inside. Tammy and both the little kids, a boy and a girl, they're all shot up. The little boy's on top of his mother – it looks like he was trying to help. The girl is ... under the bed. Trying to hide.'

'Jesus. What about Jason?'

'Gone, is all I know. Out the back door, probably, while Casey was waiting for back-up. Must have crawled across the little yard there and out the gate into a kind of alley between rows of houses. Only way I can figure. Listen, send me all my guys, Jake, we've got three bodies and a ton of physical evidence.'

'Sure. But what about Jason, have you started—'

'Yeah, I already filed an APB, all the squads are looking for him. He's on foot, you know. His old Volks is here and his mother's car too. So he can't have gone far. We'll find him.'

'OK, I'll get everybody moving from here. You called Pokey?'

'No. Will you? And BCA? Give BCA my cell number, huh? They can call me if they got any questions.'

'Sure. What else?'

'Tell Andy and Bo to bring plenty of gloves and recorders and tape, and a crime scene kit. Water, plenty of bottled water – this place gives you a dry throat. Chewing gum. Jar of Vicks. And my digital camera ... that's all I can think of right now.'

The next couple of hours were a steady sweat. I sent Ray his four investigators with two carloads of gear. They all phoned back non-stop, calling for more crime scene tape, booties, notebooks, paper evidence bags. They were working at a gory death scene with children, the hardest of all scenes to tolerate. I didn't need to see their faces to know they were stifling powerful emotions. Their messages were all succinct and stoical, but I could hear how fast their irritation built up over any mistakes or delay. A cop under that kind of stress has a tendency to go off on anybody who crosses him, even by accident. Proper support was critical now, so I fought off a powerful urge to go and see the crime scene myself. Against all my instincts, I stayed at my desk and did my job.

Calling the crime lab sometimes feels like a perverse test: how long can you stand to listen to a phone ring before a cold authoritarian voice answers and puts you on hold? But that day an accommodating female pounced right on my call and stayed with me. Then the fact that this was a disastrous family tragedy began to work in our favor: a big crime scene automatically attracts attention, even at BCA. The friendly operator checked with a couple of department heads, came back and said a team of experts would be headed our way within half an hour.

The coroner was next. He left a patient in mid-zit to take my call. I gave him the briefest possible description of the assassinated family in the double-wide. He breathed his two-note sigh, 'Ah, yah,' and took down the address. I don't know how he manages this unpredictable arrangement, but I've never known Pokey's work to delay an investigation.

As soon as all the essential jobs were done I walked across to the chief's office and brought him up to date.

'Aw, hell,' he said, when I told him about the dead children. He stacked up the papers he'd been reading and squared the corners carefully, as if tidying his desk might be a start on fixing the world. 'Ray's hunch was right, huh?'

'Looks that way.' I didn't tell him about my

wolf dream; I would never tell that to Frank. But I thought of it, as I hurried back to my own office, and an undercurrent of sneaky private relief began in my head. I garbled the message, I thought, the baby was fine all along. My instincts had planted the wolf in my dreams in reaction to a serial purse-snatcher who kept increasing the level of violence.

Most of the Property Crimes investigators were migrating busily up and down the hall between Kevin's office and the conference table, questioning Noel Utley and comparing notes on answers. I walked past a double row of empty cubicles and took a seat with a good view of the prisoner.

His looks were classically boy-next-door, very pale skin sprinkled with freckles, and hair and eyes almost matching the freckles, a shade lighter than a bran muffin. His hair was straight and cut very short, he wore jeans washed almost white and a plaid flannel shirt. I found it hard to square his guileless appearance with the devious crimes we were trying to hang on him, but Kevin wasn't having any trouble with it. He declared he knew enough to book Noel right now for grand theft.

'But since this is your first offense I'm inclined to give you the chance to help yourself out. You tell me right now which computer you used to place the orders, show me where you fenced the stuff so I don't have to search for that, I'll put in a good word for you with the county attorney when the time comes to plead.'

'Oh, that'll be swell,' Noel said. He had a slightly lopsided smile that showed one eye-tooth partly covering the other – the final, perfect touch to his quirky appeal. In Hollywood he'd get the best friend part every time, I thought. His voice was still boyish, but his attitude was hardening into poison. 'You think I'm a virgin, I don't even know when I'm getting screwed? Boy, I wish I had enough money to hire a decent lawyer.'

'Oh, come on,' Kevin said, 'you must have stolen enough for three lawyers by now.'

'Is that how this works? You hang a bunch of crimes on me and put me away?'

'I wish,' Kevin said. 'But no, I have to put you in touch with a social worker who'll help you get a public defender. As soon as you get a lawyer, though, he's going to tell you your best bet is to co-operate fully.'

'That sounds nice and friendly,' Noel said. 'Are we going to have cookie sales, too, and sing karaoke?'

My phone rang. It was Andy, at the crime scene, and I went back to my desk to make a list of his new requests. They needed triple-A batteries, he said, the big metal tape measure, Ray's warm gloves that he'd left in his desk, more water, and would I order sandwiches for Casey to pick up on the way back? I told him I'd do all that and that I'd need a status report for the news media before two p.m.

I was so busy with his order, I was only dimly aware of John Smith when he came over from the support staff, some time after ten, slipped quietly into his wobbly little paper fort, and began to point and click. He didn't seem to need any help or direction from me, which was good because I was already up to my armpits. An hour or so later, when he slid out of his jury-rigged workstation and crossed the hall to my open door, I didn't even look up.

'Ahem,' he said.

'Oh, hi there.' He had been diligent and helpful all week so I tried to think of some polite way to tell him I had no time to talk to him. I looked at my watch. It was almost eleven thirty. 'I guess you're about ready to leave us, aren't you?'

'Well, yes, but—'

'Well, hey, we owe you a big one. Kevin and his crew are down the hall right now, questioning a suspect they'd never have caught without your help.'

He nodded amiably but he didn't leave. I knew my phone would start ringing any minute. 'Do you need to talk to Kevin before you go?'

'Um ... I really wanted to see Ray, but I

guess he's at that big crime scene, isn't he? So maybe you can tell him, you know those charges he gave me to look up?'

'Yes?'

'They were for one iPod and one GPS apiece.'

'How about that?' I had cared about those charges before and I knew I would again, but not now.

'And they were all sent to that same place.'

'OK. Is that the documentation? I'll take it.' I had three messages waiting on my email and I was late returning Andy's last call.

He held out the credit card bills he'd been researching, but when I reached to take them his grip tightened on them and he said, 'Don't you think that's odd? I mean, Ray's working on a different case, isn't he?'

'He sure is.' I was on full automatic, focused on the terrible scenes my detectives were describing every time I answered the phone. I tugged on the copies a little. He let go, looking puzzled, and turned away.

Just as he reached my doorway, sleepy synapses somewhere in my brain awoke and fired. 'Wait a minute. What did you just say?'

'I said it was odd.'

'Before that. You said all the items...'

'Went to that same place. Yeah.'

'You don't mean the one where all of Kevin's victims—'

'Yeah, the Mail Boxes store.'

'Wait, now. That doesn't make sense.'

He shrugged. 'Computers just don't lie. They're all from that same one, too.'

'The same one what?'

'Computer.'

'John, they can't be.'

He shrugged again. 'The IP addresses are the same.'

'I don't speak Computer. Can you say it in English?'

He took a deep breath, wiggled his nose like a rabbit, blinked once and said, 'I know the items on the cards Ray gave me were ordered off the same computer as all the items on Kevin's cards because I checked the headers and the machine identifiers are the same.'

He got the whole sentence out in one breath, and stood there looking friendly and helpful, but unconcerned. In John Smith's world, all information is good.

In mine it's a little more complicated. He had just carpet-bombed everything I thought I knew about The Sprinter, the rummage sale and the awful tragedy at the McKay Meadows mobile home park. For weeks, we'd all been chasing our tails around two separate cases that now were melting into one. And the whole ominous mess seemed to be still in motion, manipulated by some unseen hand.

Or maybe not unseen. Maybe I'd been

looking at it and didn't recognize it. Down the hall, Kevin was trying to get his mouthy little prisoner to admit he was charging fancy electronic toys to stolen credit card numbers. Noel hadn't copped to anything yet but Kevin said it was just a matter of time. 'He thinks he can just deny he had anything to do with what happened at the store and make it go away,' he said, 'but soon as I get one of those yard sale people in here, they'll identify him and then I've got him boxed.'

But maybe we'd just been going after the small stuff with Noel Utley. I couldn't quite get my mind around the idea that his hazel eyes and matching freckles belonged in the same picture frame with a murdered family, but... Work with what you've got, I heard Frank say again.

'Will you walk down the hall with me?' I asked John Smith. 'Kevin needs to know about this.'

'Well, sure. Which way...?'

I pointed, and he went ahead of me out the door. Two steps into the hall, he collided with Curtis Brill.

'Ah, here you are, good,' Curtis said, looking at me, ignoring John Smith. 'I got the use of the church van today so I decided to come in and ask – is it true, what I just heard on TV? That someone's killed Jason Wells' whole family?'

'Yes, I'm afraid it is.'

'My God, that's terrible. Where's poor Jason, do you know?'

'No, he's – how do you happen to know Jason Wells?'

'We work together sometimes, selling cars. He's what? What were you going to say?'

'He's disappeared. Curtis, will you excuse me for a few minutes? There's something I need to do right now, but then I need to ask – can you please wait in my office?'

'Well ... maybe for a few minutes. I really should be trying to get in touch with poor Jay. He's going to need my help.' The prospect of being needed perked him up; he stood up straighter and got stronger-looking. Something about what he had just said was ringing bells in my head, but I didn't have time to think about it.

As I turned to walk down the hall with John, some kind of flurry began at the conference table, words of assent and then a scraping of chairs. Kevin and Julie and Chris got up and walked toward us, leading Noel Utley in handcuffs.

'Well, for heaven's sake,' Curtis Brill said, 'what's No-No doing here?'

Fourteen

I asked Julie to take Noel Utley back to the conference table and wait there with him.

The rest of the detectives stood around Curtis and me in the hall while we yelled at each other. He demanded I tell him right away why No-No was wearing handcuffs. I told him I didn't have time to talk to him right now. I said if he wanted more information he could wait in my office until I did have time for him.

'I can't do that,' he said, 'I've only got the van for a few hours and I've got things to do.'

'Go away and do them then. Come back later.'

'Don't you see that's out of the question for me until I've done what I can for my friend?'

'Trust me, Curtis, there's nothing you can do for Noel Utley.'

'With all due respect, Captain, you simply don't understand the nature of my ministry.'

'Maybe not,' I said, 'but I do know that unless you sit in there and be quiet for the next half hour I'm going to book you on suspicion of murder and put you in a cell.'

His face got very red. Actually, mine may have been somewhat flushed as well. Helpless and daffy as he sometimes seemed, Curtis in his ministering mode was like a steel cylinder, smooth and impervious on all sides, impossible to penetrate. He just brushed all objections aside. And I couldn't put up with that; information was flowing into the Rutherford police station faster than we were equipped to process it, and I couldn't organize it properly till I could get Curtis Brill to shut up. And shutting up just wasn't on his agenda at all.

'What on earth are you saying? You think I killed Geraldine?' He took out a handkerchief and began to mop his face. 'My God, is everybody in this building going crazy?'

'Curtis, will you just listen to me? Whether I suspect you or not, I've got enough circumstantial evidence to justify putting you on ice in a cell for a few days, and I'll do it if that's the only way I can quiet you down while I sort this out.'

He opened and closed his mouth a couple of times, like a beached fish, and finally said, 'That's all you want from me? Quiet?'

'For the present.'

'All the help and advice I've offered you – and all you want is quiet?'

'Yes.'

'For how long?'

'Half an hour.' Then, I thought, we could re-negotiate.

He walked to my extra chair and sat down, slowly. 'Very well, then. Quiet you want, quiet you've got.' He looked at his watch and added, 'For half an hour.'

'Excellent.' I closed the door. In the hall outside, I huddled with Kevin and Chris and John Smith.

Kevin said, 'What's the big deal about Noel Utley being called No-No?'

'In those first interviews – after Geraldine Lovejoy was killed? – her sister told me Curtis had three pals named Pee-Wee and No-No and Jay. Said he used to bring them home to dinner all the time, and her sister ended up cooking and cleaning for all of them. Just before you walked up here, Curtis asked about Jason Wells' family, and he called Jason "Jay". Then he saw all of you coming and he said, "What's No-No doing here?". He called Noel Utley "No-No".'

'So the bereaved boyfriend is pals with The Sprinter and the credit card thief, both? They're in a gang? I think I'm getting a case of information overload. Is Pee-Wee going to pop out of a closet in a minute?'

'I half expect it. And we have to sort this out fast, because the whole thing's coming unraveled.' I asked John Smith, 'Could you squeeze out a little more time in here today?'

'I have to ask Mary. But if it's important to a homicide, I'm sure she'll OK it.'

'Tell her I said it's very important.' I asked Kevin, 'That store manager at Mail Boxes – Shelley? She's pretty computer savvy, right?'

'Oh, sure. She runs the whole place off a software program called Simon. It tracks all their traffic with no glitches, she says.'

'Good. Give John her phone number.' To John I said, 'I want you to give Shelley the IP addresses you told me about, and ask her to check all the computers in her store. We need to know if one of them sent those orders.'

'Ah. Sure, I can do that,' John said. He wrote down the number Kevin gave him and went back to his wobbly niche looking happy.

'Now, let's talk about search warrants,' I said. We began naming the areas we might want to search: cars and residences for Curtis, Noel and Jason, as well as any sheds, garages, lean-tos or motor homes on their properties.

'Think, have we got everything?' Kevin kept saying as Chris made up the list. 'You have to ask for each specific thing by name or they'll throw it out in court.' After we'd checked it twice he sent Chris off to find a judge.

I called Ray Bailey's cell. He picked up on the first ring, talking quietly with his lips so close to the speaker that all his consonants came through as little explosions. He must have had the phone pressed hard into his ear, too, because the room he was in was full of talk and noise.

'Sorry to interrupt,' I said, 'but I need to tell you something.'

'You sure? I feel like my brain might break if I try to cram one more fact in there.'

I told him my news couldn't wait, he had to know that the two crime series we had been investigating all winter were turning into one crime stream, featuring The Sprinter and Curtis and Noel Utley, this smart-ass teenager who until now had been entirely Kevin's concern.

'Uh … my hands are kind of full here, Jake,' Ray said.

'Well, exactly. And both cases are so wrapped around each other now that I think it's pointless to worry about whose prisoner is whose. Don't you?'

'Sounds like it. Hell, Jake, if you've got both those guys there at the station, why don't you just go ahead and ask every question you can think of? Kevin too.'

'That's what I was hoping you'd say. I'll keep you informed.'

He sighed. 'If you must.'

When Kevin got back to my beachhead in the hall, I told him we had Ray's imprimatur to question everybody.

'Is it OK if we start with the preacher? I've heard what Ray has to say about him but I'd like to see for myself.' He pulled in an extra chair from the hall to my side of the desk and got ready to play observer, since he didn't fully understand yet how Curtis fit into the picture with Noel. While I walked around my desk, Curtis started to talk as if he'd never been interrupted. 'I really can't stay here much longer—'

I put my hands up like a barrier, palms forward, and said, 'Curtis, we're having what you might call a watershed day here. All hell is breaking loose and I need many answers very fast. So don't talk, please, just answer my questions.'

Curtis puffed up again. 'Really, Captain, your high-handed attitude—'

'Or if it's not possible for you to do that, I can still book you into a cell downstairs. Do I make myself clear?'

'Not really, no,' Curtis said, stiff-necked and angry. 'You said I wasn't being accused of anything, now you threaten to arrest me. Do I need an attorney?'

'Honest, Curtis, if I see you're becoming a suspect I'll let you know in plenty of time, and I'll see you get all the credit that's due you for being a co-operative witness. OK? Now, is Noel Utley a friend of yours?'

'He certainly is. Why's he in handcuffs?'

'Because he *is* a suspect. Do you call him

No-No?'

'Sometimes. It's just a silly nickname. What's he suspected of?'

'We haven't settled on the charge yet, but it's not going to be small.'

'Well, but that's what I'm trying to get across to you, Captain. That's just ridiculous, you're making a mistake here. Why, Noel is just a boy, and a very backward boy at that. He hardly knew anything when Gerry and I took him under our wing. She had to teach him table manners and he'd had no religious instruction at all.'

'That so? So No-No's one of the boys Beverly Keefe told me about, that spent a lot of time at your house and ate the suppers that Geraldine fixed?'

'Yes. Did Beverly find something objectionable about that?'

'I'm asking the questions, remember? What else did you do together?'

'He joined my church.'

'But that was after he got to know you, right? That's not where you met him?'

'No, we got acquainted at Happy Roads. The used car lot. We both work there, off and on.'

'And Pee-Wee? He works there too?'

'Yes, he's the owner's nephew, actually. His given name is, um, Peter Rhodes.'

'Does Jason Wells work there too?'

'He used to. Not much lately.'

'You call Jason "Jay" sometimes?'

'Occasionally. They all call me "The Rev" sometimes, too, when we're joking around. And we call our boss "Ol' Hap" sometimes – he even refers to himself that way, it's his, um, persona. Why are you so interested in nicknames?'

'Using nicknames, that means you're pals, right? What else do you do together?'

He put on his benign look. 'I've been helping all of those boys get ready to be born again. To accept Christ as their personal savior.'

'Ah. How about fraudulent credit card purchases? You helping with those too?'

'Fraudulent what? What are you talking about?'

'Was it your computer they used?'

'I don't own a computer. Why is it that you always talk about things I don't understand?'

I turned to Kevin. 'What say we step out a minute?' We left Curtis there, flouncing – he could somehow flounce sitting down.

Outside my door I said, 'Let's go see what Noel has to say about their wonderful friendship.'

Walking down the hall Kevin said, 'You believe him about the computer?'

'You know, I'm almost inclined to. He was the same way about VINs – he honestly didn't seem to know what I was talking about.'

'Just a babe in the woods, huh? Does it strike you this is a very odd group of guys? The spacey rev and the sociopath mugger and this kinky little thief I've got here?'

'Makes you want to get to know Pee-Wee, doesn't it?'

At the conference table, Noel was sitting beside Julie Rider, looking pleased with himself. Julie was wearing her perfect-cop face, so neutral it almost disappeared into the wall. Noel, I surmised, had been attempting to gross out the female cop, unaware that in private Julie was the acknowledged trash talker of the RPD. Just as well we came back when we did, I thought; if Julie lost patience the air might soon be blue.

Kevin and I sat down opposite each other in the middle of the table. Kevin began eyeing Noel like a prime cut, medium rare with a light glaze of au jus.

'So,' he said, 'Curtis helps you place your orders, huh?'

Caught off guard, Noel laughed out loud. 'Curtis?' He looked genuinely amused. 'You must be joking.'

'Why is that so funny?'

Noel chuckled. 'The Rev isn't the sharpest knife in the drawer, technology-wise.' He leaned a little toward Kevin and added confidentially, 'Or any other wise, actually.'

'Is that so? I thought he was your mentor.'

'Did he tell you that? Shee. In his dreams.'

'So all he does for you is store the merchandise?'

There was a tiny hesitation before he said, 'I told you, I'm not receiving any merchandise.'

'That's right, you did say that.' Kevin's smile grew toothier; he knew he'd struck a nerve somewhere. 'So when Sergeant Deaver comes back with a signed search warrant and we search Curtis's apartment, we won't find any packages addressed to those four fake names at Mail Boxes?'

'Well, I don't claim to know everything The Rev has been doing,' Noel said, flashing his elfin twinkle, 'but I sure doubt it.'

Kevin had been warm, now he was cooler; Noel was comfortable again. Kevin leaned back in his chair, tapping an uneven rhythm – thrup, thrup, thrup-thrup – on the table with the tips of his fingers.

While he thought I said quickly, 'You move the stuff in his car, though, right? Is that why you switched cars the night Geraldine was killed?' Noel's nostrils flared on the phrase 'switched cars'. He looked away and re-settled himself in his chair.

Bingo.

'I didn't switch any cars,' he said.

'Well, we'll search it all,' I said. 'Your car too – we're bringing that in from Mail Boxes now. That's the one,' I said, on a sudden inspiration, 'that you used to pick up Jason after his muggings, isn't it?' Kevin looked at me, surprised, so he missed the way Noel's face went blank on that question. Bingo again.

'We're going to search your apartment, too. I got warrants for both of you.'

'Fine,' Noel said. 'Search away.' He had himself in hand again, the little superior smile was back. Clearly, the packages were somewhere else. But I had scored with the car switch, and the pick-up after the muggings. I knew it and he knew I knew.

My cell rang. 'BCA is here,' Ray said. 'I'm about ready to hand off to them. My crew can finish up our part. What's happening there?'

'Damn near everything. OK with you if I order in some sandwiches? You and I and Kevin could eat lunch here and compare notes.'

'That'll be fine.'

'Let's clear the decks,' I said when I got off the phone. 'Ray's coming in.'

Julie took Noel down to the jail and booked him for felony theft.

I escorted Curtis to the conference table and left him there with Chris Deaver, who had instructions to ask every possible question about Curtis's life, jobs, income, last known address, family and colleagues past and present. Some of it we might never need, but Curtis was still mysterious, his past was opaque and his sources of income obscure. I wanted him to become an open book. Besides, I didn't quite have enough to hold him but I wanted to keep him in the building while two of Kevin's detectives searched his apartment. We told them to look for loose ceiling tiles, cubbies behind books, any hidey-hole. Ray had been through the place right after Geraldine's death, but he wasn't looking for electronic gadgets still in their boxes.

Kevin went up the hall to find out what John Smith had learned at Mail Boxes, and got good news and bad.

'Noel used Shelley's office PC,' John said, 'but she doesn't want to give it up.'

'She has to,' Kevin said. 'I'll call her. Oh, boy, won't she love me when I threaten to subpoena that baby.'

'Doesn't your mojo work on Shelley any more?' I asked him.

'If it wasn't good enough in the backseat of a Cutlass Supreme in the moonlight, why would it work six years later in a copy shop?' He thought about it for a few seconds, with his eyes narrowed. 'She does enjoy being admired, though. Maybe I should try a little hopeless yearning.'

Some combination of hopeless yearning and law-enforcement gravitas worked, apparently, because he came back from the phone in a few minutes saying she was ready to hand it over. John got permission from Mary to be the one who went after it. He felt he could ease the pain of parting for her and I thought he was right.

Casey appeared in my doorway about then, holding up a paper sack, saying, 'I got them meatball subs you ordered.' Ray walked in behind him, looking ruined.

'Come in and sit down.' I got him a fresh bottle of water, found Kevin, and closed the door to my office. We ate quickly, talking desultorily about the NBA playoffs. Then Kevin and I sat in wretched silence while Ray described the crime scene in precise detail.

'There's a ton of physical evidence,' he said at the end. 'The killer didn't even try to be careful. It's a rage scene, for sure. Broken dishes and furniture, blood all over three rooms, in the middle of a pool of blood a fuzzy little teddy bear—' his voice went dry as boots over gravel – 'with one leg torn off. They had a terrible fight before he started shooting, there's a broken window and a door off its hinges.'

'All those muggings, all winter,' I said, 'did you ever see any evidence that The Sprinter had a gun?'

'Never.'

'So we could be looking for a different killer?'

'Could be but I doubt it. The scene says

"family fight" to me. DNA and prints will settle it, I guess. Or we could find Jason – can you believe he's still out there?' He shook his head. 'He's on foot – why hasn't somebody picked him up? Jeez, he was right there, and Casey ... oh well, he did it by the book. I mean, gunshots ... he had to wait for back-up. But you'd think – well, no more about that.' He balled up the wrapping of his lunch and tossed it absently into the wastebasket. 'What's new down here? You said a lot's happening.'

We told him all the ways the two cases were still wrapping around each other, and about our interrogation of Noel Utley. 'I saw a tell on "storing the merchandise",' I said, 'and another one on "switched cars".'

'Me too,' Kevin said.

Ray said, 'So the purse-snatching was mainly for the credit cards like I thought.'

'Looks that way,' I said, 'but because you got so proactive about getting cards cancelled, they didn't get as much as they expected. Which explains the yard sale caper, I think; they must have been looking for a new way to go.'

Kevin said, 'You think they were all in it together all along? Jason and Noel and Curtis?'

'Jason and Noel anyway. Not sure about Curtis. Or the third friend, Pee-Wee. I've impounded that ratty little beetle of Noel's, by the way, it's being towed into the yard right now. I'm pretty sure he was Jason's pick-up man, the one your witness saw driving away from Janet Rasmussen's mugging.'

'I don't get it, though,' Kevin said, 'about this triple homicide. Where does that fit into the plan?'

'I don't think it does,' Ray said. 'It looks to me like a family fight that got out of hand.'

'That seems uncharacteristic, though, doesn't it?' Kevin said, 'for a careful planner like Jason Wells?'

'What, you think they'd all be deader if he planned it?' Ray stood up, suddenly furious, and stomped off to the men's room.

'What did I say?' Kevin said.

'Nothing. He's been looking at dead children all morning so he feels like shit. He's looking for somebody to lay it off on, don't take it personally. Be cool with him for a while, will you? I'm going to set up a debriefing for him and his crew.' I walked over to the chief's office and found him gone, but put in a request for a critical incident debriefing. Lulu, newly co-operative, helped me with the paperwork, and I saw what a powerful asset she could be when she felt inclined. I can't have a baby very often, I reflected on the way back to my office; what else could I do to stay on her good side?

Ray and Kevin were sitting beside my desk,

sharing a bag of M&M's.

'You want some?' Kevin asked me, pointing to the last two colored candies.

'No thanks.' I watched while they each politely took one. *What the hell did Kevin do while I was gone?* 'What's next?'

'We need to know more about that used car lot where they all work,' Kevin said. 'Don't we? And the guy that runs it, what's his name?'

'Happy Rhodes. Some name, huh?'

'Perfect. I wonder why they all call him Ol' Hap?'

'Apparently he calls himself that. Isn't that what he's called in those ads for Happy Roads? The ones that show him waving his hat and smiling?'

'That's right. What's that supposed to be, folksy?'

'Yes. Kind of upbeat country with a touch of hip,' Kevin said firmly.

'Jeez, you think you got it exact enough?' Ray was dry and amused, now, his flash of temper had evaporated.

'Style is Kevin's hobby,' I said, trying for a neutral tone.

'More than that,' Kevin said. 'As I see it, style is a negotiating tool. I think law enforcement people should study styles so they'd know what people are trying to tell us about themselves.'

'Now there's a fresh idea,' I said.

'You disagree?'

'Not exactly. I just think you'll get that course when hell freezes over.'

'No,' Kevin said, making his lunch wrappings into a basketball and lofting it into the wastebasket, 'when I'm chief is when we'll get it.'

I watched him preen while the dust settled around that pronouncement. In the years I'd worked with him I had considered him by turns resourceful, irritating, imaginative and ridiculously over-confident. I'd never before, for one minute, thought of him as competition. *Watch your back, Jake Hines.*

'Folksy guys can be as crooked as anybody,' Kevin said, 'in my experience. Have you ever seen that car lot, Ray?'

'No,' Ray said, 'every time Jake and I get ready to go there a bunch of other stuff happens.'

'You want to drive out there now?'

'I've got to write crime scene reports,' Ray said, looking grim again, 'for about a week.'

'Jake?'

'Maybe, Ray, if you're going to be here ... you could call me if something...?'

'Sure, go ahead. When you get back maybe you'll explain to me why people like their used car dealers folksy.'

Happy Roads was the smallest in the row of dealerships on Auto Row, and the one with the fewest customers. Three dozen plus late-model cars were lined up at the front of the lot where they showed from the street; tired old beaters huddled at the back.

'Look at all the Camrys,' I said, as we drove in the lot. 'Five ... no, six of them in a row.'

'All '99s. Identical to Gerry's,' Kevin said. 'How do you like that?'

'I'm crazy about it,' I said. 'Let's go in.'

The sales office had display space for one vehicle on a turntable, and it, too, was a '99 Camry. Along the back wall hung a big colored sign I remembered from newspaper ads, a picture of a smiling man, lean and middle-aged, waving a cowboy hat. The copy read: 'Happy Roads – the place to find a great ride!'

The salesman who greeted us as we came through the door was short and nearing forty, wearing carefully pressed slacks and shirt and a quiet tie. His back-up guy was out on the lot describing the merits of much-used sedans to a hand-holding couple wearing matching tattoos.

We showed him our shields. I said, 'That must be Happy in the ad, right? We need to talk to him.'

'Happy isn't on the premises right at this moment,' our salesman said, sticking his hand out, 'but hey, my name's Les and I'm younger and better lookin', won't I do?' Les was trying for folksy too – his smile was roguish – but his eyes couldn't quite maintain the sparkle. I read him as a second-start guy, trying to get back on his feet after a bankruptcy or maybe a booze problem.

Anyway he was anxious to please. I said, 'What's the story on all these identical Camrys?'

'Happy got a terrific deal, a fleet discount from a rental agency. It's a very nice car, reliable, gets good mileage. We had two dozen of them, but they've been moving so well, these are the last ones left. You interested in a Camry for yourself?'

'Maybe another time,' I said. 'Today we need to talk to Happy. You expect him any time soon?'

'Not really. He said he'd probably be at the farm all afternoon. Shall I give him a message?'

'No, I guess not. How far's the farm?'

'Oh, I don't, uh ... know that, I'm sorry.' He made an ironic face and added, 'Seems like he never asks me out there.' His chuckle invited me to share the joke.

I thanked him, gave him my card and said we'd come back later. Back in our Crown Vic at the curb we watched for a few minutes while nothing much happened in the car lot.

Kevin said, 'You giving odds the switched Camry came from anyplace else but this lot?'

'Nope.'

'You think the proprietor was in on the action?'

'Too soon to speculate, I guess. Since we still don't know for sure why they made the switch.'

'Well, but something about the stolen credit cards and ill-gotten merch, right? Why would a used car dealer get mixed up in that?'

'Don't know. Except ... it occurred to me once or twice that maybe Happy Rhodes put up the money to get Jason out of jail. I thought the boss might have something going with the mother. But I don't see enough business here to finance any generous gestures like that, do you?'

'Not today, for sure. So you're thinking maybe he makes up his cash shortfalls swiping credit cards? Or maybe he makes it at the farm.'

'Yeah, I wonder. I think Bev Keefe called it "a hobby farm" on the Byron road. Are you curious to know what his hobbies are?'

'You bet. Why don't you ask Ray if he's got directions to the place in his notes? Ray takes awesome notes,' Kevin said, as if he was delivering fresh gossip. The fact that Ray painstakingly wrote down all the things other people forgot was the main reason I had picked him to head People Crimes.

He didn't have the address of Happy's farm, though. 'You interviewed Bev Keefe, remember? Everything I know about her I got from you. Wait, though – isn't Curtis Brill still here someplace?'

'Talking to Chris Deaver. I hope. You're right, he might know – will you ask him?'

'OK. Listen, while I'm doing that, I'm going to put you on the line with John Smith, he's been in here pawing the floor about some electronic searching triumph that he says you and Kevin need to know about.'

I waited through some muttering and then John said, 'Man, have I got a treat for you.'

'Tell me in short English words.'

He laughed happily. 'Shelley didn't want me to take her PC, you know? So she kept talking to me, saying we could just upload what we needed on to a disc. I told her I was pretty sure we need the machine itself for proof but we could give her a loaner and upload *her* accounts on to that. That's right, isn't it?'

'Sounds OK. Is that my treat?'

'No ... but after we talked a while, she said she'd bet Noel set up an eBay account to sell the stuff he ordered, and she wouldn't be surprised if he used her computer for that too. So the two of us searched around and we found it. He had it hidden under ... well, I won't bore you with details.'

'No, God, don't say anything to take the shine off what you just said. John, you know, sometimes you're pretty good and other times you're just excellent.'

'Why, thank you!' He giggled; praise made him giddy. 'The search was pretty routine, really,' he said, trying to regain his cool. 'The good news is, I'm working with his eBay account now and his fraudulent purchases are matching up nicely with his sales offers. We can identify most of them precisely, because he's listing them NIB.'

'What's that?'

'New In Box. Don't you ever sell anything on eBay?'

'How could I? The only thing I own is a rundown farm.'

'That might be a little tricky, but you could do it.'

'Over my dead body. What's holding Ray?'

'Who? Oh, he's right here waiting.'

He had just done me a favor so I said politely, 'Put him on, please.'

'He says it's about eight miles,' Ray said. 'Take Highway Fourteen west and turn south where the sign says Salem Corners. Couple miles on that road, you'll see four mailboxes together on a wagon wheel; one says Rhodes. Turn right on to a dirt road and look for a place with a long driveway with a windbreak on the west side, two tall blue silos by a red barn. Any chance you might need some back-up?'

'For what? I just want to ask him what he

knows about Noel and Jason.'

'Well, fine, but nothing about this case so far has gone the way we expected, has it? Tell me you've got your weapon.'

'Of course I have my weapon. Relax, Ray, you just had a very bad morning. I set up a CID for you and the guys on your crew, by the way. I'll let you know the time.' He protested half-heartedly that he didn't need any counseling and I told him it wasn't optional. Law enforcement supervisors have to struggle through this boilerplate conversation after bad crime scenes now. Cops all know counseling works for other cops, but they think it's too demeaning to consider for themselves.

'That's not exactly true, is it?' Kevin said as I drove away from the car lot.

'What's not true?'

'What you said to Ray. We're going to the farm because you think the car lot looks a little hinky, right?'

'Don't you?'

'Sure. Too many Camrys that match Geraldine's, and too little anything else.'

'Exactly. Pretty lean cuisine for an owner and the two employees we saw? Yet we know three other guys that work there.'

'Part time.'

'Even so.'

'What?' he said, when I looked at his hip. 'Yes, I've got my weapon. Did Ray get you spooked? Amigo, his nerves are shot. He was ready to kick my teeth in this morning.'

'I know. What did you do to cool him down so fast? I came back ready to referee a fight and found you eating *candy* together, for God's sake.'

He laughed out loud, a happy, carefree sound that brightened the gray day. 'Soon as he came back from the can I said, "You know, I gotta hand it to you, Ray, I don't see how you can go to these grizzly crime scenes and stay so cool. I don't think I could do it." He kind of humped up and looked grouchy for a minute and then he said the stress at a homicide scene does wear on you but you have to learn to suck it up and do your job.' Kevin chuckled and preened himself.

'My, my. Almost too clever for government work.'

'Au contraire, exactly right! He was trapped inside my compliment, that's not a bad place to be! He flexed his biceps and straightened his tie, and I dug out my M&M's. While we ate dessert he told me some more about the blood spatter patterns. Fascinating stuff, good enough to make you gag.' His laugh was short and sharp this time. 'Better than fighting, anyway.'

'For sure. Help me watch for the turn now.' After five more miles we began to admit we must have missed it. In three more miles I found a tiny driveway to turn around in. It took five turns and I narrowly avoided a slide into a snow-filled ditch.

'We're going to look pretty dumb if we have to call for a tow,' Kevin said.

'Just watch for the frigging turn, will you?'

The graveled road we finally turned south on looked like it might be soft, but I figured it must be OK for us if the big blue passenger van ahead of us wasn't having any trouble. I was right; the roadbed had good drainage and we sailed right along.

Kevin said, 'Are those mailboxes up ahead of that van?'

'On a wagon wheel, sure enough.' The van slowed there too. After some hesitation it turned right around the wagon wheel, on to a narrow dirt road with serious ruts. Watching it fishtail slowly west, I debated whether to follow.

'Well, the van's making it all right,' Kevin said. He seemed to have lost his anxiety about calling a tow. I ventured cautiously into the muddy track of the vehicle ahead. We slid around some, but we kept moving forward. Half a mile ahead of us, the old blue van turned south again at the second driveway, and crawled crablike toward a red barn with two tall silos. 'Isn't this interesting? Everybody's going to Happy's place.'

I turned where the van had turned. The long driveway was very sloppy. 'Damn, I wish I'd brought my truck,' I said, fighting to stay out of the deepest ruts, throwing mud in a wide arc into the windbreak. The Crown Vic hit bottom and bounced, and I used the momentum to climb on to a crest. My cell phone rang. I ignored it and concentrated on staying in the driveway and out of the trees.

Kevin said, 'You phone is ringing.'

'It'll take a message.' I fought the wheel to stay out of the deepest rut. Somebody had spread crushed rock over a low spot at the end nearest the house; I felt the tires bite into it and stop spinning. I stopped at the far side of the patch, about fifty feet outside the gate, and watched the van pause by the house. We could see what he saw, that there were no lights on in the house and a late-model Dodge pickup parked by the right front corner of the barn.

After a few seconds the van rolled on, along the side of a cobbled path that led from the house to the barn. Tracking mud across a messy yard strewn with farm implements and spare parts, it passed a budding willow tree that stood by a bend in the path, and stopped in front of the barn, facing the Dodge.

The driver got out. Kevin said, 'Hey, isn't that the—'

'What the hell is he doing here?' Curtis Brill had climbed out of the van. 'I told Chris to keep him talking! How'd he get here ahead of us?'

'Guess he didn't miss the turn,' Kevin said. 'Aren't we going to say hello?'

'In a minute.' I rolled down the window. 'Let's see what he does first.'

Kevin lowered his window, too. 'He does not seem to have noticed us, does he?'

'No. He probably never looks in his rear-view mirror.'

Curtis was looking at the barn now, walking across the front of it, calling, 'Hap?' A padlocked hasp secured the big double doors in the center front. He walked past them to the small door near the right-hand corner of the barn, and tried the handle a couple of times. When it wouldn't turn he stepped back, looked up at the hayloft and called again, 'Hap?' There was a door up there with no lock, just a cutout in the siding that must latch on the inside. But it didn't open to his call; nothing moved.

You get used to a lot of background noise in a city, so in the country you notice the silence first and then every little sound that punctuates the silence. A jay squawked in the willow tree. An unlatched gate by the barn, rocking on its hinges, made a metallic scraping noise. Curtis walked back across the front of the barn to the left-hand corner and looked around it toward the rear, calling, 'Happy?'

A thin, weathered man with a grizzled fringe of hair under a baseball cap came around the left rear corner of the barn, carrying a tire iron. Curtis waved and said, 'Hi, Happy.'

I have often wondered about people who get stuck early in life with a descriptive nick-name. How would it feel being called Red after you've gone gray, or hearing friends call you Slim as you put on weight? I thought of it again as Happy Rhodes, a wiry undis-tinguished little guy barely recognizable from the picture in his display space, and not waving any jolly greetings now, walked toward us along the side of his barn looking seriously pissed off.

He stopped three feet from Curtis and asked him, 'You lost?'

'No,' Curtis said, putting his hand out. 'How are you, Happy? I came out because I thought you might not have heard about Jason's family and – what's the matter?'

Rhodes, facing the driveway, had seen us sitting there. He pointed and asked Curtis, 'You know these guys?'

Curtis turned and saw us, shrugged, and said something to Rhodes I couldn't hear. I put the car in gear and drove toward them. 'Well, you found it all right,' Curtis said as we stopped in front of him, 'but what took you so long?' Like a genial host, he turned toward Rhodes as we got out of the car and said, 'Happy, this is—'

'Curtis,' Rhodes said, 'what the *fuck* are

you doing here?'

'Oh – well, mostly I came to tell you...' Seemingly oblivious to the fact that his host was glaring at him, Curtis took a step toward Happy and reached out to take his arm. 'There's terrible news about Jason's family, and I knew you'd want to do something...'

'Damn it to hell!' Happy waved the tire iron and Curtis, a little alarmed finally, stepped back. 'I've told you boys more than once – haven't I? – don't never bother me at the farm! It's one thing when I invite you out for company picnics and that, but otherwise – and you got no business *at all* bringing these other people out here, who are they?'

I stepped forward. 'Captain Jake Hines, Mr Rhodes. Curtis didn't bring us, we came by ourselves to talk to you.' I showed him my shield. Kevin pulled his out, too.

Rhodes looked at our credentials carefully, comparing our pictures to our faces. 'So,' he said, squinting at me, 'Rutherford police got coloreds in the force now, huh? I heard that but I didn't believe it. We're gettin' more like the Twin Cities every day, ain't we?' He spat, deliberately, an inch from my left foot. 'Whatcha want?'

Now that DNA has traced us all back to that one cradle in Africa, people who can't get over racial bigotry usually strike me as too ludicrous to take seriously. But something was a little off-key about Happy's attack; even if he was a retro hater who couldn't assimilate current events, his hostility at this moment struck me as a little extreme. Why was he trying to offend me before he even found out what I wanted? He seemed to be trying to get a fight started. To distract me from what? An idea occurred to me and I thought, Give it a try. I said, 'Where's Jason?'

There was just one quick little flicker of his eyelids, but it was enough. He recovered fast and said, 'Hell would I know?' He re-settled his cap on his head, brought his inner arms in to his waist and hoisted his belt a fraction of an inch. He was trying to look cool because he wasn't. Why? He was in his own yard and we hadn't threatened him.

Deliberately, then, he played the race card again, turning away from me to ask Kevin, 'Must be kind of hard, ain't it, workin' alongside the blacks? Don't know no better than to barge into a man's private space and start asking dumb questions. What's that do to the image?'

Kevin said, 'What's it do to the farmer image to walk around carrying a blunt instrument and smelling like cannabis?' He was smiling, but his cover was off his weapon. He had a better nose than I did, or maybe I was too focused on holding my temper to take a deep breath. Now that he mentioned it I could smell pot too.

'Happy,' Curtis chided gently, 'are you out of sorts about something?' He smiled at us with an apologetic little shrug. 'He's usually the life of the party.'

Happy's worn, ruddy face turned briefly into a twisted mask of rage, eyes blazing, cheeks going purple. Automatically, my cop's muscles got ready to apply restraints. Then he surprised me with an amazing transition: his face went blank and smooth as a poker player counting cards, and stayed that way through four seconds of mesmerized silence. At the end of it, as if a switch had been thrown he morphed again, into the genial cowboy of his Happy Roads ads. He grinned around at the three of us, who were watching him now the way a wren watches a hawk, and said, 'You know, I think what it is, I'm all dried out and it's making me cranky. Why don't we all go set in the kitchen and have us a beer?'

Still carrying his tire iron, he turned and strode off along the little cobbled path that led toward the house.

'Well now, that's more like the Happy we all know and love,' Curtis said brightly, trotting after him.

Kevin and I looked at each other and shrugged. And that's when my peripheral vision caught the sight that had made Happy's face go blank: a sheriff's car churning up his long driveway, its rear end swaying like a hula dancer's as it threw mud into the trees.

I turned back and saw Happy still headed for his house, walking fast. Curtis was three paces behind him, talking to his back. 'I didn't have a chance to get any details of the tragedy, perhaps we could call the station—'

His conversation ended abruptly beside the willow tree, when Happy whirled and threw the tire iron at him.

And the instant the tool left his hand, Happy's right arm was reaching into the crotch of the willow tree. Before the heavy metal bar had even thudded into Curtis's belly, the arm was out again, with an automatic shotgun that he swung to his shoulder and aimed at me.

Kevin and I were already running toward our vehicle with our weapons drawn. Before we reached the cover of the car, Happy's powerful gun blew out the windshield and the driver's-side window. A million shards of glass blew toward me and his second shot sprayed more buckshot through the hole as I dived, half a second late. A burning track of pain crossed the left side of my head and the top of my ear.

Then I was on the ground, shooting under my vehicle at Happy's legs and feet. Kevin was beside me shooting too. Blood was pouring in a hot stream across my forehead and into my eye. One of us hit Happy's right leg; it flew backward in a strange way and he fell down on his face. He twisted in a break-dancer move to face us as another bullet flew into his chest, splattering blood and dirt all over him. For a few crazy seconds we were all firing right at each other under our car. Then I heard the sheriff's deputies enter the battle with their blazing double-ought buck rounds, and for a few seconds I was firing blindly into smoke, lost in the clamor and stink of armed combat.

My focus shifted abruptly when some hideous monster sunk enormous teeth into my right calf and began devouring it. I heard somebody scream and realized the voice was mine. I turned to try to shoot the monster and saw a scarecrow-thin boy fall out of the hayloft and land at my feet. A cloud came over the sun and the yard spun away from me in a sickening arc.

When I woke up the yard was back where it belonged and I was lying on it. Kevin was standing nearby, talking quietly to a sheriff's deputy whose name I couldn't remember.

I sat up and said, 'The car man was behind the whole thing, wasn't he?' Kevin came over and caught me as I started to tip sideways and the sun went dark again.

The next time I woke up he was sitting beside me in an ambulance. When he saw my eyes open he leaned over me and asked, 'Can you hear me?'

I nodded, just barely. He said, 'You got shot.' Did he really think I didn't know that? 'In the head and the leg. You've lost a lot of blood but these guys are putting it all back, see?' He pointed to tubes running here and there, being adjusted by the gloved hands of a paramedic somewhere near my head.

I tried to ask him a question but my mouth didn't work.

'You don't need to talk,' he said. 'You're going to be fine. Happy's dead, and Jason's dead, and so's that skinny kid who was shooting at you out of the hayloft.'

My mouth almost formed a word, 'Who?'

'Don't know yet. You and I walked into a nest of snakes and fought our way out, with a little help from two sheriff's deputies. Now all you have to do is lie still and look like a hero.' He smiled at me fondly. 'That might be the hard part, huh?'

Fifteen

Shaped like a girl again and smiling in the doorway, Trudy said, 'Welcome home.'

'Hold the door, Oz,' Dan Sullivan told his brother. With the two Sullivans boosting and belaying, I maneuvered my new walker over the doorsill and into the kitchen. My head looked like an ad for a war movie and my leg hurt like hell, but I was home. Ozzie pulled a chair away from the table, I flopped into it and Dan helped me swing my cast around so I could scoot up to my coffee cup.

'Did I just die and go to heaven or do I smell cinnamon rolls?' Ozzie swung his nose around like a golden retriever in pheasant country.

'Didn't I promise?' Trudy pulled a towel off a platter of pastries. 'Still warm.'

'Oh, lady, you do know how to please a country boy, don't you?'

'Oh, no, now, listen, we won't stay,' Dan said. 'You've got plenty to do without—'

'Sit,' Trudy said. 'You did all this work for me, now you get num-nums.'

'Well, if you insist,' he said, and they both

laughed. We all knew Dan Sullivan was counting on eating Trudy's baked goods just as much as Ozzie was, but he was the older brother and worried more about manners.

'I owe you guys a big fat favor,' I said, as we all dug in. 'Jeez, hauling me home from the hospital took up your whole morning.'

'Fetching you is the least of what they did,' Trudy said. 'Look here.' She got up and opened the door into the dining room. The table and chairs were gone. Sunshine streamed across our bed and the baby crib.

'My God. You rebuilt the house again?'

'Since yesterday,' Trudy said. 'It was Dan's idea. When I told him you wanted to opt out of rehab and come home, he said, "What could we do to make things a little handier for you?" And as soon as he said that I realized it would save a lot of steps if we had all the essentials on the first floor.'

'So the dining room's upstairs now?'

'Yeah, we just reversed rooms,' Dan said. 'We can change it back just as fast when you're ready.'

'You two,' I said, 'are putting a fresh shine on the word neighbor.'

'Aw, hell, we're just trying to soften you up for haying season,' Ozzie said.

We all had a big laugh over that, ignoring the hard bargaining that still lay ahead for us. Trudy and I owed them another summer's sweat equity for the extensive remodeling they did on our house. But my wrecked leg might not heal in time for haying, and with a new baby to care for Trudy couldn't possibly raise a monster garden the way she had the last two years, with the bulk of the produce going to the Sullivans. I was hoping to trade them several more summers in my fishing boat just for an extension on the loan.

But we could talk about that another day. For now it was bliss to be sitting in my own sunny kitchen snarfing up Trudy's good cooking. If I didn't move my leg at all, I had moments when I was almost comfortable. The bullet had gone through the long muscles on the back of my calf, though, so if I forgot and twitched my foot the nerve endings sent messages to my brain saying the monster was feeding on my leg again. I had promised to do at home, twice a day, the ball-busting exercises I was missing in rehab. I thought about them as I finished my second cup of coffee and I guess I must have winced. Dan saw me, poked his brother and said, 'Come on, Oz, we gotta ramble.'

When they were gone Trudy said, 'Have you seen yourself in a mirror yet?'

'I saw enough. The docs assure me it's all going to heal.'

'I know. But right now you look kind of green. Let's get you settled in bed before the baby wakes up.'

'You've got enough to do,' I said, 'I can take care of myself.'

'Please don't waste time being noble,' she said, 'I've got this all figured out.'

'Oh, well,' I said, 'if you've got it figured out there's no point in arguing, is there?'

'Absolutely none. No need for sarcasm either.'

Her mouth got that straight-line look that means you're treading along the lip of an emotional volcano. With no strength to spare for explosions, I held up my arms and said, 'Take me, I'm yours.' That got me a smile and a quick kiss before she went to work on me.

She eased my shirt off around my head bandages and helped me into a sweatshirt that zipped in the front. 'We'll call those pants your pajamas now,' she said. I'd come home in knit sweatpants cut off at the right knee to allow access to the bandages and temporary cast holding my lower leg together. The docs had cut away my bloody jeans last Friday in the ER.

She set the walker by my chair, helped me stand up and get positioned right, and walked with me to the bathroom.

'What,' I said, looking in, 'the bathroom door's upstairs too?'

'For now. We don't need the privacy and it's easier to get the walker through.' They had war-gamed everything since Monday when I negotiated this early release.

'I won't be any trouble,' I falsely promised when I made the deal, 'and I'd rather be home with you and Ben.'

'I'd like it too,' she said. 'Just give me one day to get ready.'

She ordered a lot of stuff by phone, recruited her mother and sister to shop and clean house and pressed the Sullivans into service as movers and shakers. They'd rearranged all the furniture so there were clear paths for my walker. They filled the woodbox so we could have a fire if we wanted it, laid in extra batteries and flashlights and stocked the kitchen with supplies enough for a brigade. A pad by the phone had a list of a dozen numbers she could call in case of emergency. On this calm, shiny morning in April, our house looked prepared to outlast a blizzard.

'You expecting some natural disaster?' I asked her, looking around.

'I'm expecting a quiet time of healing. But I can handle a couple of glitches if I have to.'

'You really are an awesome woman, you know it?' I leaned down to nuzzle her neck and almost fell over.

'Oops. Careful, lover.' She walked me to the bedside, piled up extra pillows, and found me a pain pill in the kit I'd brought home. 'Let's get you settled in here, because Benny's waking up.'

'Is that what I hear?' A snuffling noise was coming from the crib. I swung my good left leg into bed, grabbed the painful right one and hoisted it in after, and leaned back. 'Hey, it's fun sleeping downstairs. A little weird lying next to the buffet.'

'We decided it was too much trouble to move. You can get better acquainted with Grandma Halvorson's willow ware.' She walked around to the crib on her side of the bed, picked up the baby, brought him back and laid him in my arms. 'Here, talk to the boy while I get ready.' Ben felt like a squirming knot of hot, unhappy muscle. A shade less red than the last time I'd seen him, he chewed on his hands for a few seconds, made a couple of tragic faces and began to cry.

He still had that loud, insistent voice. It made me anxious and wracked with guilt. The two minutes till Trudy came back and took him from me seemed very long. His crying got louder and more frantic while she changed him, and even after she got in bed and put her nipple in his mouth, for a few seconds he made a comical effort to suck and cry at the same time. Trudy laughed and said, 'Jeez, kid, you can't take yes for an answer, can you?'

I fell asleep while she was feeding him. When I woke up two hours later the monster was devouring my leg again. I took another pain pill, ate a bowl of chicken soup, because Trudy told me to, and slept again. The rest of Wednesday went by like that, a little soup and a lot of sleep.

But Thursday morning at four o'clock, I woke up feeling like Mister Alert, Master of the Universe. My leg hurt some, but not bad, and it was such a treat to be wide awake after five blurry days that I put off taking a pill. Trudy was warm beside me in the bed, sleeping soundly. I stared into the dark, listening to Ben making noises in his crib like a small pig rooting for truffles. There were two pillows within reach on the floor. I propped myself up, turned on my bedside light, found a copy of *Sports Illustrated* on my bedside table. After a couple of restless whimpers, Ben began to wail.

What can a one-legged man do for a crying infant who only wants what his father will never have? I lay in a sweaty panic, waiting for Trudy to wake up. After a few minutes that felt like eternity, she opened one eye a crack and said, 'Mmff?'

'I think he's hungry,' I said.

'Juss fed him,' she mumbled, and turned her face into the pillow.

'He's crying, though.' I touched her shoulder. 'He must need something.'

She sat bolt upright, looked at me desperately, and flung herself out of bed. Scooping the baby out of his crib, she walked to my side of the bed and laid him face down against my chest. 'Hold him a while, will you? Pat his back a little. Sometimes he gets a bellyache after he eats.' She trotted back around to her side, climbed in and burrowed under the covers. 'So tired,' she murmured. In thirty seconds, she was asleep.

Ben was doing tiny yoga exercises against my chest, twisting and flailing. His noises sounded discontented but non-specific. I patted and rubbed. He twisted and kicked. Finally he let go a belch that seemed to have enough air in it for two sumo wrestlers. I stared at him in alarm, half expecting him to explode, but he quit whimpering almost at once and lay still. Soon he was asleep, drooling on my sweatshirt. I watched him in triumph till my arms threatened to fall off. When I eased him down between us, he went right on sleeping.

Trudy woke up at six thirty, found the baby next to her and looked at me, startled. We did some furtive whispering while I showed her my watch and reported on the glorious belch. Ben began trying to eat his fingers again about seven, and the entire cycle started over.

I had a part to play in this continual circus now, though – I was Baby Soothing Man. Ben had taken to nursing like a champ, but his new digestive system still needed tuning up. His meals gave him gas, and his bowel movements gave him pain. He shared every twinge with us, holding nothing back. My son was a first-class communicator; when Ben wasn't happy, they knew it across the highway.

'Come on, kid,' I pleaded with him that afternoon as he twisted and wailed on my chest, 'give us a break and poop.'

'Why does it bother you so much when he cries?' Trudy asked me.

'I don't know – he makes me feel guilty, I guess.'

'Well, get over it, will you?' she said. 'It's the only way he's got to get what he needs. Think about how you got yourself out of that dumpster the day you were born. If you hadn't had a good big voice—'

'OK,' I said hastily, 'let's not talk about *that* any more.'

'Why? You should be proud of the fact that you saved your own life before you even had your eyes open.'

'Oh, I'm OK with it. I just don't want to think about Ben in the garbage.'

'My sweetheart.' She nuzzled my neck.

I nibbled her ear and said, 'It's kind of fun staying in bed all day, isn't it?'

'Yes.' She sighed. 'I'm sorry I can't have sex yet.'

'That's all right, I'm not up to much right now myself.'

'We've got a lot to talk about, though.

Haven't we? So much happened so fast – and first I was in the hospital and then you were. Now we're both in this house for days and we're practically *assigned* to do nothing but R and R.'

'You know, I bet I can stand that.'

'Me too. Let's try for a ... what's that thing Shakespeare says? A marriage of true minds.'

'I'm kind of behind on my Shakespeare. Who says that, Romeo?'

'It's in one of the sonnets. Why do you always do that?'

'Do what?'

'Talk like a dumb bozo whenever I mention a poet or a painter? You've got a culture twitch.'

'I do? Well, I'm kind of sensitive about my bad education. I went to four grade schools and three high schools. A lot fell through the cracks. I guess when I feel awkward about what I don't know I play the fool to cover it up. It's a version of what McCafferty calls crapping upstream of the critics.'

'But I'm not critical of you. Am I? Was that a dubious look?' She made a face. 'OK, maybe sometimes a little. Not today, though. If I scoot over like this can you put your arm around me?'

I would never suggest that new fathers try to get shot in the leg; given a choice I'd skip that part myself. But ever since Ben was born I know something that I pass along free to any start-up dads I meet: pull whatever scam you have to in order to stay home with the family a while. Those days and nights together, helping our son along the path from reluctant infant to beginner human being, that opportunity will never come again. And it stays in my mind as some of my best time on earth.

We spent almost all of the first week in bed together, reading and talking and playing endless hands of canasta – we kept a running score that got up into ridiculous numbers. Every three to five hours – his schedule hadn't smoothed out yet – Ben would do his irritated pig imitation for a couple of minutes and then holler for chow.

Trudy would nurse him and hand him over to me. I clapped him face down over my heart – that was the sweet spot, I soon learned. He liked hearing my heartbeat, I think; it made him feel halfway back to that cozy retreat in the womb that he had been so disappointed to leave. Ben would twitch and claw at me with his tiny fists, grunting and whimpering till the enzymes went to work on the calories and he got comfortable. Often in the daytime, when he finally got to sleep we laid him between us with his head pointed at our feet, on top of the covers with his own blanket around him. While we talked, we watched him sleep and smooth out, get his systems working and start the transition from wrinkled gnome to well-fed baby.

'You were very good in the hospital, the day Ben was born,' she said. 'You really helped.'

'Well, I'm glad if I did, but I've got to tell you, childbirth didn't live up to its hype, for me.'

'Is that a fact?' She enjoyed that a lot. 'What in particular did you find so disappointing?'

'It's too damn hard! Why do they always show people in the movies smiling and looking happy? Did we do any of that? No – it was grim and terrifying, what you went through, and it got worse as it went along. I've never been so slavering scared in my life as I was during the last two or three pushes.'

'This from the man who just got shot in two places? You want scared, I almost fainted when they told me what had happened to you. I thought you were behind your desk in a nice clean office! Did you know you were going after a dangerous criminal when you went out to that farm?'

'Absolutely not. We'd have gone with flak jackets and a whole team – we don't take foolish chances, you know that.'

'Except this time you did.'

'Not intentionally. We just went out to ask good ol' Hap a few questions.'

'Why do you keep calling him good ol' Hap after he tried to kill you?'

'That's what everybody calls him. Curtis and his pals, and the salesmen at the car lot – good ol' Hap, they say, what a character, ol' Hap knows how to keep things humming.'

'See, now, that would make me suspicious right away.'

'Yes, well, we must see if we can't sign you on as an investigator.'

'No thanks. I'm still not sure why he shot you.'

'Well, I was standing in front of his barn full of marijuana, where he was also building a meth lab, and had a dead body in the hayloft.'

'Oh, those are all good reasons, aren't they?'

'And not the only ones at that, it turns out. Happy was already a little paranoid because his drug dealers had killed Geraldine Lovejoy. When Curtis and Kevin and I all turned up in his yard at once, and a sheriff's car followed us in, he thought we'd figured that out.'

'But you hadn't?'

'Well, Curtis certainly hadn't. Kevin and I began to smell something funny at his used car lot, but we were a long way from pinning drug traffic and murder on him.'

'You think you've got it all straight now?'

'I think I understand most of it. Ray and Kevin both came to see me in the hospital,

Bo and Rosie stopped in a couple of times, and even Andy came once. I had more social life in a week in the hospital than I get out here in an average year. And everybody that came brought me the latest news.'

'Bo and Rosie came to see me too. It's nice they're finally getting it on, isn't it?'

'You think so?'

'Well, they've been in love forever, so yes, I think so.'

'How did you know that – did Rosie tell you?

'Never said a word. But how could anybody miss it?'

'See, we really have to get you in the department.'

'With you for my boss? In your dreams.'

'What kind of a crack is that? I'm a good boss.'

'I'm sure you are, lover. But not for me. How's it going to work with Rosie and Bo on the same squad?'

'I'm going to start worrying about that as soon as my leg's better. Not today, though.'

'OK. Tell me some more about the farm – why was Curtis out there? He's the boyfriend of the girl you found on the sidewalk, right? Did he have a gun?'

'Nope. Curtis had nothing but his illusions. He may have lost a few of those. Along with several inches of his intestines and one kidney, because good old Happy punctured his gut with a tire iron.'

'Oh, that's awful – why was he there?'

'He was trying to find his friend Jason Wells, to console him for the tragic death of his whole family. What he didn't know was that Jason was the one who killed them, and now he was dead in the hayloft.'

'This gets worse and worse. Who killed Jason?'

'Happy did. Jason called him for help sometime after he crawled out of his own yard, where he somehow managed to elude a dozen or so of Rutherford's finest who were surrounding the place. Happy sent Pee-Wee to pick him up. They killed him in the barn, and they had a grave almost dug for him by the time we got there.'

'You picked a great time to go asking questions, didn't you? This Pee-Wee is the, what did you say? Nephew?'

'Nephew, gofer, bag man. Recruiter of new drug dealers, too, I guess – they were building a franchise group of Pee-Wee's contemporaries.'

'Is he in jail?'

'No, he's dead too. One of the deputies shot him when he leaned out of the hayloft and shot me. Fortunately Pee-Wee's aim was bad.'

'Not bad enough to spare your poor leg. How's it feel today?'

'Almost tolerable, when I'm perfectly still.

Tell me I have to do my exercises today.'

'You have to do your exercises today and every day from now on so you stay flexible for all the great sex we're going to have pretty soon.'

'Ah, that's what Darrell calls incentivizing, isn't it? I can feel it working already. You want to try a little heavy petting just to keep your edge?'

'I don't think so, I'm edgy enough for two people already. I hope you won't mind having a lusty wife when this is over.'

'I'm almost certain I can tolerate that.' I nibbled her ear.

She giggled, got up and refilled our water glasses, settled back against the pillows. 'Let's talk some more. What's the story on that car Jimmy got so worked up about?'

'Worked up doesn't begin to describe it. He was a complete jerk about it, to Ray and me both. How can you stand to work for him the way he is lately?'

'Oh, you just have to cut him a little slack for a while, Jake, his twins are teething.'

'Is that right? God, what perfect justice. Tell me they keep him up all night. But how come he tells you but not me?'

'He doesn't tell me anything, he pretends to be completely objective at all times. But I can always tell when he's not getting enough sleep, and besides, I'm friends with his wife.'

'You really are a born sleuth.'

'You mean gossip. I know that tone of voice. Tell me the story on the car.'

'Noel and Jason got greedy, that's what blew the whole deal. They were snatching purses and defrauding card-holders to raise cash so they could set up as dealers, you understand that part? Happy had agreed to start them in a couple of months. But then Noel had all that good luck with credit card carbons at the rummage sale. He sold a bunch of the stuff he ordered and they got their bankroll sooner than expected. So when Happy got a great buy on a big shipment, Noel and Jason pleaded with Pee-Wee to sell them some of it so they could get their campus customers started. Pee-Wee refused at first because they weren't set up with a space at the storage locker where they did their drops.'

'Drops?'

'Happy never delivered directly to his dealers, they ordered by phone and exchanged money and dope at a neutral location at different times, like spies. Noel said hey, just to get started, this one time we can use Gerry's car.'

'How did he know where it would be?'

'Curtis had found a Bible class for Noel that met on the same nights Gerry went to Accounting. It was only a few blocks from the Fisher Building. He rode with her and walked from there. Of course he didn't actually go to class, just walked in the front door and out the back. They were playing Curtis because he was useful.'

'How come Noel had a key to Geraldine's car?'

'Pee-Wee made it at Happy Roads.'

'So you're telling me these boys got all sorts of favors, meals and rides and tutoring, from this couple and then wrecked their lives without a blink.'

'Hey, I never promised you a heart-warming story. You want me to stop?'

'No, I'm hooked, I have to hear the rest. They made the deal with Pee-Wee?'

'Without telling Happy. But it had to be Friday night, the night Happy stayed late to close up the used car lot and balance the books. Pee-Wee would be alone at the farm and have access to the weed. He convinced himself his uncle would be OK with the early start as soon as he saw the money. Jason said he'd get along without a pickup. It was going to be his last mugging anyway and they agreed he'd quit if he didn't find a mark in two hours. Noel wanted him to skip it entirely but Jason said they'd need spending money till the drug biz got going good. So Pee-Wee agreed to meet Noel at Gerry's car, while she was in class, for their first exchange of drugs and money.'

'Ah. And then the class got cancelled. Isn't that what you said?'

'The one thing they never considered. She came back to the car unexpectedly, opened the door and found the two of them with open backpacks, their laps full of drugs and money. She probably keyed the door unlocked with the remote, walked up and yanked it open and was startled, of course, to find them there.'

'Would she know marijuana when she saw it?'

'Oh, everybody knows a little something these days, and I suppose the money spoke for itself. She demanded an explanation, what are you doing in my car, what's going on here? She got louder and louder, Noel says, and he panicked and grabbed her, tried to drag her into the car. Pee-Wee jumped out of the passenger seat, ran around the car and began slamming her with the door. She started to pass out and as her knees buckled she got her head between the door and the doorpost. He broke her nose and cracked her skull. She fell in on top of Noel, bleeding, and there he was, holding an inert body, with blood all over him and the car, the drugs and the money.'

'The way you tell it I could almost feel sorry for him.'

'Don't bother, he's doing plenty of that for himself. Ray says he keeps complaining that this is so unfair, it wasn't supposed to go this way.'

'Boy, that's just ... breathtaking.'

'Oh, yeah, Noel's a breathtaking boy.'

'What does he look like?'

'Your favorite boy scout. Ginger-colored hair, overbite and freckles.'

'Now *that* really *is* unfair.'

'Yeah, we've got to get Mother Nature to cut out these devious tricks.'

She got out of bed and stretched. 'Let's do your walking and knee-bends now and then I'll make us some tea.'

Twenty minutes later she was wiping salt water off my face, saying, 'Rats, it hurts so much it makes you cry, huh?'

'That's sweat,' I panted. 'Policemen don't cry.'

'Oh, that's right, I forgot. Once more around the kitchen, my sweaty valentine, and you get your tea.'

Back in bed in a dry shirt, I thanked her as graciously as I could for the big fragrant cup of tea she brought me. Every molecule in my body was crying out for a beer, but I was still taking too many painkillers to risk it. The buckshot grooves on the left side of my head were healing nicely, but the .45 slug had blown away significant chunks of my calf muscle. I was being tortured by my body's effort to refill the hole, and was humbly grateful for the pharmaceuticals that made healing bearable.

Actually, I could have been home in bed

with Trudy even if I'd managed to dodge all the bullets – Kevin was off work too, without a scratch on him. We had both fired our weapons in the course of police business, so we were on paid administrative leave until an independent investigation by a neighboring department declared it a righteous shoot. The Winona County sheriff's department was doing ours. It was totally routine and I endorsed the system in the abstract. Now that it was judging me, though, I felt the taint hanging over my career and hated it. A sore place inside my head kept yelling, You weren't even there, how can you decide?

'These are Mama's oatmeal cookies, you want one? Careful with the crumbs.' We munched in thoughtful silence, holding paper towels under our chins. She took our cups out to the sink, came back and snuggled discreetly, careful not to touch my leg. 'OK, Uncle Remus, back to the tale. What did the boys do when they realized they'd killed the car's owner?'

'They did what all losers do, picked the worst possible option. They called Happy Rhodes. He was furious, of course, but he couldn't leave them in a public place with his dope and money and all that blood. He told Pee-Wee to take off the VIN plate and license plate and bring them to the used car lot, along with all the documentation in the glove compartment. Well, and all the money and dope, of course. Noel had to stay in Gerry's car with the body – they cleaned her up a little, propped her up and draped her scarf around her head – and waited for Pee-Wee to come back with a fresh car. Then Pee-Wee was supposed to help dump the body, try to make it look like a mugging, and drive the dirty car to the farm. But it took so long to change the VIN plate, an hour went by and Noel knew people would soon be coming out of the concert. He lost his nerve sitting there alone with a dead body. Next time there was a lull in traffic he pulled out of the lot, turned right for a few feet and then backed up till he was right next to the curb. As soon as he had the street to himself he jumped out and pulled the body out on to the sidewalk. He was stooping over her, trying to make her look as if she just fell down, when a couple came around the corner and almost fell over him.'

'Oh, I bet I can guess the next part.'

'Tell me.'

'He told them he just found this girl on the sidewalk, it looked like she'd been attacked, and would they run back to the concert and find somebody to help?'

'Bingo. As soon as they were out of sight, of course, he jumped in the car and got out of there. He never even noticed that her purse was lying in the parking lot where she dropped it when Pee-Wee began hitting her with the door.'

'But he still had a terrible problem, didn't he? He was driving around in a bloody car with no license plate—'

'With blood on his clothes and hands. Yes. And his brain must have frozen up entirely at that point, because he went straight to the one place in town where he should have known he'd get killed – Happy's used car lot. But here his famous luck kicked in again, for a few minutes. Two blocks away from the car lot he saw Pee-Wee driving toward him in a nice clean Camry just like the one he was driving. He rolled down the window and waved, and pulled over to the curb. Pee-Wee did a U-turn and pulled in behind him, and they talked. Noel told Pee-Wee he was losing it, he had to go home because he was starting to shake. Pee-Wee said follow me to Happy Roads, I'll show you where my car is parked and you can leave Gerry's and take mine.'

'And they actually did that?'

'I can't believe they got away with it but he says they did and all the physical evidence bears him out. But from then on, of course, Uncle Hap was gunning for Noel and Jason, and maybe Pee-Wee too when he got around to him.'

'Jason got arrested that night, though, didn't he?'

'Right, he was safe in jail till his mother

bailed him out.'

'Did the fight at his house have anything to do with this?'

'That was mostly just good old family rage, I think. But I expect his mother was ragging on him about the things she had to do for Happy to get his bail money.'

'Oh, you mean—'

'I'm sure we'll prove Happy put up the bail money. He would have wanted Jason out of there so he could kill him. But probably he got a little taste from Mama first just for the hell of it.'

'And she would do it?'

'For Jason? In a heartbeat. Some other time I'll tell you about the love-hate affair between Jason and his mother.'

'Maybe I'll get along without that part. Why didn't they put Gerry's replacement car back in the parking lot?'

'Pee-Wee tried several times but there were always cops working there. I think I heard him once, driving by slow in the snowstorm. Finally he parked it on the street where we found it, dropped the keys under the seat and locked it up manually, and called Noel for his ride.'

'I see.' Ben whimpered between us, waved his arms and kicked at some pain or phantom enemy. We watched as his tragic expression smoothed out and he went back to sleep.

I asked Trudy, 'You think babies dream?'

'Some doctors say they dream almost constantly for the first few months.'

'But he just got born. What's he got to review?'

'Um ... thousands of years of human history?'

'Oh, you think he's still in touch with...? Aw, come on.'

'If only the little bugger could talk, huh?'

'Ozzie Sullivan says we should treasure every single day before he learns.'

'Poor Oz, his kids give him no respect.' She pondered a while in silence. 'How did Noel manage to stay alive for another whole week, if Happy was out to get him?'

'Happy was busy, I guess, getting a bloody Camry moved out to his farm, cleaning up bags of dope and money. And Noel made himself hard to find – as soon as he cleaned up that night, he packed a bag and never went near his crib again. He crashed with some buddies – a different place every night – stayed a couple of nights at the Y. He only surfaced, he says, for that one morning job at Mail Boxes. He had to keep that because the loot was still coming in.'

'Noel's telling all this to Ray and Kevin?'

'At length and in depth. Noel's turned into a major news source.'

'Why?'

'He needs a new deal. His buddies are

dead, he killed the only woman who was ever nice to him and I don't believe even Curtis will pray for him any more.'

'I still don't see why he'd confess to murder.'

'He won't. He'll plead it down to manslaughter two, or aggravated assault with mitigating ... you know. He'll find a lot of people who'll talk about his troubled childhood, his abusive stepmother. All true, probably. And it's his first offense.'

'But he sat in her own car and helped kill her.'

'True. And Milo assured him he was looking forward to charging him with murder one – Noel's the only candidate left standing and a jury will want to blame somebody for all this carnage. Happy had been scrubbing away at Gerry's car, out there in his barn, but your lab guys are hopeful they'll still find some of Noel's DNA in it.'

'If charging him with the max is so much fun why doesn't Milo do it?'

'Because he'd rather let Noel plead down so he can get the full story about what was going on. This way he gets a credible case against the rest of Happy's drug dealers, and the county can seize the farm and the used car lot. Oh, and the money – once Noel got into the spirit of bargaining he offered to lead us to Happy's stashes.'

'How on earth did he know that?'

'He's a little vague about why he did all that midnight spying out there. I suspect Jay and No-No were making a deal with Pee-Wee to knock over the farm.'

'What a grand bunch, huh?'

'I guess the feeling was mutual. Kevin says Happy's last words were something like, "Shoulda killed the whole bunch of them the day Jason got out of jail."'

'He blamed the boys for him getting shot?'

'Which in a way they did. Though we didn't know what he had in the barn. I told you, we just went out there to talk.'

'But then why did you have the sheriff's deputies follow you?'

'I didn't. Ray called the sheriff for help when I didn't answer my cell phone.'

'Why didn't you answer?'

'The driveway was muddy. I was busy driving.'

'Oh, for heaven's sake! You mean your survival's all due to pure luck?'

'Well, now, I wouldn't go that far. It also depended on a lot of people using good instincts and highly trained survival skills...'

'Horseapples. You got lucky, or you wouldn't even be talking to me right now. God—' she flounced and pushed her hair around – 'I hate that. Promise me from now on you'll stay in your office where you belong.'

'You sound like the chief.'

'Oh, the chief! That's what I forgot to tell you. He called the first day you were home, while you were sleeping. He wanted to thank you for your help with his reunion.'

'He was dreading it something awful. Did he say how it went?'

'Terrific, he said. The best thing he's ever done. He said they had a great time together, talked non-stop for two days. They're having T-shirts made that say: "McCafferty's Nine". From now on they're all going to keep in touch and meet every year.'

'Isn't that a hoot? He was sure it was going to be a disaster.'

'You think they'll actually keep in touch?'

'No. But let's not ask for perfection, it's good enough they had fun. Listen, now—' I nudged her elbow – 'what about this marriage of true minds you promised me? All you've done so far is interrogate me. When do I get to hear your news?'

'Jake, all I've been doing is making milk.'

'For the last few days, sure. But before that you were still a keen-eyed forensic scientist, right? So tell me what's new on the cutting edge.'

'See, that's the other thing you always do.'

'What? What do I always do that you wouldn't think of criticizing me for?'

She laughed, but just a little, and got right back to it. 'You always say all these admiring things about my work, but in a kind of a snide, underhanded way, as if you think I'm putting on airs about it.'

'No I don't. Do I? I'm very proud of what you do, Trudy. Don't look at me like that.'

'"Keen-eyed forensic scientist." What kind of pond-slime is that?'

'Well.' I heard myself saying it and knew she had me. 'I think it's the same slime I smeared on Shakespeare. Hearing you talk about the work you're doing now, Trudy, you know, it makes me feel like my head just turned into an anvil. Do you have any idea how daunting it is for a man to realize his wife can talk knowledgeably on a subject that's so hellishly goddamn complicated he'll never understand it?'

'Oh, come on, you understand it well enough. Maybe not the technical details, but you know what we're proving.'

'I thought I had a fair grip on it a couple of years ago, when you were showing me the alleles on these profiles of DNA from inside the nucleus. I thought, OK, there's the working diagram, half mama, half papa, and now I see the match, let's nail the bastard. But this mitochondrial stuff, not so much. I mean, it's not as precise as the nucleic stuff, I don't get why we want to mess around with it.'

'You understand that all your mitochondrial DNA comes from your mother, don't you? So it places you in a family. You remember the story about Prince Phillip, how some of his mitochondrial DNA helped prove that old bones found in Russia belonged to several members of the murdered Czar's family?'

'Because it proved they had the same maternal ancestors.'

'Exactly. It works to prove innocence, too, of course – if you're *not* in the family of the DNA at the scene you can't be a suspect. The other thing is its abundance. Mitochondrial DNA is much more abundant in our cells than nucleic DNA is. So if we only get a tiny sample, or a badly degraded one ... there's a case on record of a rape conviction that was obtained using a single pubic hair.'

'My, my.'

'Yeah. You know—' she put her head on one side and looked at me the way a robin looks at a worm – 'we haven't talked about it yet, but there's an exciting facet of this you should be thinking about, Jake. With a hundred dollars and a cheek swab, you can get the answer to a lot of questions about what your ethnic heritage is, and where your ancestors came from.'

'Yeah, I heard about that. I just—'

'What, now that you can get it you're not sure you want to know?'

'Oh ... later on, I guess ... it might make a good show-and-tell for Ben some day. But it won't tell me what I really want to know.'

'Like what?'

'Like why somebody looked at me – remember how it felt when we looked at Ben that first day? I mean, I was on his team in a second, he was *mine*. But somebody looked at me when I was newborn like that and threw me away.'

She drew in her breath sharply and grabbed my hand, and I wished I could take the words back. We had a good start now on a happy family, and I wanted to be rid of the grief I'd always felt about my parents. To blow the thought away I said, 'Anyway I know who I am now.'

'You do?' She looked at me, round-eyed. 'Since when?'

'Since the last couple of weeks.' I stretched all of my body but my right leg, a new skill I was perfecting. 'For one thing, I'm the cop most of the buckshot missed. You might want to start calling me Lucky.'

'OK, Lucky. Please don't make a habit of narrow escapes.'

'I won't.' I kissed the inside of her elbow, where she's got a place that feels like warm satin. 'I'm also the husband of a smart beautiful Swede who can nurse a baby and play canasta at the same time.'

'I must say,' she giggled, 'that has a certain panache.'

'As it were.' I watched Ben Franklin gnaw on a knuckle. 'And if that's not enough for you, it turns out I'm the man whose chest turns screaming babies to jelly.'

'Well, now there, you know, you really have got something.'

'Damn right.' I gave her the Groucho eyebrows. 'Soon as this leg heals up, baby, if you play your cards right I'll let you lie on my chest.'

'Ah, Jake,' she sighed, 'you're just too good to me.'

The three of us stayed close and warm during the days and nights that followed, eating and drinking, talking and laughing and crying when we needed to. Trudy and I healed up while Ben got used to the hard work of breathing air and digesting his food. By summer he was out in the yard with us on shady afternoons, blinking at robins.